DEADLY TRADE

Books by
SARA DRISCOLL

Echoes of Memory
Shadow Play

FBI K-9s

Lone Wolf
Before It's Too Late
Storm Rising
No Man's Land
Leave No Trace
Under Pressure
Still Waters
That Others May Live
Summit's Edge
Deadly Trade

NYPD Negotiators

Exit Strategy
Shot Caller
Lockdown
Terminal Impasse

DEADLY TRADE

SARA DRISCOLL

KENSINGTON
PUBLISHING CORP.

kensingtonbooks.com

This book is a work of fiction. Names, characters, businesses, organizations, places, events, and incidents either are the product of the author's imagination or are used fictitiously. Any resemblance to actual persons, living or dead, events, or locales is entirely coincidental.

To the extent that the image or images on the cover of this book depict a person or persons, such person or persons are merely models, and are not intended to portray any character or characters featured in the book.

KENSINGTON BOOKS are published by

Kensington Publishing Corp.
900 Third Avenue
New York, NY 10022

Copyright © 2025 by Sara Driscoll

All rights reserved. No part of this book may be reproduced in any form or by any means without the prior written consent of the Publisher, excepting brief quotes used in reviews.

Without limiting the author's and publisher's exclusive rights, any unauthorized use of this publication to train generative artificial intelligence (AI) technologies is expressly prohibited.

All Kensington titles, imprints and distributed lines are available at special quantity discounts for bulk purchases for sales promotion, premiums, fundraising, educational or institutional use.

Special book excerpts or customized printings can also be created to fit specific needs. For details, write or phone the office of the Kensington Special Sales Manager: Kensington Publishing Corp., 900 Third Avenue, New York, NY, 10022. Attn. Special Sales Department. Phone: 1-800-221-2647.

Library of Congress Card Catalogue Number: 2025937913

KENSINGTON and the K with book logo Reg. U.S. Pat. & TM. Off.

ISBN: 978-1-4967-5631-2
First Kensington Hardcover Edition: November 2025

ISBN: 978-1-4967-5632-9 (ebook)

10 9 8 7 6 5 4 3 2 1

Printed in the United States of America

The authorized representative in the EU for product safety and compliance is eucomply OU, Parnu mnt 139b-14, Apt 123
Tallinn, Berlin 11317, hello@eucompliancepartner.com

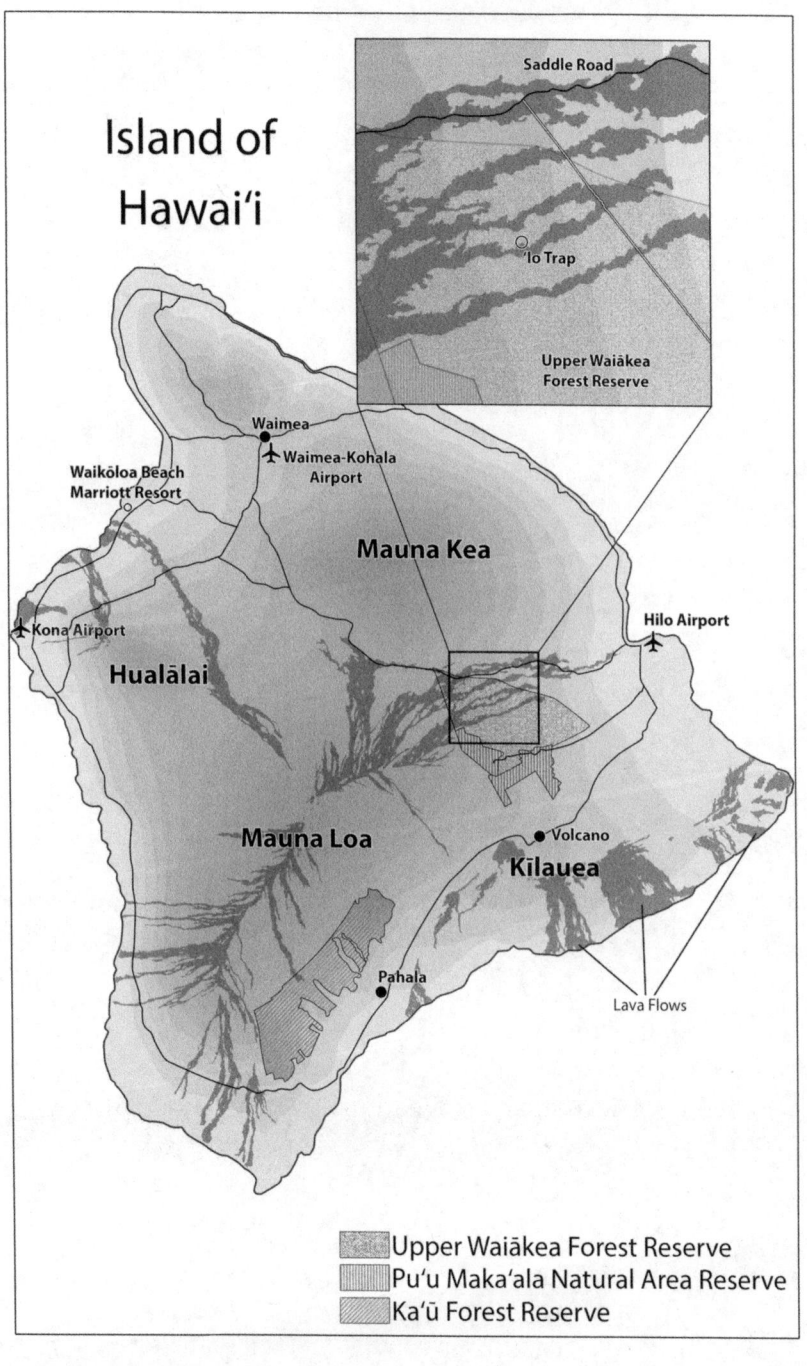

DEADLY TRADE

CHAPTER 1

Shield Volcano: A low-profile volcano with gentle sloping sides formed by numerous eruptions and repetitive layering of lava flows. The Hawaiian Islands are the summits of massive undersea shield volcanoes.

May 27, 5:49 AM
Four Seasons Resort Lanai
Lanai City, Lanai, Hawaii

In the dim light stealing between thick curtains, Meg Jennings slipped quietly out of bed. The black Labrador, curled in a nest of thick blankets beside the bed, raised his head, then stood and padded after her as she left the bedroom.

Meg paused for a moment, her hand on the bedroom doorjamb as she looked over her shoulder. Todd Webb, her husband of only a week, lay on his back, the light sheet bunched around his naked hips and one arm thrown over his head. Even in the scant illumination, his short, dark hair was tousled, and stubble shaded his jaw. A smile curved Meg's lips—it was good to see him so relaxed. Too often their life carried too many stresses.

The week on Lanai had been good for them. They both worked intense jobs—Todd as a firefighter/paramedic with

DC Fire and Emergency Medical Services, and Meg as a K-9 handler with the FBI's Forensic Canine Unit, specifically the Human Scent Evidence Team. Immediately preceding the wedding, Meg had come off a dangerous deployment in Colorado tracking a downed hijacked aircraft and the man responsible. The mission had been so treacherous, she'd nearly lost her partner, Brian Foster, to an avalanche. Thankfully, the Mountain Rescue Aspen team Meg and Brian had paired with, as well as Brian's own German shepherd, Lacey, had worked in concert to find and rescue Brian. They'd then successfully tracked the hijacker, though, in the end, Meg had been responsible for firing the shot that finally incapacitated him.

All had ended well, though, with the suspect injured—not killed—and taken into custody, and with Meg and Brian home in time to take their roles as bride and officiant at Meg and Todd's wedding ceremony. But there had been moments near the top of 14,029-foot Pyramid Peak when Meg hadn't been sure she'd make it back in time, or possibly even survive the excursion. Brian was the only member of the team who knew about Meg's fear of heights—not even their direct supervisor, Special-Agent-in-Charge Craig Beaumont, was aware—and while he'd done his best to support her, it had been an utterly nerve-rattling experience.

The Hawaiian Islands were formed by volcanoes—some still active. Hawaii's mountains were notably tall—while the peak of Mauna Kea on the Big Island was over 13,000 feet above sea level, its base was on the sea floor, making its full height 19,700 feet, taller than Mount Everest. Meg's twin goals for their time in Hawaii—besides time spent with Todd—was to relax away the extreme stress of that previous case and to stay as close to sea level as humanly possible on a volcanic island.

They were heading to the Big Island of Hawai'i next.

Their week on Lanai had been replete with sleep, gourmet food, swimming, beach walks, and hours of uninterrupted honeymoon sex, and while Meg had found the relaxation she craved a week ago, she was now getting antsy. She was used to an active life. She valued a relaxing vacation; however, at some point, she needed to get out and *do something*.

Clad in a sleep tank and shorts, she padded barefoot across the thick, plush carpet of the suite's living room toward the sliding patio door that led out to their private lanai. When they'd planned their honeymoon, they wanted their own private space, so they had booked an oceanfront studio suite for their use. Not too big, but enough space for private meals inside or out on the lanai, warm evenings cuddling on the couch, catching up on the latest mindless blockbuster, or a long soak in the deep whirlpool tub.

It had been heaven. But their active lifestyle could be set aside for only so long, and it was time to turn her thoughts toward returning to work. Lives could literally depend on them. The same could be said for Todd, though he'd slipped away a few times to hit the fitness center for a weight workout—when your survival and that of the firefighters beside you depended on being able to easily carry hundreds of pounds, maintaining that strength was crucial, even on your honeymoon.

It was time for them to get back into action, though of the vacation variety.

As if hearing her thoughts, her dog brushed against her leg as she grasped the handle of the sliding door. "Hey, buddy." She kept her voice just below a whisper, not wanting to wake Todd. She ran one hand over silky black fur as her dog looked up at her with a loving brown gaze. "Out we go." She slid the door open and stepped out onto warm tile flooring of their private lanai; even at this time of day, the temperature was close to eighty degrees Fahrenheit as the daytime temperatures only varied from the mid-seventies to the mid-eighties. She stepped over to the glass-fronted lanai railing and braced her forearms on sun-baked metal as she looked out at the scene below.

The resort was on the south face of the island of Lanai, perfectly situated to take in both sunrises to the east and sunsets to the west. They were on the second floor of the wing closest to the ocean, directly facing the turquoise and cerulean waters. Below the balcony, between the sturdy trunks of towering palm trees, gardens spread lush and green all the way downhill to the rocky ocean shore below. When she turned toward the east, Hulopoʻe Beach stretched wide—all white sand and crashing waves, where they'd enjoyed exploring the sea life in the tide pools.

Past the beach, a stunning sunrise was just breaking over the horizon, lighting the wispy clouds above in tones of mauve, fuchsia, and fiery ochre as the edge of the bright ball of sun peeked over the rolling waters, visible from her high perch. "Isn't that gorgeous?" Meg loosed a long, contented sigh as she took in the stunning colors, while a white-tailed tropicbird, its underside pure white, with black eye bars and long white tail streamers, soared overhead, its *keck-keck-keck* cry echoing over the rocky shoreline. A light, warm breeze ruffled her dark hair, streaming loose over her shoulders.

She jumped as a warm arm circled her waist, pulling her in against a hard body, while soft lips found the side of her neck. Light fabric brushed against her bare legs.

"Good morning." Todd's voice was low and raspy, still threaded with sleep.

Meg closed her eyes, tipping her head to the side to allow him better access. "Morning." The word slipped out on a hum of pleasure.

He pulled her in tighter, his cheek pressed to her temple as they looked out on the glorious sunny morning. "You snuck out of bed." His hand slipped under her tank top to stroke a thumb over her belly.

"I was awake and you were still sleeping. I didn't want to disturb you. I'm not there yet, but you seem to have finally switched over to this time zone."

"Five hours difference . . . it took a few days. Not that I minded getting up in the dark and watching night turn to day. Pretty spectacular." He chuckled. "Especially when I could then coax you back to bed."

"Oh, yeah, that took a lot of effort." She turned to face him, threading one hand through the hair at the back of his skull, and drew his mouth down to hers for a leisurely kiss. "I'm not sure how you managed the struggle."

He grinned at her. "You know us firefighters. Nothing stops us."

"A characteristic I've always appreciated when you're assisting with our cases." Her smile faded a bit as her gaze dropped down to Hawk.

"Hey." He waited until she met his eyes. "What's all that?"

"All what?"

He lightly tapped an index finger to her temple. "Whatever's going on up here. What were you thinking about when I interrupted you?"

"You didn't interrupt me." She turned in his arms to face the stunning vista before them. "I was appreciating the view."

"Undoubtedly. You'd have to be blind not to. And?"

Meg reminded herself that Todd's ability to discern her thoughts, allowing him to thoroughly understand her, was one of the reasons they worked so well. Any man who would partner with her had to understand the importance of her dog in her life, had to understand that Hawk was her canine soulmate—her heart dog. Many men would be jealous and would come to resent Hawk as a result. Todd was not one of those men.

"I've loved our week here together. It's been amazing. Relaxing, sexy"—she looked over her shoulder at him and gave him a wink—"with great food and wonderful scenery."

"But..."

"But I'm getting itchy. It's just been so..."

"Inactive," Todd finished for her. "I can see it in you, just like I feel it in me."

Suddenly the trips to the fitness center made more sense to Meg. "When you went to work out on the machines, it wasn't just about getting your reps in."

"It was, but it was also just working my body. You and me, we're not staid and inactive people. We're doers. And I agree, the week has been amazing, but I think a week of this kind of relaxation is all you and I can take."

Meg released a pent-up breath. "I'm so relieved to hear you say that. I didn't want you to think I wasn't loving this trip."

"I know you're having a good time. We've both enjoyed the break. And now it's time for us to start thinking about what we're going back to in a week. What do you have in mind?"

"You up for some parkour?"

"Absolutely."

"I need to get Hawk moving. The break has been good for him, too—that Colorado deployment took as much out of him as it did me with the physiological challenges of altitude—but I don't want him to lose his edge." Her gaze dropped to find Hawk staring up at her, his eyes full of both love and trust. He'd follow her anywhere, even over a cliff if she asked it of him—the trust went that deep. "As a team, we're nothing without him."

"The team is nothing without either one of you. He's

the nose, the driving force behind your searches, but he can't function without you to get him to where he needs to work, to read his signals, and to make sure he stays on course. Individually, you're both good. Together, you're amazing."

"Now you're just buttering me up to get me back into bed."

"I don't need to butter you up to do that." He waggled his eyebrows at her. "I can do that in so many other ways." He laughed when she turned and pressed both palms against his bare chest as if to push him and his confidence away, while his arms remained locked around her. "But I do know that kind of partnership needs constant work. Yes, it needs rest so you can recharge, but it's like any other muscle—it needs exercise to stay in shape. So let's keep it in shape. Works for me too. Lifting is great, but I admit I'd love a cardio workout. Parkour where?"

"We fly to the Big Island tomorrow for four days before we head to Oʻahu. From the research I did before we left, there are numerous places for hiking. We'll have a four-by-four to get us around, so we can hike a crater at Volcanoes National Park, or there's a nature reserve I want to check out, or there's a hike down to the ocean on the north end of the island." She grimaced. "Or we can hike up Mauna Kea. The visitor center is at eleven thousand feet, and you can drive or hike all the way to the top at thirteen thousand feet."

Todd cocked a single eyebrow at her. "Do I need to give you the altitude illness speech again?"

Meg laughed. "*No.* That one is last on my list. We just did a big mountain, so I'm happy to skip that one. I just wasn't sure if you'd like that experience. If not, there's lots more to do *much* lower down." She wound her arms around his neck. "You're really okay with us getting out there, rather than enjoying our privacy?"

"We've had a week to enjoy our privacy. And don't get me wrong, I *have* enjoyed it. But the important thing is we have another whole week to spend together." He dropped a hand from her hip to run it over Hawk's head. "With Hawk, of course."

"He's going to miss his time here. He's such a celebrity." Normally, the resort only allowed dogs up to fifteen pounds, but Meg had made special arrangements for Hawk as a law enforcement canine, and they essentially classified him as a service dog, allowing him to go anywhere on the resort as long as he was leashed with Meg or Todd, and was as well-behaved as Meg claimed him to be. Hawk went everywhere with them, always walking at heel at Meg's knee, or lying under their table on the patio at meals or by their chairs when one of them was swimming in one of the resort's two pools.

Guests were tickled by Hawk's presence and continually approached to greet him. Hawk loved people and clearly adored the attention, and he constantly won them over when Meg had him say hi—he would sit and politely offer a paw to shake—especially children, many of whom returned again and again to pet and praise the black Lab. He loved every second of it, and Meg was happy to let him bask in the adoration. If they wanted privacy, they could eat in their suite, and by and large, people were good about not disturbing them too much.

"I'm sure he'll be a celebrity when we settle at Waikōloa. Hiking and parkour on the Big Island starting tomorrow, after one more day of peace, quiet, and laziness here. Does that sound good?"

"It does to me."

"Excellent. Starting now." Bending, he slipped one arm under her knees and one behind her back and lifted her off her feet.

Meg's small gasp of surprise rolled into a laugh. "What do you have in mind?" She purposefully echoed his own words back to him.

His laugh was deep and rife with anticipation. "How about I show you?"

Her laugh trailed behind them as he carried her into the suite and toward the bedroom, leaving the sliding door open, allowing Hawk to follow whenever he was ready.

CHAPTER 2

Preparation phase: The first stage of a volcanic eruption where magma rises from deep in the earth to fill the magma chamber beneath the summit of a volcano.

May 29, 9:37 AM
Puʻu Makaʻala Natural Area Reserve
Volcano, Hawaiʻi

"Watch your head." Meg pushed the enormous fan of a fern branch high over her head and ducked under it to continue down the trail.

The Department of Land and Natural Resources' definition of an established hiking trail wasn't entirely accurate. Deep in the Puʻu Makaʻala Natural Area Reserve, there often wasn't a visible footpath. If it wasn't for the very occasional blue band tied around a tree trunk or fern branch—some now tumbled to the ground—Meg wouldn't be sure they were still on the trail.

Armed with her satellite phone with GPS and mapping functions, she wasn't concerned; they'd find their way out. They'd purposely left their hotel early that morning to make sure there was plenty of daylight to guide their steps. With a two-hour drive there and back, they'd wanted an early start to give them plenty of time to explore.

This deep into the forest, daylight was surprisingly scarce, blocked by not only the towering canopy, but the thick understory. The surrounding plants were mostly ferns of different shapes and sizes—from small ground cover ferns, bursting from the soft loamy soil, to huge tree ferns, their stocky trunks four or five feet tall before they exploded into a mass of thick stalks, each two or three inches across and bearing a fern frond six or eight feet long. Fiddleheads, some two or three feet high, pushed through mounds of dried, brown tangles of dead fronds to reach skyward. Hardwood trees stretched tall, their canopy high above the ferns, their leaves seeking the sun. Overhead, bursts of red flowers dotted the treetops as the backlit silhouettes of birds flitted between branches, their high-pitched calls filtering down to ground level. The forest carried the odors of rich, damp soil and vigorous plant life, the humidity-drenched air touched with the organic scent of the dead and dying foliage.

Meg patted her thigh twice. "Hawk, come."

Hawk ran unleashed, giving him the freedom to move around obstacles without being tied to his handler. Meg was comfortable with the arrangement as the Lab was extremely responsive to voice commands. Even more so if Meg used his "don't-mess-with-me" name—Talon—only ever used during urgent times of unquestioning and immediate compliance, usually when lives were on the line.

Hawk had briefly paused to sniff at a pile of downed fern fronds; he now trotted to catch up to Meg, with Todd bringing up the rear.

Meg climbed over the trunk of a large, downed tree. It was awkward hopping over it rather than stepping on it when it lay at an angle, jammed between a pair of hardwoods. Deep in the forest, nature ran its course—trees fell, ferns wilted, wildlife died, all remaining where they fell, slowly breaking down and returning to the earth, as nature intended. Which meant Meg couldn't be sure if the tree could hold her weight. This was definitely not the location for an injury, even if she was accompanied by a paramedic. Todd shouldered Meg's go bag backpack with basic supplies for all three of them, including Meg's first aid kit, but he wasn't carrying his professional med kit.

Meg checked the ground on the other side of the obstruction, finding it clear. She slapped a hand on the log, covered with thick green moss, which oozed retained water under the force of her palm. "Hawk, over." Meg stepped back, allowing Hawk to leap over the log, only skidding slightly as he landed in the muddy soil on the far side. Taller than Meg's nearly six-foot frame by several inches, most of it in his legs, Todd stepped over the log with considerably more ease.

The life that surrounded them was a vivid, lush green. Here on the windward side of the Big Island, the clouds came often, carried on trade winds from the east, forced upward by a pair of thirteen-thousand-foot mountains, where the water vapor they carried condensed and fell on the east side of the mountain, often torrentially. The two sides of the island were diametrically opposed environments—desert-like lava fields stretched for miles on the western side, dotted with explosions of feathery desert pili grasses, while the eastern side was a verdant jungle.

Deep in the forest, the quiet was almost otherworldly. The wind only seemed to touch the very treetops; here on the ground, there were only the sounds of their boot steps, breathing, the jingle of Hawk's collar, and the call of birds high above. Otherworldly, but extremely peaceful.

Meg took another step, her waterproof hiking boot sinking deep into wet mud on the narrow, winding hint of a path. Her weather app had told her the preceding few days had brought over five inches of rain, and it felt like much of it had collected in this nearly 19,000 acres of protected land.

"Entertain me while we're doing this." Todd's voice came from behind her. "What is this place? When we were planning this trip, I remember you saying it's not on any hiking trail app, but any other details got lost in the rest of the chaos around your deployment and the wedding. How did you find it?"

"I could have filled you in over the past week, but you seemed... distracted." She turned and flashed him a smile.

He met her smile with his own. "Can you blame me? By the time we get back, we'll be a boring, old married couple. Had to take advantage while I could."

"With our lives, do you honestly think we're going to be boring?"

"Good point. So, this place? I get Volcanoes National Park—where else are we going to be able to walk an active volcano, even if it's not currently erupting?—but this place is utterly deserted."

Todd wasn't wrong. Their driving directions had come from a website that listed the three old-growth forests on the Hawaiian Islands; Puʻu Makaʻala—which translated to "watchful hill"—was the only such forest on the island of Hawaiʻi. After driving through the town of Volcano, just outside of Volcanoes National Park, they'd driven northwest until they ran out of road and pulled through gates where a sign buried in foliage announced they were entering Hawaii's Department of Land and Natural Resources reserve. From then on, it was twin dirt, tooth-rattling tracks for a half mile before they entered a small green space, fenced in on all sides except for the entrance they'd used, with signage, a wood ladder angled into an inverted V over the wire wildlife fence, and a self-closing raised metal gate for anyone who thought the ladder looked too rickety.

Meg, Todd, and Hawk had all opted for the gate.

The most notable aspect of the reserve was undoubtedly the isolation. Civilization was approximately a mile away in the form of occupied homes and farms, but deep in the forest, they felt very much alone. No one else was at the reserve that morning, and the moment they passed through the gate separating the small clearing and the forest proper, it was obvious not many people ever visited Puʻu Makaʻala.

"I was looking for less-traveled places for us to hike." Meg pitched her voice loud enough that Todd could hear as she pushed her way through the fronds that blocked their path and reached out to catch at her ponytail. "Places where I could let Hawk run off leash. You and I know he's safe off leash, but your average hiker doesn't, and could flip out and make trouble. Some of the places we're visiting, we'll have to contend with crowds. In places like Volcanoes National Park, I have permission to bring him, again classified as a service dog, as long as he remains leashed at all times and isn't detrimental to the park ecosystem management, which he won't be."

"Not a chance."

"It's an exception, however, as that's an area where pets aren't allowed. They made it clear dogs have been lost going over cliffs after birds or have gotten into trouble falling into steam vents around the park in the past, so pets aren't allowed. It's a privilege to bring him with us, and I know it. I wanted to find a place where we could get his unleashed parkour workout in, and Puʻu Makaʻala seemed perfect. It's protected because it houses a number of endangered and threatened plant and bird species and is kind of off the beaten path. And though the trail is clearly marked and hiking is allowed, none of the major hiking apps include it, maybe because of the protected status."

"I've never been on a hiking trail before where there's a boot brush station so you can clean your boots before going in to avoid carrying in any invasive plant species."

"They're careful, and you can't blame them for it. Also, did you see the sign at the entry gate? This is a sacred space to the Hawaiian people, which is why all this acreage is fenced off to keep the feral pigs and goats out. And to protect the endangered native plant species."

They had yet to see a feral pig during their time on the islands, but wild goats were visible scattered over the lands surrounding the highways on the west side of Hawai'i and over the long run of Saddle Road, which wound between Mauna Kea and Mauna Loa's peaks.

"You'll keep Hawk to the main trail." Behind her, Todd paused, and Meg imagined he was scanning their surroundings. "Such as it is," he finished.

"Such as it is. We have rocks and the scattering of rubber steps the Department of Land and Natural Resources put in for the really tricky spots, as well as some fallen trees I can see are intact. He's getting his workout. And so are we because we're making our way up the lower reaches of Mauna Loa. We've probably climbed close to a thousand feet by now, and are probably about five thousand feet above sea level. I'd say we're about a third of the way up, but it's all part of the exertion." Meg rolled her shoulders and shook out her hands. "This is my way to climb a mountain."

"Feeling good?"

"Absolutely." Meg turned to look down at Hawk—his eyes bright, his steps quick, even in the soggy mud, and his fringed tail high and waving happily. "So is Hawk. He loves this. He's not officially working, but his nose hasn't stopped since we went through the gate."

"It must be a kaleidoscope of scent here. Maybe not so much in the way of fauna, but the flora is over the top."

"That's an understatement."

They reached a winding series of steps that cut into a steep rise, crosshatched black rubber platforms nailed into place with sturdy spikes. Meg hoisted herself up the first few steps, steadying herself on a thick fern stem. But on the next step, her muddy boot slipped. She reached out with her left hand for another stem, but it immediately gave way under her grip, its dead, hollow length not able to carry her weight. She lurched sideways just as Todd's warning call of caution sounded, then her hand closed around a live stem and she steadied herself.

She turned around to find that Todd had stepped in front of Hawk, positioned to catch her if she windmilled backward.

"You okay?" he asked.

"Yeah, sorry about that. My boots are muddy and I slipped." She reached up and ran a hand over the back of her neck where the thick humidity had sweat trickling. "Can you stay behind Hawk in case he does the same?"

"Sure."

"Hawk, up. Come!"

The dog managed better, his pads giving him traction. As Meg mounted the steps to the top, Hawk took them at a run, coming to stand beside her, his tongue lolling joyfully from his panting mouth, his eyes sparkling with happiness.

"You're having a ball, aren't you?" Meg bent down and dropped a kiss on the top of his head, then straightened and took a step back. "Come, Hawk. Todd, you're clear."

He joined them, taking the stairs carefully to avoid any mishaps, and then they hiked farther up the path, its length nearly invisible, hidden beneath a carpet of dead tree leaves and a blanket of soggy brown fern fronds, long fallen from their stalks.

Sudden silence made Meg pause—several long seconds

where the constant chatter of the birds above fell eerily silent. She cast her eyes skyward. "Do you hear that?"

"Hear what?"

"Exactly. The birds have gone—"

The earth suddenly rolled beneath her feet, a strong vibration that had her sidestepping as she was thrown off-balance.

Earthquake!

CHAPTER 3

Volatiles: Chemicals present in magma that expand rapidly during a volcanic eruption, increasing the eruption intensity. This class of chemicals includes water, carbon dioxide, sulfur, and chlorine.

May 29, 10:06 AM
Puʻu Makaʻala Natural Area Reserve
Volcano, Hawaiʻi

Meg caught her balance, bracing herself in a wide stance, instinctively turning to plant one boot beside her dog and dropping her hand onto his back to keep him close. His apprehension and uneasiness radiated through the tense muscles under her fingers and the raised line of fur running between his shoulder blades. A quick glance behind showed Todd similarly braced, his gaze scanning the trees and ferns around them. They swayed for only a handful of seconds, and then the ground quieted again as they all remained locked in place for an extended moment.

Seconds later, birdsong filled the air.

"Was that . . . ?"

"An earthquake? Yes." Todd stepped closer to them, as if preparing for an oncoming wave. "A fairly strong one, too, though I doubt enough to damage any of the local buildings. Kainalu wasn't kidding. I thought he was exaggerating a bit. Spinning a tale."

"He's done that a few times already for the entertainment of guests, so you wouldn't have been off base taking it that way."

They'd been leaving that morning when Kainalu—one of the outside attendants at the front door—had wished them a good day. When they'd told him where they were going, Kainalu had cautioned them he'd seen on the news that Mauna Loa was grumbling and the southern section of the island was experiencing tremors. He'd described it with the same grandiose flair of his other tales, making it seem like another larger-than-life story.

Apparently not.

Mauna Loa hadn't erupted for thirty-five years. In the decades before that, the volcano had erupted roughly every five years, and the locals recognized they were more than due for Mauna Loa's fire. Nearby volcano Kīlauea had erupted catastrophically only the previous year, with Fissure 8 on the eastern tip of the island opening and wiping out hundreds of houses and displacing thousands of residents as molten rock spewed and surged inexorably downhill toward the ocean.

"I'm regretting not paying enough attention to that last eruption when it was on the news," Meg said. "Might have been helpful now."

"Me too. It's not the same volcano, but the geology will be extremely similar this close together. I remember the news stories, remember no one died, but there was catastrophic damage. It seemed a long way away when we were home in DC." Todd looked down at the fallen fern fronds ground into the dirt under his boots. "It's hitting a little closer to home now. For everyone's safety, we better bone up on some emergency measures in case we need them."

"Agreed. Chances of it being a problem likely approach zero, but we both like being prepared, so let's do it anyway." Meg dropped down to a squat, balanced on the balls of her feet to be eye-to-eye with her dog as she ran her hands over him. He'd relaxed somewhat but was still braced as if expecting another tremor. "It's okay, Hawk. All done." She squinted up at Todd. "He was behind me. Do you think he sensed it coming?"

"He paused for a minute, but I assumed he did because you did."

"I did because the birds went quiet. They must have known it was coming. Pretty sure Hawk did too. Maybe he could hear the vibrations coming before they hit."

"If so, they must have been at a frequency only he could hear because we certainly missed it. He's still on alert. Think he can still hear something?"

"Possibly. But it must be fading fast as the wave moves away from us, unless there's a second wave headed our way." She looked up at Todd. "We were lucky we weren't in a more vulnerable position. Quakes have aftershocks. Or that might have just been a warning shot across the bow. We need to keep that in mind." She smoothed the fur down Hawk's back with one hand, glad to see his body sway slightly; he was relaxing. She pushed to her feet. "Let's keep going. I know you're already keeping an eye on him to make sure he doesn't run into trouble, but watch for him to react to something we can't see. It could give us a few seconds to prepare in case that was Mauna Loa's opening volley."

"Will do."

They continued down the trail, Meg confirming every so often they were on the right track by the blue bands still appearing sporadically. Through the thick forest, over rocks, squeezing between tree trunks and around stands of giant ferns, they delved deeper into the natural area reserve.

"I think Hawk can hear something."

Meg stopped dead at Todd's words. She swiveled around to look at her dog—rather than tense and braced, he seemed alert and intrigued, his head turned to their left. She followed his gaze, but all she could see was sunlight-dappled fern fronds reaching ten or twelve feet high, with smaller ferns and dead stems filling any open space beneath, and slender tree trunks climbing higher above them. "I don't think it's another tremor. That startled him. He'd react negatively to another one. Right now, he just looks interested." She studied her dog for another long span of seconds. "He's either hearing something, or he may be picking up some scent."

"It doesn't feel like there's enough air movement down here for that."

"The wind is definitely in the treetops, but I agree, it's pretty quiet at ground level. Still, there may be enough minimal air movement to carry something to him." A flash of memory came to her and she grimaced.

Todd's look was pure suspicion. "What?"

"The last time he caught a thread of scent like that, it led to Rita Pratt's dead body, my suspension, and the risk of Hawk being taken away from me."

"You think he's scenting a dead body?"

"No." Meg blew out a breath and peered through the greenery again. "I mean, what would be the chances?"

Todd leveled her with a pointed look. "I'd say not terrible based on past performances. You think he's hearing other hikers? It's extremely isolated out here—how likely is that?"

"Not impossible, but most hikers would be like us and

sticking to the path. This is clearly off path. And from studying maps of the areas when I was planning, we're toward the west edge of the natural area reserve. The chances of the path veering further west at that angle versus continuing on into the greater reserve is essentially nonexistent, but I can't discount he's picking something up. Possibly someone lost or in trouble. Why else would they be out here in this remote area off what little of the path we're following?"

"We're equipped to find our way back if we get lost in this jungle, I assume?"

"For sure. I can note this location on the GPS and get us back to it. Or take us directly to the car, because I noted that too. We won't get lost."

"Normal hikers wouldn't have your technology. Cell phone coverage could be spotty this deep into the reserve, even if we're not really that far from civilization. Anyone lost in here could easily wander deeper into the jungle rather than coming out of it."

"You want to go after them. I can hear it in your tone of voice." Meg's statement wasn't accusatory—it was a direct statement of fact. She knew her husband, knew how his mind worked.

"Well . . . yeah. If someone needs help . . ."

"It's what we do, and we're currently equipped to do it. Or could call for assistance if we're not." She eyed the dense, tangled underbrush. "It's not going to be an easy hike. And I have no idea how Hawk would even manage to work a scent cone in here."

Scent particles diffused downwind of a target object in a cone shape—narrow close to the target and expanding in ever-widening waves with greater distance. A trained K-9 walking into a scent cone would move perpendicular to the wind, following the cone to the edge of scent and then turning to traverse to the far side of the cone, each pass getting smaller and smaller until the dog closed in on the target object. There was no way to work the scent cone in the usual pattern in this jungle.

"Chances are extremely high we're going to walk out of the scent cone, and he may not be able to pick it up again."

"And if he's not smelling something, but hearing something we're not?"

Meg studied Hawk, his ears perked high as he leaned on every sense. "That would help give him directionality."

"I'm willing to try, if you are."

"I am."

Hawk passed his weight from paw to paw, as if holding himself back from leaping into the ferns because he didn't have Meg's permission yet.

"And so is Hawk. He's going to want to take off like a cork coming out of a bottle. I'll use voice commands to keep him with us because I don't want him getting separated from us in this. Leashing him off the path is an even bigger no-go than on the path. Too much risk of getting jammed up. If worst comes to worst, I have the whistle for longer-distance recall, but I'd rather not have to use it." She looked up at Todd. "Ready?"

He bounced on his toes once to resettle the backpack. "Ready."

"Here we go. Hawk." Meg waited as her dog quieted in response to her tone, his eyes raising to hers. She could read his enthusiasm and anticipation in their depths, as if he'd spoken his wishes out loud. "Find, Hawk. Find whatever has your attention."

Hawk burst into motion like a sprinter out of the starting blocks, arrowing into the thick ferns to the left of the path. Meg mumbled a curse as he seemed to pick the thickest stand of greenery and then followed directly behind him. "Slow, Hawk. Slow. Stay with me." She didn't need to check to see if Todd was behind her; she could hear him hacking his way through the foliage.

It was slow going in the extreme, forging a path where none existed. Even Hawk, who had the advantage of being able to wind around the trunks of fern trees—whereas Meg and Todd had to push through the thick fronds on stubborn woody stems above—had difficulty maneuvering through the lush plants. Even worse for the dog were the snarls of dead ferns close to the ground. Meg had to push forward to stomp down several tangles to allow her dog to proceed on the path only he could detect, one he clearly didn't want to deviate from.

Ten minutes in, Meg called for a break. "Hawk, stop." She caught up to him, breathing heavily. Even for someone in top physical condition, this was a solid workout. "Let's get you some water. You haven't had any since we started this hike. Todd." She made a twirling motion with her index finger, and he turned his back to her, allowing her to extract Hawk's collapsible water dish and one of the sturdy plastic water bottles they'd filled at the hotel before departing. She poured water into his bowl and set it on a flat level patch covered with a swath of narrow, twisted dead leaves. As he lapped, she downed a long series of swallows, then handed the bottle to Todd to do the same.

A sheen of sweat covered his forehead and his breaths came harder, but, like her, he was nowhere near winded. "Are we getting closer? Can you tell?"

"He's very focused. He stopped on command, but I can tell from how restless he is he's still on the scent.

Likely more so than at the beginning." Hawk finished his water, and she repacked the dish and bottle. "Okay, Hawk. Find."

The search continued.

Fifteen minutes later, Meg was confident they hadn't left the natural area reserve, as they had yet to hit the wire fencing containing the protected space, but she suspected they were getting close. The environment was nearly identical to the area surrounding the path, though the birdsong seemed louder, more varied. The birds possibly felt safer in this area, left fallow to allow protected species a safe space to thrive. She could only hope she, Todd, and Hawk weren't doing significant damage in their quest to help some poor, lost soul. They were doing their best to leave as few footprints as possible, but it was impossible not to make an impression. As it was, a search that should have taken them likely under ten minutes was taking easily four times that.

Hawk abruptly stopped, the fur on his back rising in alarm.

"Brace yourself," Meg threw over her shoulder to Todd as she planted her boots, ready for the tremor Hawk was signaling to hit. Yet as long seconds passed and the earth remained still, Meg second-guessed herself. Returning her gaze to Hawk, she realized his stance was one bordering on aggression, not fear. "Hawk, stop," she ordered. "Sit."

Hawk paused, clearly torn.

Apprehension crawled up the back of Meg's neck. This was very unlike Hawk; he wasn't the aggressive type, so for him to behave this way meant only one thing.

She had a brief mental flash of Hawk soaring through the air to latch his teeth onto Daniel Mannew's wrist, just above where he gripped the gun fixed on Meg. Then of Hawk bursting from behind their office door to leap on

Lou Giraldi's back as he straddled Meg, sinking his teeth deep into her attacker's flesh before he could sexually assault her, then beat or strangle her to death on the floor of her own home.

Hawk had saved her life multiple times, and would always rise to the occasion when required. The only time he ever broke from his usual easygoing temperament was when he was defensive of *her*. Which meant he sensed something ahead was dangerous.

"Hawk, sit." There was no mistaking the command in Meg's tone this time.

The Lab sat, but his unease didn't waver.

"What's going on?" Todd asked.

"I'm not sure." Meg kept her voice low, suspecting it wouldn't carry through the tangled stalks, trunks, and branches, but not wanting to take any chances. "Something's making Hawk uneasy. At first I thought it might be another tremor, but his attitude is all wrong. He's not scared; he's on the defensive for some reason. Stay here with Hawk. I need to see what's going on."

Todd grabbed her upper arm before she could take a single step, holding tight. "He's gone defensive. That could mean trouble. And you intend to walk straight into it? I know you can take care of yourself, but you're not carrying."

"No, I'm not. But now I suspect something is wrong, I can't just stroll away without checking it out." She met his gaze so he couldn't doubt her determination. "I won't take any chances, I swear. If it's something I'm not prepared to take on, I'll pull back. Then I'll be able to call for assistance if it's needed."

She could see the battle warring in his eyes, but he released her nonetheless.

This was part of their relationship—the understanding between them that they both did dangerous activities as part of their day-to-day lives. Todd regularly ran straight into infernos everyone else was trying to escape; Meg handled dangerous search scenarios and tangled with criminals as part of the team's work with the FBI. Their agreement was that neither would ask the other to step back from what they considered their duty. Meg had once been a Richmond Police Department K-9 patrol officer with her late K-9 Deuce, who was lost in the line of duty. Her grief over his death had driven her out of the force, but she'd never lost her law enforcement sensibilities. That same sense of duty drove her now.

Todd didn't like it, but he understood. Still, his eyes held deep unease.

Meg turned to her dog. "Hawk, stay with Todd. *Stay.*"

Her dog let out a low whine of unease, but sat at Todd's side.

Meg turned away from Todd before the look in his eye coerced her to let it go. She pushed into a thicket of especially dense fern fronds, yanking free the greenery that caught in her hair, and forced her way through. She spluttered as a fern stalk slipped from her grasp, the wide frond bouncing back to slap her in the face, clamping down on the knee-jerk instinct to react vocally. Not being sure what she was walking into, silence—as hard as it would be in this environment—was crucial.

Silently spitting out a fern leaf, she pushed the stem down and to her left as she stepped around it, sliding another branch out of her way as she slipped to the right.

She moved as quietly through the forest as she could, careful of every step and how each branch groaned as she tried to clear a way through. All around her were normal forest sounds—birds calling and the gentle rustle of leaves overhead—but nothing indicated a problem.

Holding on to a tree trunk, she stepped over a felled tangle of dead stems and leaves, then pushed through a dense mass of lush fronds.

And stepped out of the shaded wall of greenery into an unexpectedly open clearing.

Her blood went cold despite her overheated body. Since she'd set foot in this jungle, minus the narrow, winding hiking trail, there hadn't been an open space larger than a few feet, as nature always filled a vacuum. Now here was a huge section, open almost all the way to the canopy that continued to shade the forest floor below.

She jerked to a halt, trying to take in everything in a single lightning-fast scan.

She stood at the edge of a space about thirty feet wide, one clearly constructed without care for any of the reserve's protected species. Trees formed a rough circle around the area, while the more pliant ferns and underbrush that filled the shallow gully had been ruthlessly hacked down and carelessly tossed in a pile or trampled cruelly underfoot. A single fern tree lay toppled near its stump, its top stalks just beginning to brown, telling how recently it had been felled.

As horrifying as the damage was to the fern forest, it was the two men across the clearing who riveted her attention.

One man was bent toward the ground, examining something with his back to her, while the other stood in front of a row of swaying cloth bags hanging from a sturdy rope strung between tree trunks. Both whirled upright and around at the sound of her unexpected entrance.

The ex-cop in her automatically cataloged their traits.

Blond, short-cut, just over six feet, 220 pounds.

Brunette, longer hair, five nine or five ten, 180 pounds.

Both wearing heavy boots, dark pants, and unzipped, lightweight jackets over dark shirts.

The air around them felt soupy with humidity as the panicked calls of birds rose stridently over the silence of three humans staring at each other.

The dark-haired man darted a hand inside his jacket, and Meg caught a glimpse of the pale strapping of a shoulder holster tucked under his left arm.

Armed and apparently ready to shoot or at least threaten without a single word of warning or question.

Run!

She whipped around and launched herself at the greenery, pushing through as hard as she could, wanting to disappear into the forest on her feet so when she went horizontal once she was hidden, they'd be shooting over her head.

She knew it was a risk, but she had to warn Todd and Hawk. *"Talon, down!"*

She knew it was the only command she'd need. Hawk would immediately go down. Todd would instantly understand her use of the "don't-mess-with-me" name and would follow suit automatically. Knowing her husband, as soon as the order was given, he'd be splayed over her dog, just as she would have had he been with her. They'd both protect Hawk at all costs.

She cursed as the thick stems and leaves slowed her pace as she pushed against them with all her might, any thought of protecting the environment forgotten. She was in real trouble if she couldn't lose herself in the jungle simply because it was too thick to penetrate.

Bullets would have no such trouble.

The sound of the first gunshot blasted through the air, and bird calls exploded along with the din of scores of flapping wings and disturbed branches as any bird in the area took flight in a desperate attempt to escape.

A blinding flash of pain ripped through Meg's left arm, agony flaming like someone had stabbed her with a red-hot poker.

The thought ricocheted through her brain with the speed of a bullet.

She'd been shot.

CHAPTER 4

Magma: Molten rock within the earth's core from which igneous rock is formed after cooling and solidifying.

May 29, 11:05 AM
Puʻu Makaʻala Natural Area Reserve
Volcano, Hawaiʻi

Meg couldn't hold back the involuntary cry of pain, then immediately clamped her jaw shut, not allowing any other sound that might further pinpoint her position.

Far enough into the thick foliage or not, she had to take cover before the next bullet was a headshot. She also needed to know how badly she'd been hurt, but that would have to wait. The severity of that shot wouldn't matter if a second shot pierced her skull or heart. She dove into an explosion of fern fronds, crushing the tender plants as she fell, hitting the ground belly-down hard enough to knock the wind from her lungs, her arms thrown up to protect her head. The shock of the impact rattled her frame, and she nearly screamed as burning pain radiated into her torso and down to her fingertips, but somehow managed to swallow the outburst.

Four more shots rang out, each *crack* immediately swallowed by the thick foliage, followed by the sound of crashing into the forest.

Not in this direction, thank God.

The crashing gradually grew more distant.

Meg lay on the ground, panting through teeth gritted against the pain, every sense on overdrive, ready to spring to her feet to launch herself into the fray and retreat to protect her partner and dog. Though it wouldn't be much of a fight, as she'd already been hit and she lacked a deadly weapon.

Luckily, that sacrifice would not be required.

Pain radiated from just below her shoulder, stabbing fiery arrows down her arm and across her back. She drew in a deep breath, trying to fight back the agony. She forced her breathing into a measured inhale and exhale, and slowly, the waves of pain receded slightly.

She waited thirty seconds with no indication of human life before she raised her head, listening intently. Shrill bird calls still filled the air, but the sounds of man had entirely disappeared.

Rather than pursuing, they'd fled? The whole situation was odd—the two men had come armed into the middle of a protected forest region, had pulled out lethal firepower at the first sign of discovery, and then had fled, rather than pursuing their target?

What had she walked into? What had they been doing that they felt they needed to shoot, cut, and run? There was no doubt in her mind she'd stumbled across something illegal.

Only one way to find out. But first she had to make sure Todd and Hawk weren't hurt.

She grimaced. *Todd.* She was injured—again. He was not going to be happy.

She pulled up a bit higher, craning her neck to see as much of her left shoulder as possible. Bright scarlet drenched the entire length of her athletic tee's sleeve down to her wrist. It was cooler at this altitude, and she'd thought it wise to stay covered when pushing through the jungle, so she'd worn one of the usual wicking athletic shirts she standardly donned for searches. But now the length meant she couldn't flip up the edge of the sleeve to see the injury. She grimaced at the sight of so much blood and the long tear that shredded the sleeve where it curved around her arm, but she couldn't see the extent of the injury.

Using her right hand as she held her left arm close to her body, she pushed back from the ground, folding into child's pose with her thighs over her calves and her torso stretched long—*Thanks, Cara, for all the yoga sessions*—and held there for a moment. The pain in her left arm was fading slightly, but she wasn't about to jostle it by rushing.

She slowly straightened to a kneeling position and, grasping her left elbow, tried to rotate her arm to get a better view. Pain rocketed through her body, and she bit back a curse. She let go quickly. Better to let the professional assess her and do his thing. Best thing she could do now was get him here.

It was quiet in the direction of the clearing, but it was also quiet where Todd and Hawk still sheltered. Not necessarily too quiet—Todd would be keeping Hawk down and safe—but it was time to confirm all was well. She wasn't bleeding so copiously she thought a major blood vessel had been hit, but she wanted to play it safe and let them come to her.

She dug into the right pocket on the side of her yoga pants and pulled out a short whistle.

It was a skill they almost never used, and usually the whistle rolled around at the bottom of her go bag, but Hawk was trained to recall at the sound of three short whistles. Normally, they were never separated by so great a distance that she simply couldn't call him back. However, deep in the fern forest, she'd worried he'd have trouble hearing her voice if they split up. The whistle, on the other hand, was at a frequency that could cut through the terrain and would still be audible to him, so she'd slipped it into her pocket that morning, just in case. More than that, if the men were still around, they might not be able to distinguish the whistle from the sounds of the birds.

She raised the whistle to her lips and blew three sharp, clear tones. Then she dropped her hand into her lap, the whistle wrapped in her fist, and waited. She'd give them up to five minutes to find her, and then she'd whistle again, but she suspected it wouldn't take that long. The sound would be Hawk's cue to get up, even if that meant scrambling out from under Todd, and immediately following her scent. Todd would gamely follow along, knowing Hawk was reacting to something Todd couldn't sense. Todd might have even heard the sound himself and not identified it as human-made, but he would know to trust Hawk.

Two minutes later, thrashing came from south of Meg's position and she slipped the whistle into her pocket. It was too much volume for it to be just her dog, which loosened some of the knot in her gut. Her arm had calmed down to a burning throb, and she was glad Todd would be here soon to look at it, even as she dreaded the worry she was about to cause him.

Seconds later, Hawk shot through the ferns and nearly fell over her, then danced around her in joy at their reunion, despite the small space. It only took a moment for the smell of blood to cut through his joy and to register that something was seriously wrong. He calmed down as if a bucket of water had been tossed over him.

When Todd pushed his way through, he found Meg kneeling on the bed of crushed fern fronds, her right arm draped over her dog. His sharp gaze swept over her, his relief at finding her in one piece shining in his eyes until he moved in far enough to see her left arm. Then his expression morphed to a mix of concern and clinical assessment.

He dropped to his knees beside her, shimmied out of the backpack, and gently cupped her left elbow, quickly examining as much of the wound as he could see through her blood-soaked sleeve. "I'd ask what you found, but I think that's going to have to wait for a minute. Are we safe here?"

"Yes. Best I can tell, they took off."

" 'They'?" Todd pulled Meg's first aid kit from the backpack. He opened the kit and pulled on latex gloves, then laid out the supplies he'd need before beginning the process of carefully pulling the fabric of Meg's sleeve away to fully assess her wound.

"I interrupted two men." She sucked in air through gritted teeth. "In a clearing to the north of us."

"A clearing?" Surprise and disbelief rang clear in Todd's tone. "Here?"

"Not a natural one. They chopped down a bunch of ferns to open up part of the forest. I didn't have time for more than a cursory look before one of them went for the gun he wore in a shoulder holster under his jacket. That ended the conversation before it began. I dove for cover in the forest just before the first shots." She looked down at her arm. "I didn't get far enough in, and I didn't have time to get down before the bullets started flying. How's it look?"

"Like you were shot." His hands bloody, he reached for the scissors in her first aid kit and made quick work of snipping the sleeve off above her wound, then sliding the material down her arm and off her hand. He dropped it onto the broken branches beside him.

"You sound pissed."

"That someone did this to you? Of course I'm pissed."

"Are you mad at me?"

He was silent for a prolonged moment, then exhaled. "At you? No. At the situation? Damn straight. You were shot on our honeymoon."

"You know me, always getting into some scrape." Meg tried to make light of it, but knew her words fell flat from the set of Todd's mouth. She laid a hand on his forearm. "I'm sorry."

"There's nothing for you to apologize for. It's not like you planned this. Just wrong place, wrong time." He paused for a moment. "This could have been so much worse." His fingers tightened on her arm, a silent acknowledgment that she could have been killed.

"I think it would have been worse for anyone who didn't react as quickly as I did."

"You . . . an ex-cop and current FBI contractor? You'd sum up a situation in milliseconds and make the call to get the hell out. A normal person would have paused for an extra three seconds and then might have frozen at the sight of a gun."

"I never saw the actual gun. The shoulder holster was enough to get me moving." She hissed with pain as he drew a ragged, blood-soaked thread from the wound. "How bad is it? I couldn't get a good look at it. Bad angle. Did the bullet go through? I don't think it hit bone. I can still move the arm—it just hurts like someone set it on fire."

"GSWs are excruciating. Lucky for us, it's not even a through and through. The bullet carved a meaty trough out of the outside of your upper arm, but never penetrated. It didn't hit your cephalic vein, or your brachial artery, or we'd be in big trouble all the way out here. You've lost more than enough blood, but it's all from smaller vessels."

"I'm afraid to ask, but does it need stitching?" She paused for a moment. "Did you bring supplies for that?"

"Of course I did. From the bigger first aid kit at home. I started stocking the kit at home differently after Giraldi's attack. In this case, however, there's really nothing to stitch. It's more like a long burn. I'm going to clean and dress it and apply a compression bandage to control the bleeding. Then you need to call 911. You don't need medical, but you do need law enforcement."

Meg groaned. "I'm sure they're going to be thrilled to hear from me. They always love it when the Bureau sticks its nose in."

"This is hardly sticking your nose in. You're carrying your ID?"

"In back, in my waistband pocket, as usual. When Hawk and I are out and about, I never know when I might need to justify taking him somewhere. Or if I need official ID to assist if a situation pops up on the fly. But let's wait on calling. I'd like to see what I interrupted before I call so I can tell the locals what we're looking at."

"I get that." Todd met her eyes. "I'm going to irrigate your wound with sterile saline and then disinfect it with povidone-iodine. It shouldn't hurt too badly, not like it was alcohol, but I'm still washing out an open wound, so it's going to be uncomfortable."

"Good thing someone who knows what he's doing and is always prepared keeps my first aid kit stocked."

"And then some for this trip. I've learned to always expect the unexpected with you and Hawk. This is just another example." Todd's gaze dropped to where Meg sat with her arm still looped over Hawk. "You might want to let go of him, rather than risk squeezing him too tight. If I had my full med kit, I'd treat with lidocaine before doing this, but there was only so much I could pack into your little kit, knowing we were going to be on the move."

"It's the thought that counts."

"Remember that sentiment in about thirty seconds."

She pulled away from her dog and ran her hand down his back. "Good boy, buddy. Now sit and keep me company." She took a deep breath. "Do it."

"Yes, ma'am." He shifted backward a foot, then cupped her elbow, raising her upper arm to be parallel to the ground and then carefully rotated it outward so all fluids washing over the wound would fall into the scattered fern fronds on the ground. "Hold still like this. I'll be as quick and gentle as possible, but I need to clean this out or you risk infection with such an open wound."

"You'd never let that happen. Let's get it over with."

True to his word, Todd was quick and gentle, but the process was still painful. Meg stayed frozen as he worked, her head bowed and both hands clenched into fists, her ragged breathing the only active sign of her discomfort. When he was satisfied the wound was well cleaned, he soaked a line of sterile gauze with povidone-iodine and packed the wound, then followed it with dry gauze and rolled the compression bandage around her upper arm.

"That's the same procedure you had us do on top of Pyramid Peak to First Officer Jon Slaight after the plane crash, isn't it?"

"Different kind of injury, but the same need to flush and disinfect a wound with what someone would be carrying in a first aid kit. It's fast and efficient, though you don't need to be splinted like Slaight." He used two clip fasteners to secure the end of the bandage and then rubbed a hand up and down her back. "All done."

Meg sagged against her dog, who'd crept close during the process. "Thanks. I know that wasn't fun for you either."

"Causing you pain isn't high on my list. But when you constantly need me resetting your dislocated shoulder, pulling glass shards out of your knee, gluing shut a gash on your forehead, icing your face after some bastard tried to batter you to death—"

Meg stopped his words by laying a hand against his cheek. "I remember. You don't need to keep a mental list." She stroked her thumb over his skin. "But I know you do because it bothers you. I'm sorry to have added to it."

She studied her arm as he repacked the first aid kit, then rolled up her bloody sleeve and tucked it into her bag. Dried blood trailed down her forearm and the back of her hand in rivulets, and a beige bandage circled her arm just under the cap of material that still remained after he'd amputated her sleeve. She looked up when he stood, shouldered the pack, and then offered his hand. She laid hers in his and let him pull her to her feet as carefully as possible.

He stared down into her eyes, assessing her, not releasing her. "You're okay?"

"Yes. I mean, it hurts, but I'm okay. Really." She went up on tiptoe and pressed her lips briefly to his. "Thank you for patching me up. Again. What is this? Number twenty? Twenty-five?"

Her obvious exaggeration made him chuckle. "I've lost count."

"Me too. Probably better that way." She looked over her shoulder, back toward the clearing, and then down at her dog. "Let's go through, but I don't want Hawk wandering free this time. I want him with me so he can warn us if anyone comes back. Hawk, heel. I know it's going to be hard, buddy, but let's do our best. Heel."

Returning to the clearing was easier simply because she'd already passed through the area twice, as attested by broken branches and crushed shoots. In just a few moments, they stepped out into open space.

Todd whistled. "They did a number on this area. Just razed it, totally without care. Now the question is why?"

Frantic motion caught Meg's eye, and she squinted at the spot of bright red seemingly thrashing in midair. Moving toward it, she realized it was a bird. *How on earth was it suspended in midair like that?* As she closed in on it, she focused on what had been invisible to her on the far side of the clearing—a fifteen-foot length of netting stretched between trees, its mesh so fine, it was camouflaged against the green foliage beyond. The net had four heavier horizontal lines that stretched from side to side, suspending extra material so the netting formed a pocket below the next line. The bird—bright scarlet with a long, curved bill, black wings and tail, and vibrant orange legs—must have flown into the net, fallen into the pocket, and become snarled in the mesh. It was struggling to free itself, its frantic squeaks and whistles accentuating its distress.

Reaching the net and maneuvering the rest of her body to keep her left arm as still as possible, Meg cupped both hands, slipping her right hand under the net so she could close both hands over the bird from each side of the net, careful of its extended, snarled wings. "Todd, I need a hand. Hawk, stop. Sit. I need you to give us a little space. It's already terrified enough."

Todd jogged over. "What do you—" He cut off abruptly. "A net? They strung a net in the forest?"

"To catch this, I assume." Meg tipped her hands open just far enough to reveal the bird, no longer struggling, lying exhausted in her grasp. "It's that same bird we saw on that big sign when we first entered the trail, the one about 'Hawai'i's Watchable Wildlife.' The red bird with the curved beak."

"The honeycreeper. How badly is it tangled?"

"Pretty badly. I could try to untangle it, but I suspect it's snarled, and we'd risk harming it."

"I think you're right." He ripped open one of the Velcro pockets of his athletic cargo pants and pulled out a gray canvas pouch. He flipped it open, and a Leatherman multi-tool slid into his palm. "Better to do it our way."

" 'Our way'?"

"On the job, time is always of the essence, so we tend to brute-force our way into all situations. And we always carry the tools needed to finesse a situation." He flipped a tiny set of scissors out of one end of the multi-tool. "This will be safer than any of the blades. One wrong cut and we've killed it rather than saved it. Let me go around your other side."

Todd was a quick and efficient worker, instantly sizing up how the bird was snared and calculating the fewest number of cuts to free it while ensuring they didn't leave any bits attached, something that could slowly kill the creature over the next few days. It was as if the bird knew help had arrived; it didn't struggle, and as successive strands were cut, it pulled its wings in to rest comfortably in Meg's hold. Todd would occasionally wrap his hands around hers to change their position, but otherwise worked silently and swiftly.

In short order, the bird was entirely disconnected from the net, which now bore a large hole from Todd's surgical extraction. "Give me another minute." Todd dug into his pants pocket, this time pulling out a small LED flashlight he turned on to shine the beam into the hollow of Meg's hands. "I want to make sure it's totally free. I pulled out pieces as they came loose, so we should be okay, but I'd rather confirm." Ten seconds passed as he examined the bird in its human enclosure. "All good. Now, before you let it go . . ." He snapped open the largest blade on the Leatherman and made quick work of cutting all four ropes securing the netting, letting it fall to the ground.

"You realize you just tampered with a crime scene, right?"

"We don't want more birds to get caught in it. Especially this one. We just freed it; we don't want it getting caught in the same net a second time. Whoever comes to see what happened can examine it on the ground. We can tell them how it was arranged when we got here."

"There's that firefighter practicality again. It goes bone-deep." Her smile conveyed her approval. She checked on Hawk, who still sat exactly as commanded, but she could sense his curiosity. "Hawk, stay. Almost done. I know this is interesting, but it's scared enough." She walked another fifteen feet away from her dog to give the bird some space. "Letting it go now."

She opened her cupped hands. For a moment, the bird crouched motionless in her palms, and then, with a rising two-note call and a flutter of crimson wings, it flashed skyward to disappear into the trees.

"It looked good," Todd said. "Moved easily. I'm no expert, but it doesn't look like the time in the net harmed it."

"Thank goodness." Meg turned to look at the cloth bags suspended from the rope. They were made of a loose weave fabric—likely cotton in her estimation—to allow the birds to breathe. "Now we need to check those bags, and if it's more birds, free them if they're unhurt. When we call it in, incoming teams would prefer we keep them as evidence, but it could be hours before anyone comes. And who knows how long they've been in there?"

"You're going to call 911 for the locals?"

The idea that had been niggling at the back of Meg's brain roared to the forefront. It was all adding up, and that meant the locals were the wrong level of law enforcement. "No, I'm going to call Craig."

"You're going to call Beaumont from the middle of a Hawaiian jungle?" Todd's eyes narrowed on her thoughtfully as he followed her train of thought. "You think this is a federal case."

"Everything I'm seeing here leads me to believe we just interrupted a wildlife trafficking ring."

"It would be unlikely that these guys were hunters. What hunter goes after small forest birds? Larger birds like pheasants, sure, but not songbirds."

"No. And I actually looked into that. When I go into a new area with Hawk, I check to see if we're going to be crossing over with hunting seasons and territories, because that can put us at risk. But it's springtime on the Hawaiian Islands, meaning moms and babies of all species are off-limits. The only thing you can hunt right now on Hawai'i is rams in a specific area north of Kona on the west side of the island. Otherwise, no hunting."

"Doesn't mean no poaching," Todd pointed out, "but, again, songbirds? Doesn't play."

"No, it doesn't. We have two men who illegally destroyed protected land and hung a net to catch birds. When I discovered them, they moved directly to deadly force, then cut and run, abandoning their catches to die, as far as they knew."

"My bigger question is why did they cut and run? Why didn't they go after you? If you were a threat, why didn't they make sure you were neutralized?"

"I can only assume they were cutting their losses. I barely had a chance to see their faces before it was clear they were a threat. A normal person wouldn't have catalogued their characteristics like an ex-cop would, so they wouldn't assume I'd seen as much as I had. And what if I wasn't alone? Did they hear me call for Hawk to get down? Did they think I was with a group? They may have considered it safer to ditch the birds they'd caught, ensure their own safety, and find a new spot to try again."

"The sound of gunfire would carry and would bring

people to investigate, so they might have been done the moment they opened fire. Whatever the reason, it's pretty clear they didn't really care that the birds they'd abandoned could very well die."

"They never hesitated. Just abandoned ship without a second thought." She glanced at her watch. "I need to call Craig. If he wants me to call local law enforcement after that, I will. It's nearly five thirty there and I'd bet money he's still in his office at the Hoover Building. If not, I'll catch him on the way home."

"Not to mention you need to let him know you were shot."

Meg tried to refrain from rolling her eyes, but from Todd's expression, some of her reluctance must have showed anyway.

"You need to let him know," he insisted. "You may be on vacation, but he has a team member who is now on the DL because of an illegal act."

"I'm *not* on the DL."

"Who may be on the DL depending on how she heals. Luckily, she lives with a paramedic who will do everything in his power to get her back in the game ASAP."

"I'm not out of the damned game," Meg muttered. "And yes, I'll let him know. After we deal with the living creatures."

Todd pulled out his cell phone and held it up. "How about I take video of you as you release them? Then they'll hopefully be able to identify which birds they are. We know the type we just let go."

"That's a good plan."

Meg crossed over the rope line, where a quick count showed her six bags suspended from the rope, three of which were still, three in motion. Frantic bird calls came from behind the material. Wincing as her left arm burned, even as she tried to minimize its use, she untied one of the swaying bags, kneeling down and setting the bag carefully on the ground before looking up at Todd, who stood about five feet away with his camera app ready. He gave her a nod, and she loosened the bag's drawstring. There was an explosion of wings, and a bird with a dull olive back and wings, a grayish belly, and a curved black beak rose skyward, blending into the foliage above, sailing back to life.

"Got him." Todd stared down at his screen, using his thumb and index finger to enlarge the video. "We can grab screen caps off this video if they need photos."

"Perfect. Covering all bases—cataloging the evidence while letting the wild birds return to their environment. Next one."

The remaining two active bags all held birds that took to the trees as soon as they were released—one with an olive-green back, pale belly, and yellow chest, and a brown bird with a white chin with black splotches and upward-angled white and black tail feathers. Of the three remaining bags, one bird found his escape the moment the bag opened and took wing as a flash of vermillion, but the remaining two birds—one a dull green, and one a bright red like the bird rescued from the net—were either too exhausted from struggling or were injured. They were alive, but clearly needed assistance.

Meg closed the bags and rehung them, being careful to keep her left arm as motionless as possible to keep the pain from spiking any further. "I don't want to mess with these birds if they're not well. I definitely don't want to release them by tucking them under a fern to recover and make it on their own. I'd rather someone who knows what they're doing look at them and make that call."

"Agreed. Now . . . Beaumont?"

"Next on my list." Meg pulled out her cell phone, checked it, and was pleased to find a decent signal. "No need for the sat phone here. My cell works fine."

"We're working our way up Mauna Loa, giving a straight line of sight to any cell tower in Volcano."

"Works for me." But she hesitated.

"Problem?"

"No." She took a breath to beat back a sudden, unexpected tingle of irritation. "I'm just annoyed." She lowered her phone to look up at him. "I'm sorry. This isn't how I expected to spend our honeymoon. I'm irritated we're being interrupted by this. You must be too."

One corner of Todd's lips tipped up in a half smile. "Am I thrilled about it? No. Am I mad as hell you got hurt? *Yes.* Am I surprised? Actually . . . no. Trouble always seems to manage to find us. But we deal with it and we do what needs doing. And that starts now." His gaze dropped to her phone, his message clear.

He was right, as usual. And it warmed her to know he had her back no matter what.

She placed the call, putting it on speaker so Todd could hear, then stood in the now peaceful fern forest, waiting for the next blast to come her way via Washington, DC.

CHAPTER 5

Inflation: The swelling of a volcano as molten rock accumulates beneath it in the magma chamber.

May 29, 11:33 AM
Puʻu Makaʻala Natural Area Reserve
Volcano, Hawaiʻi

Meg imagined Craig sitting in his office in the Forensic Canine Unit, looking out through his glass wall into their bullpen, which was likely deserted at this hour. His instantaneous suspicion at her name being displayed on his phone. His lunge for the handset, assuming the worst. Why else would she call in the middle of her honeymoon?

"Meg, what's wrong?" Craig's tone was a mix of concern and alarm, and his lack of a salutation told her she'd read him correctly and he'd immediately leaped to a conclusion that wasn't particularly far off the mark.

"I'm okay." At Todd's pointed stare, she prevaricated. "Well, mostly okay. I have a situation. *We* have a situation—Todd and Hawk are with me, and you're on speaker."

"On Lanai?"

"No, we're on the Big Island now. Currently in the Puʻu Makaʻala Natural Area Reserve."

"What's the situation?"

"I believe we interrupted wildlife traffickers poaching in a protected space."

"Interrupted? Explain."

His next few words were muffled, like he was talking to someone, but Meg couldn't make it out. "Craig? Everything okay?"

"My door was open to the bullpen, and Brian was apparently eavesdropping."

"He's still there, this late?"

"He was just packing up to go home after getting some paperwork done." Craig's tone held an edge of annoyance. "Heard me ask if you were okay." In the silence that followed, Meg could imagine Craig leveling Brian with an icy stare. "Now he won't leave my office."

"The office was quiet, so I could hear your every word." Brian's voice came from the background. "Meg, are you all right?"

The second Brian caught wind something was wrong, he'd make sure he wormed his way into the information chain. Not that she could blame him; if it was her and she had suspicions he was in trouble, she'd be doing the same thing. Theirs was a solid partnership, and partners held each other up. "Why don't you put the call on speaker? He's only going to hound you for information until you break down and tell him. Let's do this in one shot."

"Your call." There was a pause, then Craig's more distant voice said, "You're on speaker."

"Hi, Brian."

"You're okay?" Brian's voice was clearer now.

"I'm talking to you. How could I not be okay?" Meg hoped the smile in her voice reached him. It really was good to hear his voice.

"You're calling from your honeymoon," Brian retorted. "What should be two weeks of sleep, sex, and sand."

Meg couldn't see it, but she knew Craig was rolling his eyes. She and Brian were close enough he'd always straight-talk her without embarrassment.

"You're not supposed to talk to us for nearly another week," Brian continued. "Why are you calling? What's the situation?"

"The short story is we came to a protected forest to give Hawk some parkour time. He sensed something off the main trail, so I went to investigate. I found two men in an area they'd illegally clear-cut, trapping protected forest birds."

"You have the men?"

"No, they took off into the forest."

"They just took one look at you and ran?" Brian asked.

"Not exactly." *Might as well get this over with.* "I stepped into the clearing, startling them. One of them cut right to the chase and pulled a handgun." Meg met Todd's eyes, and he nodded in encouragement. "I dove into the foliage, trying to take cover, but I was hit."

There was a brief spate of Brian and Craig talking over each other so loudly Meg couldn't follow any of it and could only shrug in Todd's direction.

After a second of silence, Craig came back on the line. "How badly are you hurt?"

Todd moved a step closer. "I can answer that. The bullet carved a furrow out of the outside of her upper left arm. It never fully penetrated, but has still left a significant injury, though not one that's life threatening. I made sure we had medical supplies on hand because we were going to be so remote. The wound has already been cleaned, disinfected, packed, and wrapped. We'll need to keep an eye on it, but she's going to be fine."

"Thank God." Brian's voice came from a slight distance, as if Craig had told him to take a step back.

"Thank you," Craig said. "I'm extremely glad you were

on hand to make sure she got the care she needed. Is anyone else injured?"

"No, sir," Meg said. "Hawk and Todd were far enough back they weren't in the line of fire."

"Any idea of what they used?"

"I didn't even see the handgun, just the shoulder holster."

"Craig, from what I saw, I'm going to estimate it was a 9mm or a .40 caliber bullet," Todd said. "No true entry wound to estimate size—just from the dimensions of the furrow. It certainly wasn't a .22 or a .50 caliber, but something more midrange and typical for a handgun."

"They fired five shots in total," Meg added. "Not that there's any way to find any of the bullets for forensics in here. But I'll be fine, so let's move on. It's the birds that are important."

"You say they're protected birds?"

"Yes. We're in the Puʻu Makaʻala Natural Area Reserve, a remote, old-growth fern forest protected by the Department of Land and Natural Resources here on the Big Island. Both the plants and wildlife inside the entire fenced reserve are protected."

"If it's truly wildlife trafficking, that's within our jurisdiction. Or at least shared jurisdiction with US Fish and Wildlife."

"That's why I didn't call local law enforcement to report both the shooting and the poaching."

"Local law enforcement needs to be at least informed of your shooting, but I'll take care of that for you once we have everything else settled. First, I want all the details." Paper rustled in the background, and Meg knew Craig was flipping to the next page in the yellow legal pad that always sat on his desk for note-taking. "Go back to the beginning and tell me everything in order so I can pass it on to the Honolulu field office."

"As I said, we came to Puʻu Makaʻala Natural Area Reserve because after a week of"—she imagined Craig turning beet red at *sleep, sex, and sand* and changed tack—"relaxing, we wanted to get out and explore. And keep in shape."

"Spell the name of the reserve for me."

Meg did, then continued. "It's eighteen-thousand-plus acres of protected forest and birds, totally off the beaten path and deserted, especially at this time on a weekday. We'd been hiking for over an hour when Hawk alerted to something off the trail. I use the term 'trail' lightly because it's barely a path at all. If it hadn't been for the occasional colored flag, I'd have thought we'd left the trail just past the gate. Anyway, I couldn't tell if he could hear something or smell it, but something definitely had his attention."

"You couldn't see anything?" Craig asked.

"It's hard to describe how dense this area is. Hang on." Meg flipped to her photo gallery, sending Brian four images she'd captured during their hike. A moment later, she heard the chime of his phone alerting to an incoming text. "Check your phone, Brian, then show Craig. You'll see what I mean."

There was a moment of silence, then Brian whistled. "That's a lot of foliage."

"That's what it's been like since we entered the reserve. The entire space is packed with plant life, to the extent there's barely wide enough clearance for the path in some sections. Todd and I discussed it, and we both had concerns someone might be in trouble, which could be bad in an area this isolated. Unless you're less than two feet off the trail, no one would just happen across you."

"Any possibility Hawk was attracted by the natural wildlife in the area?" Craig asked.

"We're on an archipelago. Wildlife is extremely limited compared to our experience on the mainland, with a few exceptions. It's simply too far out in the ocean. There aren't any foxes or wolves or bears. No alligators or big cats. There aren't even any native snakes. Many birds got here naturally, as well as marine life, but most other creatures are invasive and introduced by man. Keeping all that in mind, as we were trying to figure out what Hawk might be sensing, the thing that made the most sense in this area was a person or persons. And I'd spent enough time studying the maps to know the trail didn't go in the direction Hawk was indicating."

"So you thought someone was lost or hurt," Brian extrapolated. "Which is about the last thing the two of you would walk away from."

Meg met Todd's eyes and smiled. "Pretty much. We both agreed it needed to be checked out. If someone was hurt, we could lend aid on the spot or call in local first responders, if needed. I let Hawk follow the scent trail but kept him close. I didn't want him getting away from me in the dense forest." A thought occurred to her, and she backtracked. "Actually, I left something out—about twenty minutes before Hawk detected something off the path, we were caught in an earthquake."

"A *what?*"

"Well, maybe 'tremor' is a better descriptor. The important point is Hawk had a few seconds' warning it was coming and reacted. Raised hackles and everything. He must have been able to hear some frequency of the vibration before we could feel it. As we followed whatever it was he was sensing, cutting through the jungle as best we could, he reacted a second time. At first I thought it was another tremor. Then, as the seconds passed and nothing happened, I began to suspect it was something else."

"Hawk reacts like that when he's protective of you," Brian stated. "He knew something was wrong up ahead."

"That's what I thought too. At that point I asked Todd to stay back with Hawk, and I continued on to investigate.

I tried to move through the jungle as quietly as possible. Then, suddenly, I stepped into an extensive open area. A quick glance showed the underbrush had been chopped down creating a roughly thirty-foot open space under cover of the treetops. Standing in the space were two men. I only had about two seconds to take everything in before they turned on me, then one of them went for his gun. At that point, I dove into the ferns and tried to disappear, hoping to hit the ground before the shooting started. I didn't quite make it."

"Did you get a look at the men?" Craig asked.

"Quickly. One was dark-haired, one blond. Dark hair was about five-foot-nine, one-eighty. Blond was about six feet, two-twenty. Both were wearing hiking boots, long pants, and lightweight jackets, all black." She paused, hearing the scratch of Craig's pen in the background as he wrote down every detail. "Got all that?"

"Got it."

"On to my current concern, then. After the shooting, I could hear the two men retreat into the forest. After I reunited with Todd and Hawk and he'd patched me up, we went back to the clearing. No sign of the two men, but it was immediately evident what they were doing. They'd cleared the area so they could string a nearly invisible net between the trees, and they were catching birds as they flew through the open area. There were six bags of individual birds they had hanging from a rope off to one side."

"These are the protected birds," Craig clarified.

"Here's the thing—there was a sign near the beginning of the trail that showed pictures of some of the birds in this reserve, most of which are endangered. Those were the birds they were catching. It's not just poaching. Not just trafficking. They planned to remove endangered birds from this reserve. That has deeper implications."

"It certainly does. US Fish and Wildlife is going to be all over this."

"Good. One other thing. We freed a bird we found in the net and brought the net down to avoid any more birds getting tangled and possibly hurt, then we opened the bags to free the captured birds. Of the six, four flew away, but two are injured, so we need someone who can rescue injured birds. Especially if these are endangered species, we can't let them die."

"I agree. And they're the only evidence you have left."

"Not totally. We didn't want to hold on to the bagged birds if they were uninjured because they could be harmed trying to escape a closed bag or die without food and water, but Todd videoed me freeing each one so they can be identified. Sorry, Craig, it was the best we could do. It could be hours before anyone gets here because of the location, and we didn't want any of them to die in the meantime. I'm not sure about the injured ones as it is, but I didn't want to risk healthy birds."

"No argument here. Okay, I'm going to make some calls. I'm sorry, Meg, but I'm going to need you to sit tight and maintain the crime scene. I need to start with us, and the only full field office in the state is in Honolulu. That's hours away from you by air."

"You don't have to apologize. I brought this to you."

"It's your honeymoon. You didn't plan spending hours of it sitting around waiting for a field agent to arrive to take over from you."

Meg stifled a chuckle as Todd rolled his eyes, but then softened it with a wink. "No, it wasn't the plan, but somehow this still feels like us. Update me as soon as you can. It was good hearing both your voices. Brian, let Craig do what he needs to do."

"I will. You be careful, you hear me?" Brian called.

"Yes, Dad."

"And Todd, you make sure that arm heals."

"Count on it," Todd said.

"Talk soon," Craig said. And then he and Brian were gone.

Meg tucked her phone into the side pocket of her yoga pants. "Guess we have a little time on our hands now." Meg's shoulders rose and fell on a sigh of frustration. "Again, I'm sorry."

"You say that like this is something you did purposely. We both know it's not."

"I still feel bad, though." Meg turned in a slow circle, scanning the edge of the clearing before she selected the largest exposed trunk—about ten inches across and with a scattering of freshly fallen ferns as a cushion. "We can wait over there."

Todd crossed over to the trunk, slipped out of the backpack, set it down, and sat with his back against the tree, shifting his feet apart to make her a space between his thighs. He patted the ferns in front of him. "Join me?"

"You're taking the uncomfortable seat, and I get to lean on you?"

"You're injured. Seems like the right order to me."

Clearly, there would be no budging him, so Meg lowered herself into the lee of his legs, leaning her back against his chest. "Hawk, come here, boy." Hawk ambled over, and Meg patted the ferns beside Todd's right leg. "Down, buddy. You might as well have a rest while we wait, too." Hawk lay down beside them and propped his chin on Todd's thigh, looking up at her with big liquid eyes. "Good boy." She smiled when he let out a gusty sigh. "I wish I could relax the way he does."

"No kidding." Todd slid one hand over Meg's belly, snugging her in tighter, but the other loosely cupped her arm just under the compression bandage. "How's it feeling?"

"Like I'm one of Hawk's chew toys he's actively gnawing on."

"I can help with that." With his left hand, he unzipped the pack, then lifted out the med kit and opened it. He drew out a prescription bottle, then reached back into the pack for a water bottle. "Hold this." When Meg took the water, he opened the smaller bottle in front of her using both hands as he peered over her shoulder. He shook out two white tablets. "Take these."

"What are they?"

"Acetaminophen and codeine. You know it as Tylenol 3. Stronger than ibuprofen, and I think you could use it. And likely will for at least the first twenty-four hours."

"Where'd they come from?"

Todd turned the bottle around so she could see the name on the label—Clay McCord.

Meg stared at the label, trying to figure out why on earth her sister Cara's romantic partner and her invaluable contact at *The Washington Post* would have left his drugs in her first aid kit. "Those aren't a normal part of my first aid kit."

"No, but you told me to make sure it was stocked with whatever we might need in a remote area with no easy medical team access. I knew McCord never finished his last bottle of pain relievers after his hands were crushed last summer, so I asked him if he still had it. He did, so I borrowed it."

Meg had a mental flash of McCord lying in a hospital bed in Philadelphia, hooked up to an array of beeping equipment, his broken nose reset and bandaged, and the fingers of both hands crushed by the repeated blows of a mallet as a Mob method of extracting information, splinted and bandaged. He'd come so far in the intervening nine months, anyone not in the loop would never know he'd been so grievously injured. The only good to come from their case had been the Pulitzer Prize for Journalism, Investigative Reporting, awarded to McCord the week before for his story on blood diamond racketeering by the Philadelphia crime family, including his personal experience in the investigation.

Sometimes good came from the very bleakest of days.

"Thank you, McCord." Meg popped the pills into her mouth and downed them with several swallows of water. She closed the bottle, set it on the ground beside her, then tipped her head back against Todd's shoulder and laid her hand over Hawk's back, letting herself focus on the peace of the moment—the birdsong high in the trees, the complex scents of the fern forest, the silky texture of Hawk's fur under her fingers, and the steady rise and fall of Todd's chest.

"Have I told you today that I love you?" Todd's question was a low murmur in her ear.

"Not today."

Trying not to jiggle her upper arm in an effort to keep the worst of the pain at bay, she laid her left hand over his, where they lay clasped over her stomach. Todd had been mostly stoic about her shooting thus far, but this was him letting a little of his stress over the situation float free.

She ran her fingertip over the smooth silicone of his metallic copper-tone wedding band. Their rings had been chosen partially based on their jobs: Todd had specifically designed a bezel-mounted diamond engagement ring for Meg she could wear out on searches. However, firefighters couldn't wear metal bands on the job, so most either wore no ring, got a ring tattoo, or wore a silicone band. Todd had selected the silicone ring as a safe symbol of their love.

"You don't have to say it," she said. "I know you do. And I love you too."

She smiled as he pressed a kiss just behind her ear.

Knowing they had a while to wait, she relaxed back into his arms and let her eyelids flutter closed.

They'd survived yet another crisis. Who knew what was to come, but for now, it was just the three of them at peace.

CHAPTER 6

Residual melt: Liquid magma that remains following partial crystallization during the cooling process.

May 29, 2:22 PM
Puʻu Makaʻala Natural Area Reserve
Volcano, Hawaiʻi

Hawk was the first to know the cavalry had arrived. Craig had called about fifteen minutes after they'd settled in on their long wait with an update—he'd contacted the Honolulu field office, and they were dispatching Special Agent Jeremy Hale. Additionally, Agent Hale was bringing a US Fish and Wildlife officer who had experience in Hawaiian wildlife trafficking, as well as with the birds themselves. Hale and the wildlife officer would be covering the 216-mile trip via helicopter, a slower air vehicle, but one that would still allow them to arrive faster than a scheduled island-hopping flight between the Honolulu and Hilo airports. This also gave them the freedom to land at Mountain View Airstrip, a private airstrip with a single gravel and asphalt runway, only twenty-five minutes away from the entrance to Puʻu Makaʻala Natural Area Reserve instead of the hour it would take to drive from Hilo's airport via the Hawaiʻi Belt and Volcano Roads.

Considering the hour-long hike into the reserve on top of the trip, minimizing airtime was imperative if they had any hope of saving the injured birds. They had a car ready to meet them there, so they'd immediately be on the move.

It was just short of three hours later when Hawk went from relaxed to alert, lifting his head from his paws, his ears perked, eyes bright, and body poised to leap to his feet.

Meg stroked her hand down his back. "It's okay, Hawk. Stay down. I think our reinforcements have arrived." She climbed carefully to her feet, holding her injured arm close to her body, her muscles tight after sitting for so long. "I can't see it being the traffickers coming back, and I know it's the right time for Craig's incoming response, but we need to be prepared."

Todd stood, looking considerably looser than she felt. Granted, he hadn't had hours of trying to ignore the misery of a bullet wound. The pills had certainly helped—now, instead of a fiery burn, the pain was a dull, aching grind that slowly whittled away at her as the minutes marched on.

"Agreed." He brushed dead leaves off the seat of his cargo pants, then checked his watch. "Just under three hours. It seems long, but they made good time considering the distance between the islands, and the challenge of getting to us here."

"Thanks for your patience with this."

"No thanks required. I'm just glad you wisely packed provisions for us."

Meg swept her gaze down his large, muscular frame, then back up again. "Two energy bars could hardly be called 'provisions' for a man of your size. The plan was a late lunch in Volcano with those as a snack to fill the void until then. Not for them to *be* lunch."

"Hey, it was better than nothing. To say I'm ready for more is an understatement, but we won't be out of here until dinnertime."

"I think Hawk was the only one satisfied with his snack." Meg never went anywhere without her go bag packed with everything she and Hawk might need for a long search—including high-energy kibble for Hawk and energy bars for herself. It certainly wasn't gourmet dining, but it got the job done.

The sounds of someone fighting through the greenery filtered through the forest toward them.

"FBI and US Fish and Wildlife!" A female voice drifted through the fern branches, slightly to the south of them.

Meg nodded in approval. "That definitely confirms they're our team. The traffickers wouldn't know anyone had been sent in, especially not that combination. Though they're a little off course."

"Can you blame them? Navigating this morass is a challenge."

"Definitely is." Meg cupped her hands around her mouth. "We're over here! Aim a little farther north."

"Thanks!" A male voice this time.

In just over two minutes, a set of hands parted the stalks of fern on the edge of the clearing, and then a man stepped through, straightening as he cleared the foliage. Meg estimated he matched her own nearly six-foot height with a sturdy, muscular build under his casual athletic clothes, neatly trimmed straight dark hair, and warm, sun-bronzed olive skin speaking to his Pacific Islander heritage.

His smile was reflected in his dark eyes as he stepped forward extending a hand. "Special Agent Jeremy Hale." He pronounced the Hawaiian surname as "ha-lay."

As Meg stepped forward, hand outstretched, her gaze shot over his shoulder to the woman stepping into the clearing. She was the yin to Hale's yang, petite where he was tall and broad, light to his dark, with pale, freckled skin, her blond-shot red hair pulled back into a ponytail, with her green eyes fixed on Hale in a nonplussed expression.

Both newcomers were dressed in hiking clothes and carried backpacks. As well, to Meg's critical eye, both were armed under their zip-front light windbreakers.

"I told you I couldn't keep up with you and your long legs," the woman said, but her tone was exasperated rather than angry.

As Hale released Meg's hand, she strode up to Meg. "Special Agent Maeve Byrne, US Fish and Wildlife Service, Office of Law Enforcement. You're Beaumont's K-9 handler?"

Meg shook hands with Byrne. "Yes. Meg Jennings."

Byrne's chin cocked in the direction of Meg's bandaged arm. "Beaumont told us you'd been shot."

"Yes."

"He also said you don't require medical care. We'd really like you to get that looked at. Bullet wounds aren't scratches."

"Craig omitted some info, apparently. I don't need professional medical care because I already had it." She waved Todd forward. "This is my husband, Todd. Or rather, Lieutenant Webb, DC Fire and Emergency Medical Services. He's a dual-trained firefighter/paramedic. *He* packed the first aid kit he used to treat me, so we had everything he needed."

Both agents shook hands with Todd.

"Thanks for insisting on treatment," Todd said. "You couldn't have known she'd already be covered."

"How bad is it?" Hale asked.

"The bullet didn't penetrate, just carved a path across

her outer arm. It's cleaned and we're treating for pain. Insufficient treatment, I suspect, but the best I can do with what I have on hand currently."

"I'm fine," Meg insisted. "When we get out, we'll get whatever else we need, and Todd will keep an eye on it moving forward. It won't slow the team down. And speaking of team..." Meg extended a hand toward her dog, who still lay near the tree as commanded, but his head-up posture, bright eyes, and perked ears showed he was alert to the strangers, his attention fixed on Meg. "This is my K-9, Hawk. Hawk, come. They're friends. Come say hi."

The newcomers both chuckled when Hawk approached, sat, and politely extended a paw. Byrne was closer, so she bent down to shake Hawk's paw. "I love him already."

"Hard not to," Meg agreed. "And as well-behaved as he is, Hawk is a solid live-find dog. He's what got us here."

"Beaumont told us about what happened and how you encountered the two men. You didn't pursue them when they escaped into the forest?"

"I briefly considered it. Hawk could have followed them through the forest without any trouble. That's what we do—track and trace. But I'm on vacation and not carrying like I normally do if a search calls for it. We could be walking directly into a trap with no way to defend ourselves. Or they could circle around and pick us off as we followed the trail. Not to mention, I can't communicate to Hawk that we'd need to be as close to silent as possible as we moved through the forest. All in all, I thought it was too big a risk to both of us."

"Agreed. You weren't prepared for what you walked into."

"I can't take chances with Hawk that way. He gets injured, the team is done and I wouldn't be able to live with myself. I have to make decisions based on both of us." Meg was relieved to see no judgment on either agent's face. "Now, before we get into anything else, Agent Byrne, can you look at these birds? I'm concerned they might not be doing well."

"Yes, please, show me. Beaumont mentioned you had injured birds."

"They're here." Meg indicated the two suspended bags.

"Can you keep Hawk away? I need to keep their stress levels as low as possible. And that includes keeping them separate from what they'd see as a predator."

"Absolutely. I was keeping him away before for just that reason. Let me settle him back where we were sitting waiting for you. We'll give you a few minutes to figure out what we're looking at here."

"Thanks." Byrne opened her backpack and pulled a pair of blue nitrile gloves from a pocket, donned them, and extracted supplies—two paper bags, two shallow, square containers, some soft cloths. She set up the paper bags with the other supplies arranged inside, then stood to unhook the first bag.

Meg settled Hawk—having him lie down and giving him the command to stay—then walked over to where Todd was showing Hale the downed net. Hale was crouched down on the balls of his feet with the net draped over his gloved hands, examining the hole. "Sorry about that. We were less concerned about maintaining the evidence than freeing the bird without injuring it. Just so you're aware, we handled the net with our bare hands because we were working to quickly free the trapped bird."

"Understood. It's not like you came into the reserve prepared to maintain a crime scene. I don't know a ton about birds, but from your description, it sounds like an 'I'iwi. You have actual footage of the bagged birds?"

"We do. And yes to the bird, as long as that's a honeycreeper."

"It is. Byrne would know the status better than I. Byrne!" He raised his voice.

On the other side of the clearing, Byrne didn't raise her head but turned it toward them to hear better. "Yes?" She kept her voice low to avoid startling the bagged birds.

"Conservation status of the 'I'iwi?"

Byrne knelt on the ground with the first bag, her back to them. "IUCN Red Listed as vulnerable. One step up from endangered."

"IUCN?" Todd asked.

"International Union for the Conservation of Nature. The world body on species extinction and endangerment. The 'I'iwi is federally listed as threatened, but the state considers it endangered on O'ahu and Moloka'i. Now this little beauty is another story." She turned so they could see a small bird wrapped in her hand. She held it loosely, with its head between her index and middle finger, and her fingers and thumb wrapped around its body. Only its olive-colored head showed, with a straight, pale beak, a black mask over his eyes, and a white throat. "This is an 'Alawī, one of the most endangered birds in Hawai'i. It's found only on the Big Island in a few locations and has been listed as endangered since 1975, when there were only twelve thousand five hundred of them. It's now listed as being at most ninety-three hundred mature adults, and that number is continuing to fall."

Meg took a few steps closer, but then stopped, not wanting to frighten the small creature. "Is he okay?" She considered the bird again. "She?"

"He—too bright for the female. He's injured his wing. I think it might be broken, but I'm not the person to make that call, especially not right now. I'm trained on recovery, but the real rehab people do the hard work. For now, he's shocky and dehydrated, so that's my part. Heat, hydration, safety... Those are the hallmarks of initial recovery." She picked up a slender, capped syringe filled with water. "You can't force birds to drink by shooting water into their mouths, not without simultaneously flooding their lungs and killing them. If they can't drink themselves out in the field, best we can do is to add a drop of water on the tip of their beak, and they'll drink it that way. Can you give me a hand here? Come closer, but don't make eye contact with the bird; it will think you're a predator." Byrne extended the syringe toward Meg when she dropped to her knees beside her. "Pull the cap off for me, please."

"Sure." Meg carefully wiggled the cap off, then watched as Byrne placed a single drop of water on the tip of the bird's beak, then held it out for it to be capped again.

"I'll monitor him and give him more if I need to. You just don't want to overdo it. Once he's at the rehab facility, they have a number of safer ways to rehydrate—by IV, for example—if he's not drinking on his own. But for now, it's all about minimal handling and managing his sensory input."

"That's why the paper bag?"

"Yes. It's darker in there, and quiet, and plain paper is breathable, so it's safe to hold them in there. Injured birds are stressed already, so it's all about how to minimize that stress."

"So don't handle them and keep them in the dark."

"You also want to keep them warm, so I have a loosely packed cloth in the bag, draped over a small raised lip of a plastic container so the bird has something to perch on to feel more secure while the cloth keeps him warm and padded. We're going to have to hike these birds out and we can't afford for them to be tossed around." After ensuring the drop of water was gone, she pulled one of the bags toward her and gently lowered the bird into the bag, then slowly pulled her hand free. "That's it, my boy. You just snuggle in there. We'll get you some proper care as soon as possible." She folded over the top of the bag twice, pressing a sharp crease into the paper in case the bird tried to escape. "He shouldn't be able to fly with that wing, and should settle down into the warmth and softness of the bedding material, but just in case."

Byrne untied the second bag and opened it just enough to peer into. "This one is bleeding. I'm going to need to make sure it doesn't panic and try to fly off while I figure out what's going on. It may have gotten sliced during capture. You said they used a net?"

"Yes." Hale walked to the downed net and lifted a handful off the ground so Byrne could see it. "This stuff."

"Mist netting. It's what conservationists use to catch and band birds in field studies. But if you don't know what you're doing, you can injure the bird. Meg, can you dig the styptic powder out of the front pocket of my backpack? White screw-cap jar that says, FIRST AID FOR BIRDS. Then put on a pair of gloves. I could use a second set of hands."

"Of course." Meg pulled the bag closer to search for the requested item.

"Might also kill the bird," Todd said from where he crouched down near the edge of the clearing. "There's a dead bird here."

"Goddammit." Even with her head down and her voice slightly muffled, there was fury behind Byrne's single word as she slid a hand into the cotton bag to pull out the same kind of bright red bird they'd retrieved from the net. "My hands are full here. What's it look like?"

"Red. Slightly curved black beak, black wings and tail.

White from the legs back to under the tail. From the awkwardly unnatural position of the head, I think its neck was broken."

"It's an 'Apapane, thank God." Byrne looked skyward and blew out a breath. "And that sounds terrible. We don't want any of the birds to die, but that one isn't endangered. We can't afford to lose any of the endangered species, especially now, in nesting season. Remove the breeding adult, and the chicks in eggs die due to lack of incubation, or the nestlings or fledglings starve to death, further decreasing an already plummeting and fragile population." She glanced sideways at Meg. "It looks like it's a single, long laceration angling over the back from one shoulder to below the opposite wing. I'm going to apply a little light pressure, but then I need you to get a pinch of the styptic powder between your fingers and sprinkle it down the line of the injury." She carefully passed the bird from facing out in her left hand to facing into her right, meticulously placing her fingers to apply gentle pressure for about thirty seconds, then revealed the wound for treatment.

Meg stared down at the dark smear staining the bright red feathers. Some of the blood had dried, but more now spotted Byrne's gloves. "That's a honeycreeper, like the one we pulled out of the net."

"An 'I'iwi, yes."

"Male?"

"Can't easily sex this one. Males and females look very similar, with the females being only slightly smaller. This isn't the time for measurements."

"Definitely not."

"Sprinkle the styptic powder onto the wound where it's still seeping blood. If you're not sure if it's actively bleeding, treat it anyway."

"How fast will it work?"

"Within a couple of minutes. Once I'm sure it's stopped, I'll hydrate and bag this one."

Todd walked back to the circle of the clearing. "Meg called it, then? We're looking at wildlife trafficking?"

"Definitely," Byrne agreed. "And it's not the first we've seen of it here."

"Most people think of wildlife trafficking as the trade in animal parts," said Hale. "Rhinoceros horns, shark fins, bear gallbladders. Many of these animal parts are used in Eastern medicine or are considered delicacies. But what happens is animals are killed, or worse, stripped of those parts and left to die a slow and agonizing death. We don't have as much of that happening here because we're a remote archipelago. Our wildlife either flew, swam, or were brought here as an invasive species. We don't have the kind of desirable land mammals a lot of wildlife trafficking revolves around. We don't have pangolins, rhinoceroses, or elephants. We do, however, have seahorses and endangered sea turtles. Then there's the birds."

"They're trafficking the birds for parts?" Meg asked.

"It's not all about parts of animals." Hale came to stand behind Byrne, his eyes on her hands. "There are streams of wildlife trafficking. Some animals are used as food delicacies—shark fin soup, pangolin meat, or eels as unagi, a celebratory treat that's supposed to increase stamina. Some are used in medicine—bear gallbladders, seahorses, and pangolin scales, bones, and heads."

"Sounds like it's unlucky to be a pangolin," Todd murmured.

"It's why they're nearly extinct." Byrne's tone was scathing. "It's a tragedy. And their value is incredibly overblown. There's no scientific evidence it's effective medicine, yet they continue to die." She paused for a moment, her body stiff and her shoulders rigid. "Sorry, wildlife trafficking is a personal soapbox for me."

"No need to apologize," Meg said, staring down at the injured bird still held lightly in Byrne's fist. "We totally understand this is a red flag for you."

"For both of us," Hale said.

"We don't like it either. You guys have worked together before?"

"Oh, yeah, many times." His smile spoke volumes about that not being a hardship for him. "When Beaumont called me, I called Byrne directly rather than going through channels. I knew who I wanted with me today."

"He knew he could drive me crazy out-hiking me," Byrne retorted. "He could step over fallen trees with his absurdly long legs; I had to scramble over."

"Just giving you your workout. No need for the gym today."

She threw him a look over her shoulder from under her lashes. "Thanks for that?" There was an edge of humor in the lilt of her intonation.

"You're welcome. So, the trade encompasses food and medicine," Hale continued, as if their byplay had never happened. "There's also a mass market in tropical birds, like parrots, and in amphibians, as well as a commercial market in decor and adornment goods—elephant tusks and rhinoceros horns for display, as well as rosewood furniture, made from the endangered hardwood tree. Then we come down to the last category—the specialist market for live animals and plants. In this case, scarcity is a moneymaker. The rarer the item, the more desirable it is. Rare and endangered orchids or succulents in the plant world. Rare and endangered reptiles and amphibians in the animal world. And birds in the avian world."

Todd looked toward the smudge of red lying in the

fallen ferns. "But clearly live birds. This isn't a taxidermy thing."

"Oh, that exists too. If there's a market for any kind of item, someone will fill the void." Hale followed Todd's gaze to the dead bird. "That's evidently not what these two men were doing. They were looking for live specimens and weren't prepared to store and transport a dead one without decomposition spoiling their prize."

A slideshow of images shot through Meg's mind, birds of various colors and shapes escaping their net and fabric cages—red, olive green, and orange. "When we freed the birds, they weren't all the same kind. Would they have had more than one target?"

"Hawai'i is known as the extinction capital of the world, so they could easily have had multiple targets. Today shows how well they did." Byrne looked up at Todd. "Beaumont told me you guys only got married a week ago. I guess you didn't have endangered bird rescue and rehabilitation on your list of vacation activities." Her gaze dropped to Meg's. "But I appreciate the help." She examined the 'I'iwi. "Looks like the bleeding stopped." She administered a drop of water, and gave the bird a minute to drink it in, and then gently deposited it into the paper bag and sealed it inside. She stripped off her bloody gloves inside out so the blood was contained, balled them up, and tossed them into her open backpack before donning a fresh pair. "I want to check out their netting system." She pushed to her feet, strode over to the net spread across the ground, and picked a length of it up in her gloved hands. "Classic mist net used by ornithologists and chiropterologists for bird and bat research. But there's a real skill to removing a specimen from the mesh without injuring or killing it." Byrne's gaze slid to the dead 'Apapane. "One they obviously don't possess." She stood and dropped the net. "As far as having a target, I suspect they came here, to this location in particular, because there are so many rare birds in this area. Whatever they could recover alive, they could sell."

"Who are they selling to?" Meg asked.

"To whoever's the highest bidder. There's a booming private zoo trade among some of the richest on the planet. It's not enough to have a knockout house or houses on magnificent grounds. You have to deck out that house with the finest furniture and the most expensive art. For some, that art is living, so they have extensive private zoos. And if that zoo contains rare specimens, even better." She met Todd's eyes. "And if one of those rare specimens dies in good physical condition, then you have it taxidermied, and it simply moves to a different collection."

"Do they at least care for the animals while they're in their possession?" Todd asked.

"Usually, yes. I'll give them that. They paid a lot for their treasures, so they want them to live a long time so they can be shown off. But many creatures don't do well in captivity, or they aren't being supported on the correct diet or in the correct conditions, and they don't survive. Worse, they're removed from the breeding population when we're struggling to keep that population alive and reproducing. Are you familiar with the 'Alalā—the Hawaiian Crow?"

Todd shook his head.

"It's officially listed at this point as extinct in the wild, but the 'Alalā Project has taken thirty of the approximately one hundred twenty-five birds they have in their care and have released them into Puʻu Makaʻala over the past few years in hopes they'll survive and breed in the wild again. So far, they've been holding their own against the 'Io, the Hawaiian Hawk. In fact, week before last, they announced a breeding pair of juveniles had built their first nest together. Now, juveniles don't tend to be successful in their first year, but it's a chance, and they need every chance they can get. The 'Alalā are an example of how bad it can get. They don't truly exist in the wild, only experimentally, and the Project is ready to pull the plug at a moment's notice, if needed." Byrne's gaze dropped to the two paper bags. "We don't want to get to that place with these ones because they usually can't recover from there. The super rich and powerful will just have to find some other toy to play with." Byrne took a breath as if to calm her rising temper, then turned to Hale. "Let's get this documented and get that net bagged for evidence. Then we have a choice." Byrne turned to face Hawk. "He can follow a scent through the jungle?"

"Yes."

"I'd like to know where they went. How they got in here, what sort of transportation they used."

"I would too." Hale scanned the surrounding area. "They lost their prizes today. If this wasn't just a field trip to see what they could catch to sell but was a mission to fulfill an existing, extremely lucrative order, they'll need to try again. You don't take that kind of money without producing the product."

"Not without threat," Byrne agreed. "How about we divide and conquer? I need to get these birds out of here and over to the Hawai'i Wildlife Center in Halaula on the northern tip of the island. But we also need to find out where those men went. Meg, would you and Hawk follow the trail with Hale? I'm sure they're long gone, but if not, Hale is armed and will protect the team. Todd, if you could assist me hiking these birds back to the entrance, I can take them from there."

"That's no problem." Todd met Meg's gaze, caught her

nod of agreement, and turned back to Byrne. "Then, if you take the birds, I'll wait to hear from Meg and can pick everyone up once they're done. Wherever they are."

"That works for me." Meg looked up at the sky. "We need to start now. This isn't the place to be after nightfall, and we have no idea how long the search will take." She walked back to where she'd left her go bag and opened it. "Hawk, come." She laid out a high-energy meal for him and a bowl of water. "Give Hawk two minutes, and we'll be ready. Then let's track these men. If we can figure out where they went or how they got here, that could begin to lay the foundation to catch them."

CHAPTER 7

Spatter: Droplets of molten lava ejected from a lava fountain.

May 29, 9:07 PM
Waikōloa Beach Marriott Resort
Waikōloa, Hawaiʻi

Todd used his key card to open the door and then stepped back to let Meg and Hawk precede him.

"Come on, buddy, in you go. I need to make a call, then we're going right into the shower."

Todd closed the door behind them and slipped Meg's go bag off his shoulder to set it on the floor. "Who are you calling at this hour?"

"Craig."

Todd's gaze shot to the clock on the microwave in their tiny kitchen. "They're six hours ahead of us."

"Those were his instructions. When I called him at home at the end of our search to update him, he told me he wanted me to call him when we got back to the resort to make sure I was okay, and you hadn't had to drag me to the hospital."

"We told him it wasn't that bad. If it's going to get infected, it's way too early for that. Besides, it was promptly treated."

"I told him that. I told him it would be two or three in the morning by the time we called him, and it could wait until morning. He insisted, because by the time we called him when we were up, it would be afternoon there. This time difference makes it hard to manage communications. We hit a sweet spot earlier today."

"Call him after you've showered. Two in the morning versus three in the morning won't make much difference overall. You're going to be waking him up either way. Later might actually be better because if you wake him up and he can't go back to sleep, that puts him closer to his own workday."

"Good point. Shower it is."

"You're sure you don't want to eat first?"

One look at her dog answered that question for her. "Hawk's filthy." She took in her own mud-caked yoga pants. She'd brushed off the dried mud before getting in their SUV and then some remnants in the resort parking lot, but too much of it was ground right into the weave of the fabric. "I'm filthy. I need to make sure he's clean and comfortable and fed. Then I'll eat." She frowned down at the mud under her nails and discoloring her single remaining cuff.

"You can shower together. Two birds, one stone. You'll feel better."

Meg glanced down at her bare arm, only covered by the compression bandage. "Can I shower with this?"

"The bandage is also filthy, so it needs to come off anyway. I only brought one of that size, so we'll wash it and hang it to dry. I'd like to see you continue to use it when you're out doing anything active, like a search. But I want another look at your wound in brighter light to make sure it's clean. Tomorrow, I'll get a waterproof dressing for it.

Once you're all set, I'll step out and get us some dinner. Any preferences?"

She bent down to unlace her hiking boots, then toed them off. "I'm so hungry I could eat a horse. Or a cow in this case. A burger?"

"Works for me." He opened her go bag and extracted the first aid kit. "Let's get you cleaned up, then you can relax. You must be exhausted."

"As searches go, that one was a lot of work simply due to the environment. And then the ride home felt challenging. I'm so glad you handled it and not me. It helped that you had two perfectly fit arms in case we ran into trouble."

They'd dropped Hale off at the Mountain View Airstrip so he could coordinate picking up Byrne from the north end of the island and then had hit Hawai'i Belt Road, headed for Saddle Road to cross back through the mountains. But it was a much different westward drive in the dark, as opposed to their morning trip going east. Some of the country's finest astronomical observatories were situated on the top of Mauna Kea, just north of Saddle Road at approximately the halfway point. To maintain a perfect sky without light pollution, Saddle Road was completely without illumination, and only the reflectors built into every line of the road guided their way with the help of the vehicle's headlights. She'd never seen such stars as she had on the last section of Saddle Road—there was simply so much light pollution in DC, this was a revelation. But add in the speed limit of sixty miles per hour, approaching drivers with their high beams on occasionally blinding them, and the suffocating blanket of fog they drove into as they rose into the mountains, leaving them with only about twenty feet of visibility at most, and it was a long and stressful drive back to the west side of the island. Todd had handled the SUV perfectly, but it left Meg even more tired because she hadn't felt like she could relax until they came down into civilization.

"You're no doubt also tired yourself after what had to be an incredibly careful hike back carrying an injured bird," she continued. "Then that drive, where you had to be at full attention one hundred and ten percent of the time. Thanks for offering to get dinner when I'm sure you'd also like to put your feet up."

"Not a problem. We'll have time to relax together after we eat. Come on. Let's get you cleaned up."

Now situated in Waikōloa on the Big Island, they had taken an oceanfront suite at the Marriott Resort situated directly behind ʻAnaehoʻomalu Beach. The suite, featuring a small kitchen and a comfortable living room, as well as a private garden lanai, was perfect for their needs. Night had long fallen by this point, but their west-facing view highlighted stunning sunsets, as they had witnessed last evening while curled up on the padded couch under the cover of the pergola and surrounded by lush tropical plants. It had been lovely and romantic.

Which was a sight better than exhausted and filthy.

Meg looked down at her dog. Hawk stood at her knee, his head drooping and tail low. Grit abraded her palm as she ran it down his back. "We definitely need it. Hawk, come."

She trudged past the living room, into the bedroom, and straight into the adjoining spacious bathroom with Hawk at her knee and Todd following behind.

She pulled her phone out of the side pocket of her yoga pants, sliding it onto the counter behind her toiletries bag. Then she stripped down, dropping her clothes in a compact pile on the bathroom floor beside the deep soaker tub. "Just leave these for now. The hotel has a laundry, so I'll send them down tomorrow. Normally I wouldn't bother, but these are beyond dirty."

"There are bags in the closet. I'll bag them so they're ready to go." He set the first aid kit down on the bathroom counter. "Turn this way. Let's look at that arm." He removed the clip fasteners and carefully unrolled the dirty compression bandage, dropping it into the sink. He turned her so she could see the side of her arm in the mirror. "The outer bandage was dirty, but the gauze beneath is still clean and in place. And you haven't bled through. Also good." He pulled a roll of wide, breathable surgical tape and a pair of medical scissors from the first aid kit. "I'd like to look at the wound itself, but let's leave that until after your shower so all the dirt is off you and nothing will wash into it. This will hold things in place in the meantime." He made quick work of cutting off several lengths of surgical tape and securing the gauze.

Just the pressure of the tape application made Meg clamp her jaw shut and turn away from the pain. "Do you have any more of McCord's magic pills? The last ones wore off hours ago. I have to say, I'm not sure I could have done the search without them."

"I have more, and you're more than due for another dose. If you take some now, it will be well kicked in by bedtime, so you'll be able to rest. Get Hawk into the shower, and I'll grab you some water." Todd tucked the tape and scissors into the kit, then headed out to the suite's kitchen.

Meg pulled her hair tie out and let her ebony hair fall past her shoulders, only to find two small fern leaves snagged in the strands; she plucked them out and tossed them in the garbage. Then she unsnapped Hawk's collar, pulling a broken twig out of the breakaway buckle, and dropped the mud-smeared collar into the sink for handwashing later. She turned on the shower spray, and grabbed the travel-sized bottle of honey and oatmeal dog shampoo from her toiletries bag as she waited for the water to warm.

"Here." Todd returned with a glass of water and two tablets, which he dropped into her palm before passing her the glass, waiting as she took the pills, then taking it back. "You're good?"

"Yeah."

"I'm headed off to get us some food, then. Back soon." He dropped a kiss on her forehead, picked up her pile of dirty clothes, and left the bathroom, pulling the door shut behind him to contain the warm air.

Meg stepped naked into the shower and called her dog, pulling the sliding glass door closed behind him.

She gave herself fifteen seconds to stand in the spray, letting the water pound on her scalp, her wet hair streaming down her back, before wiping the water from her eyes and changing the water over to the handheld showerhead. Careful to keep the direct spray out of his eyes, she wet Hawk down, then applied a generous amount of shampoo and lathered him with her right hand only as she held her left arm still and close to her torso. She loosened the grit and grime with her fingers before spraying him down, the suds and dirt streaming down the drain. She did a second lather and rinse before flipping the water over to the main showerhead and starting on herself as Hawk happily waited for her.

She swallowed a groan—she didn't want to alarm her dog—as she automatically tried to lift her left arm to wash her hair with both hands as she normally did. One-handed it was. If she couldn't do a great job, Todd could help tomorrow.

As she stood under the spray, she reflected on the day.

She'd thought the hike into the reserve had been challenging. The second hike through it had been worse.

Hawk had unerringly led them along the trail only he

could smell. Meg had spotted where the two men had fled through the ferns, breaking branches as they went, and Hawk had picked up the scent.

Normally, Hawk found a subject by head-up trailing—following the scent via the air or ground—and having the independence to follow the shortest path to the end point. But this was a straightforward head-down tracking method—following the direct path through the muddy fern forest to track exactly where the men had gone, or more specifically, where they exited the forest.

Staying on the exact path was sometimes clear as a bell to both Meg and Hale—footprints in the soft mud, mostly formed but sometimes skidding, broken branches, or felled dead stems. But sometimes, they had to rely on Hawk to get them through. The first part of the search was the hardest, slogging through the thickest part of the fern forest, and Meg had to adopt an angled approach to protect her injured left arm, pushing through with her right hand and arm. They lost much of the altitude she and Todd had gained in their hike into Puʻu Makaʻala, which gave them a different difficulty. Hiking up Mauna Loa had been good cardiac exercise, but hiking down on muddy soil led to slipping.

At one point, while leading the way, Hawk's feet had slid out from under him on a sodden downward patch of mud hidden under fallen fern branches. He'd tried to stay upright—he had a better chance on four feet with a lower center of gravity—and had almost made it before skidding sideways and going down on his left side. Rather than using her usual caution, Meg scrambled after him, needing to know he was uninjured, then slipped and went down on one knee and both hands into the soft mud. She'd nearly screamed as agony shot through her injured left arm and had to take a full ten seconds sucking in air through gritted teeth to be able to even answer Hale's question from above if she was okay.

Bringing up the rear, Hale came down much more slowly, moving from tree trunk to sturdy fern stem, the rest of the way down the slope. Hale had noted that marks of a similar slide lay just to their right, so it looked like one of the men had made it down on his feet, the other oriented in some way against the ground.

They'd been moving roughly northwest in the hour since leaving the clearing, but then they suddenly broke from the trees to a rough, twin track road, allowing them to pick up their pace. Hawk stayed firmly on the trail, and with no impediment to a faster speed, they covered approximately two miles in half the time it had taken them to cover about half that distance to the tracks. When they reached the deserted paved road, they knew their search was over when Hawk lost the scent at the side of the road.

Meg hated when a search ended where a vehicle had been parked. Sometimes they'd discern some details about the vehicle that allowed their target to get away, but not this time. The edge of the road was covered in the thick stubble of dried, wild grass, meaning there was no hope of discerning tire type or chassis size.

They'd come up entirely empty.

By this point, Todd had seen Byrne safely off with her injured charges and had pulled out his phone to track where Meg and Hale might exit the area. Based on their direction when they left the site, he'd extrapolated where the men might have entered Puʻu Makaʻala—Stainback Highway, a road that ran southwest from Hawaiʻi Belt Road for about twenty miles, running between Puʻu Makaʻala Natural Area Reserve and the Upper Waiākea Forest Reserve.

He'd driven back east along Hawaiʻi Belt Road and northwest up North Kūlani Road to then go west on Stainback Highway. He'd pulled off to the side of the road to wait there, not knowing where they'd come out of the reserve and not wanting to go too far in the other direction.

Meg had called a half hour later, and she'd been thrilled to hear he was so close when she'd expected him to take nearly an hour to get to them. They'd still be on Saddle Road now if he hadn't had the intuition to figure out where they'd be.

She gave herself one extra minute to stand under the warm spray before turning off the water. She quickly wrapped both her hair and her body in towels, then stepped out and slid the door shut behind her, leaving Hawk inside.

"Okay, Hawk, shake."

Hawk braced his feet on the tiles and gave himself a hard shake, water flying everywhere, droplets briefly striking the glass with the staccato rap of heavy rainfall.

"Good boy." Meg opened the door again—now it was safe. "Out, Hawk. Mat."

Hawk stepped onto the bath mat and stood patiently as she dried his fur with a fresh towel, then released him to wander their suite. She dried herself, brushed out her hair and left it loose to dry, then went into the bedroom to dress. She went casual, with a T-shirt and a soft pair of shorts. After scrubbing Hawk's dirty collar and leaving it on a hand towel on the bathroom counter to dry, she washed and hung the compression bandage, then went out to the kitchen to feed and water Hawk. Leaving him to eat in peace, Meg wandered through the living room, then stepped out the sliding patio door and onto the garden lanai.

Even though it was nearly ten o'clock, it was still almost seventy-five degrees Fahrenheit with the gentle breeze still carrying an edge of warmth. She walked to the short lava rock wall that separated their lanai from the rest of the property, and gazed out over 'Anaeho'omalu Bay, where the moon hung close to the horizon, leaving a long trail of moonlight to shimmer over the calm waters as it reached out to caress the shore. Casting her face skyward, she took in the canopy of stars; even though here in Waikōloa there was some light pollution, the starscape overhead was still a vast improvement over DC, and allowed her to peacefully enjoy the night sky in a way she hadn't been able to through the passenger window of the SUV when they'd come through the fog. Here there was no fear they'd take a turn too quickly and risk driving off the road and into a rocky lava plain.

A soft brush against her right leg accompanied by a fragrant waft of honey and oatmeal told her she was no longer alone. "Hey, boy. All done?"

She turned and moved to the padded sofa, backed by fat pillows, and dropped down on it. She patted the sofa beside her. "Wanna come up?"

Hawk didn't need to be asked twice. He jumped up, turned around three times on the cushion, then curled into a ball with his nose resting on his front paws and partially tucked under his back leg. He exhaled heavily, and Meg could practically see his residual stress seep away as his muscles relaxed. In seconds, he was out.

Meg lay her hand on Hawk's side, lulled by the steady rise and fall of his ribs.

You need to call Craig.

She groaned with the realization that her phone was still inside on the bathroom counter. She could get up and grab it, but she'd wake Hawk, who pressed against her leg and would likely follow her unless she commanded him to stay. Maybe if he was a little more deeply asleep, she could sneak away and not disturb him. She'd just give him a few more minutes.

She crossed her ankles and tipped her head back, studying the stars through the slats of the pergola. The pain meds must have kicked in—while her arm throbbed, the pain was at a low ebb, finally letting her relax without tightening up to fend off the discomfort. Her eyes felt heavy and gritty, so she let them drift closed. *Just for a minute. Then I'll call Craig.*

She slid into sleep.

CHAPTER 8

Crater: A bowl-shaped depression resulting from either explosion or collapse.

May 29, 9:38 PM
Waikōloa Beach Marriott Resort
Waikōloa, Hawai'i

"Meg."

Meg jerked awake at the sound of her name, shooting into an upright position, then groaning with pain and slipping her right hand just under her wound to keep her arm still.

"Whoa." Todd hurriedly set two stacked takeout containers on the long, low table beside the stone wall and crouched down in front of her. "Sorry, I didn't mean to startle you. I didn't realize you were asleep; I thought you were just relaxed."

Meg blinked a few times until he came into focus. "Guess I was more tired than I thought. I put my head back for a minute, and I must have dropped off."

"Did you call Craig?"

"Not yet. I left my phone inside, and then Hawk curled up against me and I didn't want to disturb him."

"Where is it?"

"Bathroom counter."

"I'll get it." Todd disappeared through the open patio door and returned shortly with her phone in his hand. "Here you go."

"Thanks." The scent of beef and bacon floated over to her, and she inhaled deeply. "That smells amazing. Where did you get it?"

"Downstairs at the restaurant. The kitchens were just closing, but I sweet-talked them into making us a couple of burgers and fries in takeout containers so I could bring them up to the suite." He grinned down at the unconscious dog. "I think we can thank Hawk for our dinner. We're memorable because he is. And I told a bit of a sob story about how hard he worked today, being called in to work with law enforcement on his vacation and all."

"Making friends everywhere he goes, especially with such a sad tale. Want me to shift him so you can sit here?"

"Let's not wake him. He worked hard today. Hold these for a minute." He handed the containers to Meg, then moved the table closer to the couch and carried over one of the padded wicker chairs from the far end of the lanai. "This works." He looked at Meg quizzically when she set the containers down on the table and then beckoned him closer with a curved index finger. He moved closer. "What's up?"

"Just this." She slid her fingers around the back of his neck and into his hair, drawing him in, and settled into a long, slow kiss. He was smiling when she drew away. "That's for letting my dog sleep. And bringing us food."

"Anytime, if that's my reward. What about Hawk? Did he eat?"

"Right after our shower."

"Figured as much. Back in a second." He disappeared

into their suite, then returned a minute later with an open beer for himself and an iced tea for Meg. "Sorry, no cocktail for you tonight while you're on those meds."

"Poor me." She opened the can, took a sip, and smiled her appreciation. "Still, a decent consolation prize. You're the very best of husbands."

"Remember that the next time I do something that pisses you off." He grinned and sat down in the chair, then grabbed the top container, flicked it open, peered inside, and handed it to her. "That one's yours." He opened the second container and then settled back into the cushions after popping a fry into his mouth. "Still hot. I'm glad I tipped so generously."

"Not only thanks for a job well done, but insurance against the next big ask."

"You bet. With us, you never know when that will be."

"I'm going to eat, then I'll call Craig. As you said, I'm going to be waking him, so why not bump it a bit later?"

They both bit into their burgers, and a minute passed in companionable silence before Todd breached it.

"You didn't say anything about the search when you got in the SUV other than they'd gotten away. Which we assumed would happen. But you came back covered in mud, so something happened. You seemed tired, so I didn't want to push you on it right away."

Meg swallowed her bite of burger. "It was pretty much what I expected, minus the slide down a muddy incline. And losing them wasn't surprising. I didn't want to discuss it in front of Hale because you're not FBI personnel and he has no idea how many cases you've worked with us. And then I didn't want to distract you on the drive over Saddle Road because the conditions were, shall we say, challenging." She took him quickly through the majority of the search. "When we got to the end of the twin track road, we found the same metal gate closing off the wire fencing with an identical sign for Puʻu Makaʻala being under the care of the Department of Land and Natural Resources that we saw at the parking area when we entered. Like that second gate at the parking area, it was locked shut."

"The lock was still in place? They hadn't cut it and driven in?"

"No. In the first place, Hawk wouldn't have still been tracking them if they had. Also, if they'd done that, they could have driven in the two miles to where it was a shorter trip into the reserve. The road was pretty muddy from the recent rain, but there was no sign of tire tracks."

"It's probably a maintenance road for the Department of Land and Natural Resources to use because it's so hard to hack your way through the fern forest. But they were probably wise not to use it—if anyone came in behind them, they'd have been trapped."

"A single vehicle blocking the gate on the roadside would accomplish the same goal. They needed a clean getaway, so the service road, while it might have made their lives easier, might also have been a problem."

"What's the general idea? They parked on the side of the road, left their vehicle, hiked in, set up and waited, caught birds, hiked out? Or in this case, got interrupted and lit out of the reserve to where they left their vehicle because once shots were fired, there was a real risk of their escape being cut off by law enforcement?"

"That's what it looks like and is likely why they didn't come after me. Couldn't afford to lose that time. The side of the road is mowed grasses, and the ground was mostly dry, as the plant life around it absorbed much of the water and the rest ran downhill from the paved road. There were no distinguishable tire tracks."

"And you'd think the weather would have been in our favor."

"What do you mean?"

"You told me about how weather patterns on the island are driven by the trade winds. While we didn't see rain yesterday on this side of the island, we know they had significant rainfall on that side because the clouds get blocked by Mauna Kea and Mauna Loa and just hang there, dumping their load instead of spreading it out. But from our point of view, it was either too much rain or too much runoff from the road." Todd jammed a couple of fries into his mouth and chewed thoughtfully before swallowing and washing it down with beer. "Speaking of the road, there's something you and Hale might be missing because you only rode east down Stainback Highway once I picked you up."

"What's that?"

"It's a public road only up to a point. There's a minimum-security correctional facility farther west from where I picked you up."

"Seriously? In the middle of Pu'u Maka'ala? That seems like an odd place for it."

"It's on the border of Pu'u Maka'ala, not in the middle of it. And it might not be such an odd place from an escape perspective. Anyone who gets out of the facility would have two choices—being entirely visible on the road or getting extremely lost and bogged down—pun not intended—in the fern forest. Not to mention it's isolated, so no risk to the community around the facility. It actually makes sense."

"I guess. What are you thinking?"

"I waited off the road fairly far east of you because I wasn't sure where you'd exit Pu'u Maka'ala and didn't want to overshoot you, not knowing what the roads would be like farther into the wilderness. After you called and I headed in, I went past a sign warning that, past that point, the road was for authorized personnel only and everyone else was trespassing. From what I'd seen of the map, that likely makes the last approximately six or eight miles leading to the Kulani Correctional Facility for authorized use only. I wasn't worried that I was trespassing because once I had Hale in the vehicle, he could talk our way out of any law enforcement trouble."

In a flash, Meg understood the direction of his thoughts. "Which means that if they parked a vehicle at the side of the road as we hypothesized, leaving it there for hours, even on a relatively untraveled road, they'd run the risk of being discovered."

"Exactly. I think you need to assume there's at least one more person in this ring. Likely way more, truth be told, but one more for this particular excursion. You had a cell signal; so would they. At some point as they rabbited, they called for a pickup. The chance of being caught while in motion for the fifteen or twenty minutes it would take to drive both there and back is considerably lower than leaving a car unattended for hours right by a gate leading into the reserve."

Meg set down her burger, picked up her phone, and opened a browser window.

"What are you looking for?"

"Reasons to be on that road." She ran a quick Google search, instantly finding what she was looking for. "As I thought. Kulani Correctional Facility has visitation for its inmates, so traffic in and out on that road beyond the expected staff isn't unheard of. Get caught, and all you have to say is you're on the way to visit someone at the facility. You're right; that's what they likely did—called for a pickup by someone who was waiting for them, just like you did for us. That person drove in, picked them up, and they disappeared."

She finished the last few bites of her burger, had a few more fries, and then pushed her container toward Todd. "I'm stuffed. Want the rest?"

Todd hooked an index finger over the lip of her container and dragged it a little closer. "Like you need to ask."

Meg chuckled, but then her smile slid away as she glanced down at her phone. "Time to ruin someone's sleep."

"He wants you to make the call."

"I know, but I still feel bad." She speed-dialed Craig's number, waiting as the phone rang once, twice, three times.

Craig picked it up just before it would have flipped to voicemail. "Beaumont." His voice was low and sleep-slurred.

"It's Meg. I'm sorry to wake you."

"I asked you to. Hang on." There was a full thirty seconds of silence, where Meg knew Craig was creeping out of his bedroom so he didn't wake his wife. "Sorry about that."

"No worries."

"How are you? Do you need additional medical care?"

"Todd says no. Do you want to hear it from him personally? He's right here if you don't believe me."

"I believe you. There's no way he's going to let something happen to you if he can help it. He'll hang over you more than I would. I just wanted a check-in to make sure you hadn't had a setback."

"It's not comfortable, but I'm managing, and he's going to clean and dress it again before we go to bed."

"Any updates on the recovered endangered birds?"

"Last we heard, Byrne was taking them to the Hawai'i Wildlife Center, but that was hours ago. The goal is to rehabilitate and release back into the same area."

"Good, good."

There were a few seconds of silence, and Meg felt Craig's

tension across the five thousand miles separating them. "Craig? Everything okay?"

"You're not my first call tonight. I heard from Hale about two hours ago."

"Bad night for you."

Craig's laugh echoed with exhaustion. "Not a great one for sleep."

"Why did Hale call? He was with me when I updated you when we finished the search. That was before you went to bed."

"He had a request." Craig's heavy exhalation carried across their connection. "Are you private?"

"We're out on our private lanai, and I doubt anyone is close enough to hear, but I can't guarantee it."

"Move to somewhere private with Todd. You're just going to tell him anyway, so he might as well be in on this from the start."

"We're that predictable?"

"Pretty much." There was no accusation in Craig's tone, just easy acceptance. "This team keeps adding extra people, and Todd's been one of them too many times to count. It's fine."

"Hang on a minute, then." Meg drew the word out as she met Todd's questioning gaze. She dropped the phone. "He wants us to move inside to talk to both of us." She tried to slip sideways out of the couch without disturbing Hawk, but her dog snapped awake instantly. "Sorry, buddy. Now you're awake, come inside with us." She stood, waved for Todd to follow, then walked back into the suite with Hawk at her knee.

Todd entered behind her and slid the door closed.

Meg put the phone on speaker and sat down on the couch beside Todd. Hawk flopped down on the rug just inside the lanai door. "We're inside. What's going on?"

"You really impressed the hell out of Hale. Byrne, too, apparently. Both of you, for your presence of mind in the crisis, willingness to assist trapped wildlife, and dedication to jump into a search at a moment's notice. Then how you and Hawk successfully tracked the suspects until you hit a dead end. Hale's never worked with a K-9 team before, and he was extremely pleased with you and Hawk."

"I'm happy to hear he approved." Meg's tone was dry. She already knew they were a kick-ass team and didn't need her approval and acclaim to come from external sources.

"You might not be in a second," Craig retorted. "He wants you to work this case."

"You told him I'm out of the office?"

"You bet I did. His response was you stepped out of your office and into his. He and Byrne both want you. They've always known the area is a hub for wildlife trafficking, but what they've lacked is boots-on-the-ground proof. Birds have been found in other countries that must have come from Hawaii, but they've never caught the traffickers in the act. You changed that today. This is the proof they needed to launch a full investigation."

"They assume since these guys didn't get their prizes, they'll try again?"

"Yes. So they've requested your services. I told them I wasn't going to order you to help. Normally I would have no problem deploying you, but you're on your honeymoon. I offered him Brian and Lacey, but he wants to start tomorrow, and I can't guarantee I can get them there that fast. The morning would be impossible. Even the afternoon, your time, would depend on if I can get him now and then get him on a plane in about two hours."

Meg met Todd's eyes, reassured she didn't see anger. But she wasn't sure she didn't see disappointment. "Todd? Thoughts?"

"Obviously, I'd like our honeymoon to continue," he stated flatly.

That was that, then. They had so little time to themselves—he with his schedule at the firehouse, and she constantly living on the edge of a deployment. This had been time set aside for *them*. And now her job was threatening to pull her away. They only had days left. Maybe Craig could send Brian now and she'd work the case for the next day or two only until he arrived. Then, if the investigation was ongoing once the honeymoon was over, she could—

Todd's hand fell over hers where she unconsciously gripped her knee. He loosened her fingers and wrapped his around them. "That being said, days could make all the difference here. Maybe it doesn't seem like much—they're just tiny birds—but a life is a life. Just because it doesn't weigh a ton and have tusks doesn't mean it's unimportant. You and Hawk could make a real difference. Could contribute to saving a species, maybe more than one. We've all saved lives; there's not many who can say they've saved an entire species. It has to stop, and you and Hawk can help."

There were a few seconds of silence, and then Craig said, "So, I'm telling Hale yes?"

Meg held Todd's gaze, making sure what he was saying went gut deep. And what she saw there settled any question. Her shoulders relaxed, and she gripped his hand back: "You can tell him yes on two conditions. One—you get Brian and Lacey on a plane ASAP to help share the workload so maybe I'll get a few more hours of honeymoon with my husband, but I'll start things off for the teams if there's a delay getting him to Hawaii."

"That's more than fair."

"Two—Todd is part of every aspect of the team. I'm not wandering off with my dog on my honeymoon and leaving him here all alone. He comes along, Craig. Every meeting, every deployment. You know as well as I do, he can keep up through any conditions we can handle, and his skills make him a useful member of the team. Call him a civilian consultant or mutual aid, however you want to work it, but that's a deal-breaker for me."

"You don't have to sell me on including Webb. I've seen him in action."

"He'll only add to our skill set out there. That's what you tell Hale; those are my conditions. Otherwise, he gets Brian and Lacey."

"Done. I won't call you back; you'll be heading to bed yourself soon. Check for a text from me with further instructions when you get up. Thanks, Meg. I know Hale is going to be pleased."

"Then he'll agree to my terms. Thanks, Craig. Go back to bed."

"Once I roust Brian out of his and get his flight arranged. Then, third time's the charm. Night." And Craig was gone.

Meg swiveled to face Todd. "You're sure you're okay with this?"

He clasped her hand in both of his. "I meant what I said about the good you could do here. I was okay with just you and Hawk doing it. But I appreciate the inclusion even more."

"You're never anything but an asset to our cases. I'd be insane not to use you." She took his hand, looped his arm over her head, and nestled back against him. "Speaking of insane, not to use . . ."

Todd's chest vibrated with his laughter. "I know exactly where this is going. McCord's next on your list?"

"Well, I did tell him not to rest on his Pulitzer Prize–winning laurels for too long. I gave him a little over a week."

"You're going to call him at this hour? I mean, Craig told you to call, but McCord?"

"That would just be mean. I'll send him a text to find in the morning. I don't know if he knows anything about wildlife trafficking—"

"With McCord, you never know."

"Seriously. If he doesn't, he'll have a deep dive started before we make contact in the morning." She sent him a long text message with all the details, and told him she'd reach out to him when they were up in the morning. She didn't include the details of her injury. She'd rather tell him and her sister about it over the phone so she could answer all their questions and reassure them she was okay. "That's done. Now I guess you want to clean and bandage my arm again?"

"Yes. Then I think you're ready for bed."

"I wouldn't say no to that. I'm bushed."

"You had a busy day. Add on wrestling with the pain of a gunshot wound? Draining, to say the least."

She rose and followed him into the master bathroom so he could deal with her wound.

But her mind was already racing ahead, strategizing how the teams could help change the course of this investigation.

CHAPTER 9

Tilt: The change in the slope of a volcano during inflation as magma swells its surface.

May 30, 1:52 PM
Daniel K. Inouye International Airport
Honolulu, Oʻahu

Meg craned her neck as the security doors slid closed again after belching out a crowd of travelers dragging suitcases behind them. "I think I caught a glimpse of Brian."

Todd checked the time on the arrival board. "It's been long enough for him to have disembarked and picked up his bag. He and Lacey would be the first ones off the plane, as they're on Bureau business."

"That's what usually happens when we fly. Craig always paves the way so the airlines know we're in a time crunch." She glanced down at Hawk, who sat quietly on her left side. So far, holding his leash in her left hand hadn't pulled on her injured arm because Hawk was so well-behaved. Todd had checked and repacked the wound that morning after pronouncing it clean and starting the healing process. She found the pain manageable as long as she kept her arm down at her side and didn't make any sudden movements. "Hawk will be overjoyed to see Lacey. He loves hanging out with us, but I think he missed her after a full week."

"They're like an old married couple, those two."

They were standing inside the arrivals area of Hawaii's largest airport. Unlike the smaller airport in Kona on the Big Island they'd flown into—where most of its facilities were essentially outdoors, comprising large swaths of covered seating to let in the warm island air—Honolulu's airport felt like it could have been in any large metropolitan city on the mainland. It was another brilliantly sunny west coast island day, and a chorus of mynah birds in the tall palms outside echoed off the bare walls inside each time the double outer doors slid open.

The doors to baggage claim opened and another crowd of people stepped through.

"There he is," Todd said.

Meg's gaze found Brian's dark head. Tall and athletic, he was dressed in their standard uniform of casual clothes—in his case, running pants and an athletic T-shirt—wore his go bag over both shoulders, and carried a duffel as Lacey trotted easily at his side on a loose leash. He looked tired, his hair a little messy and the lines around his green eyes a little deeper than usual, but Meg chalked that up to an extremely early start to his day and travel fatigue. The text she'd found from Craig upon rising had said he had Brian booked on an American Airlines flight leaving Dulles at 7:18 AM EDT and landing in O'ahu at 1:34 PM HST, with an hour-long stopover in Phoenix, Arizona. She knew from her own experience a week earlier that it was a long flight to Hawaii, but a stopover around the halfway point was imperative when traveling with a dog, as they couldn't use the tiny onboard restrooms like the humans could.

Thank God for airports with pet-relief stations. Craig would have planned Brian's flight accordingly.

Meg waved her right arm over her head to draw Brian's attention, and he brightened, the lines of exhaustion disappearing as he grinned and waved back. Meg was about to tell Hawk that Lacey was coming, when the words died on her tongue as Brian turned to his left, his lips moving in speech. Then a second man leaned forward to peer around Brian, searching the crowd, and her jaw dropped. "McCord?"

"What about him?" Todd asked.

"He's here."

"What?"

"He's with Brian."

Todd shook his head with an amused smile. "Why am I not surprised? I guess we now know why his answer to your text was only that he'd reach out when he had more information. Apparently he's going to reach out personally and do his research on-site."

"Sneaky man. Come on, Hawk. Let's go meet Lacey. Heel."

At the sound of the German shepherd's name, Hawk shot to his feet. He fell into step with Meg, but was practically vibrating with anticipation. Not that she blamed him. She was happy to see both men—not just because they were valuable work colleagues, but because they were essentially family.

Brian grinned as he slipped between people milling near the arrivals security door. "How's my favorite newly married couple?" He dropped his duffel on the ground and opened his arms to Meg.

"Glad to see you. Watch the left arm." She stepped in and hugged him back.

Hawk, in an unexpected moment of enthusiasm, lunged for Lacey. Meg cried out in pain as her arm was jerked, and she released the leash to avoid further injury.

Directly behind Brian, McCord was the first to react, letting go of his rolling suitcase—which crashed to the floor—as he grabbed for the leash, catching it in midair. "I have him. Hawk, buddy, calm down."

Brian loosely clasped Meg's shoulders, holding her steady as air sawed through her gritted teeth. "You okay?"

"Give me a minute and I will be. Check on the dogs?"

Brian spun away to deal with the dogs, and Todd was there, holding her arm gently with one hand, his other arm around her waist. "Do I need to look at it?"

Meg shook her head. "No, he just gave it a jerk. Totally my fault. I should have anticipated he'd be so happy to see Lacey that I needed to tell him to stay and then release him when it was clear." She looked over to where Brian held both dogs' leashes as they sniffed and danced circles around each other excitedly. "They're so happy to see each other. Just as I'm happy to see you, Brian."

Brian tossed a grin over his shoulder. "Ditto, babe."

Meg turned to McCord. "And you. Thank you for catching my dog." She leaned into him to give him a one-armed hug with her uninjured arm, then pulled back to take him in. Like Brian, he was dressed casually, though for McCord that meant faded blue jeans, white sneakers, and a black T-shirt that read REGARDLESS OF WHAT YOU SAY, "IRREGARDLESS" IS STILL NOT A WORD in white block letters. *Grammar geek.* He didn't look as exhausted as Brian, but that might be nothing more than a steady stream of caffeine, knowing McCord. His blond hair was unruffled, and his blue eyes behind the wire-rimmed frames of his glasses were as sharp as usual. "I didn't expect to see you. Hear from you, yes—see you, no."

"Did you really think I'd turn down an excuse to go to Hawaii?"

"I didn't think you'd be able to talk Sykes into the expense."

There was a devilish twinkle in McCord's eye that matched his grin. "I caught him at a weak moment." The grin faded as his gaze dropped to her arm. "Brian told me about your arm on the way in. Have you told Cara?"

Meg's cheeks warmed. "No. I didn't want to worry her. And I didn't think you'd be here to rat me out."

"I won't rat you out unless you don't call her and tell her before she goes to bed tonight. Otherwise, all bets are off."

"You drive a hard bargain, McCord."

"Always. You sure you're okay?"

"It hurts like crazy, but it's not serious."

The expression on McCord's face said he wasn't sure if he should believe her. "Webb?"

"She's going to be fine. A few inches to the right, we'd be having an entirely different conversation. But she was lucky. The bullet skittered across the outside of her arm, but never penetrated the arm proper."

"She *was* lucky."

Meg rolled her eyes and leaned hard on her patience. "*She* is standing right here, you know."

"Oh, we know." McCord grinned, breaking the tension. "So . . . my impromptu trip. I woke up when your text came in, and hit the ground running."

"Cara must have loved that."

"I did it quietly downstairs."

As Cara and McCord lived in the identical other half of the duplex they'd purchased with Meg and Todd, Meg could very well imagine McCord sneaking downstairs with his laptop from his office tucked under his arm to settle at the kitchen table to start making plans.

"You said Brian was going to be flying out, so Brian was my first call. He was up and getting ready to go, as Craig had already booked him on an American Airlines flight leaving Dulles at seven eighteen. I got all the info and then called Sykes."

"I remember how much Sykes hates mornings."

"Abhors early morning calls, so that had him off-balance already. Then I played the Pulitzer card."

"Brilliant. I'm impressed." Brian's smile was full of approval. "You'll only be able to pull that lever so many times, though."

"Exactly. I figured I should shoot for the stars, especially while Sykes is riding high. A *Post*-sponsored trip to Hawaii? With the same team that brought us the Pulitzer? Seemed perfect to me. He wasn't immediately onboard, but I convinced him."

"Probably didn't hurt that he wanted to go back to bed," Todd said.

"That also played in my favor. Once I wore him down enough for him to rubber-stamp it, I called Craig."

"Had he gone back to bed by that time?" Meg asked.

"No, he was still making arrangements. All I wanted was a confirmation of flight numbers, but Craig told me he'd handle it and just to get ready to leave. Twenty minutes later, I had my ticket and boarding passes in my inbox."

"Craig is an organizational wizard."

"He really is. He got me on the same connecting flight and even got us booked together to give Brian some freedom during the trip."

"I normally travel with Meg, so if I need to sneak off to hit the head, she watches Lacey, and vice versa. Traveling alone is harder, so having McCord there as backup was great." Brian rubbed the back of his neck like it had a kink in it. "It's a long series of flights." He dropped his hand to stroke Lacey's head. "But you were great, weren't you Lacey-girl?"

The German shepherd sat up taller and thumped her tail on the tile floor.

"We would expect nothing less." Meg met Brian's eyes. "Did Craig tell you about the deal we made with Special Agent Jeremy Hale, out of the Honolulu field office?"

"That Todd is in on the investigation?"

"Yes. That was my requirement for him interrupting my honeymoon. The inclusion of my husband."

"Who is an asset to any investigation." Brian held up a hand to Todd, who high-fived him back. Then he looked sideways at McCord. "We're not going to be able to do that for you."

"At least not at the beginning," Meg agreed. "Sorry, McCord. You're going to have to sit this meeting out."

McCord's expression clearly stated he knew he'd be on the outside, at least to start. "See if you can introduce the concept of me to them. I mean, I can work from the outside, but you know how much better it goes if I work from the inside with you."

"Preaching to the choir. Leave it with us." Meg checked the time on her fitness tracker. "We have about a half-hour drive to the Honolulu field office, but the meeting isn't until three o'clock, which gives us a little wiggle room. Do you need a coffee? A meal?"

"All of the above for me. Have you eaten airplane food?"

"I have—that's why I asked. Brian, does Lacey need anything?"

"Not a thing now she has Hawk. I'm with McCord, though. Just hit a drive-through for a burger or a sandwich and coffee strong enough to stand a spoon in. I've been awake for fifteen hours, traveling in some capacity for about thirteen, and it's only midafternoon here, so I need to last at least another five or six. Caffeine is a must. Lacey slept on the plane, so she'll be fine. *I* need a boost."

"Ditto," McCord said.

"Okay, food and strong coffee. Check." Meg held out her hand for Hawk's leash and then gave Brian a pointed look when he hesitated. "I'm ready for him now. I just need to remember to rely on voice commands a bit more than usual for the next week or two. I'll be fine. Thanks," she said as he reluctantly handed over Hawk's leash.

Todd grabbed Brian's bag, waving away his protests. "You manage Lacey, I have this. McCord can manage his own because he doesn't have a dog. We're in the parking structure across the road. This way."

McCord took two steps to follow then stopped dead. "It's just occurred to me that you didn't know I was coming." He sounded suddenly unsure. "You'll be able to fit us all into your vehicle?"

Meg wagged an index finger at McCord. "This is what you get for being a smart-ass and not telling us to expect you." The finger swung toward Brian. "You could have said something too."

"I wasn't aware you didn't know until we were back in the air after the stopover in Phoenix. I assumed someone had looped you in."

"Nope." Meg gave McCord a pointed look, then let him off the hook with an easy smile. "Lucky for you, we had Hale arrange for us to pick up a seven-seater SUV with a third row once we landed on Oʻahu so we have plenty of room for everyone and their luggage with the dogs. We'll be fine. But if we don't get moving, we won't have time to get you that coffee. Hawk, come."

"When did you get here?" Brian asked as they moved as a group toward one set of exit doors.

"About forty-five minutes before you. That gave us time to pick up the SUV, circle around to the airport, park, and come back to the terminal to meet you. What's the plan after the meeting?"

"I haven't checked my email since we landed, but Craig said he was going to book us on the same flight you had going back to Hawai'i. And he said he got us into the same resort as you guys as well, so we can all travel together. Though he told us we weren't getting a fancy suite like you had." Brian jolted slightly, like he'd just remembered something. "Oh, yeah, and he said to tell you Uncle Sam is going to pick up part of your stay on the island and he's extended your current suite at your resort. He wanted you to know you're now on the clock, and that means accommodation, as well. He said to take the money you would have spent and save it for a fancy weekend away on your first anniversary to make up for this."

"Sounds like Craig's feeling guilty."

"He is."

"That's silly. It was our choice. I could have turned down the assignment and left it to you." She waved an index finger between herself and Todd. "We chose to pitch in."

"I know. Still, he feels bad. Milk it for all it's worth, I say. This gives you some leverage the next time you need a favor."

"Like an extra day off for my one-year anniversary trip."

"Now you're talking."

They walked out of the terminal and into sunlight, tropical breezes, and birdsong.

Brian inhaled deeply through his nose, his head tipped back, and his eyes closed. "Oh, God, just smell this place."

"Hawaiian car exhaust smells like DC car exhaust if you ask me," quipped McCord.

Brian threw him a nonplussed look, and then his gaze shifted past McCord to the tropical gardens that lined the front of the terminal. "I'm smelling that. What is that?"

"No idea," Meg said. "But it's lovely." She pointed across the busy roadway that curved in front of the arrivals doors on the ground floor. "We're over there. Coffee and food, then let's find out what the Bureau and Fish and Wildlife have in store for us."

CHAPTER 10

Caldera: A large crater created following a volcanic eruption when the roof of the magma chamber below collapses.

May 30, 3:01 PM
FBI Honolulu Field Office
Honolulu, Oʻahu

Meg's first thought as they were ushered into the conference room by a junior agent was that it didn't matter where in the world you were, every Bureau meeting room looked the same. The only difference was instead of the surrounding gray brick and stone buildings of DC, here in Honolulu, the view out the window was of waving palm branches and the lush green spread of a mountain range in the distance.

"Nicer than cramming into Craig's office," Brian murmured as he sat down.

"Maybe when he gets that conference room he keeps talking about, it will have a view this nice," Meg retorted.

Brian snickered, then bent to unleash his dog, who stood beside his chair. "Only if we hang tropical vacation posters on the walls. You know he's never going to get that conference room, right? He's going to keep wishing for it, and it's never going to happen."

Meg pulled out the chair beside Brian. "I know. In his heart, I think Craig knows too. He just doesn't want to admit it because that's the end of the dream. Hawk, sit." She unleashed Hawk, coiled the leash, and set it on the table in front of her chair. "Go lie down with Lacey." She pointed to the far end of the conference room, under a mounted whiteboard.

The dogs wandered to the end of the room and flopped down side by side, their heads on their front paws, angled together to touch, a picture of contentment.

Todd leaned in as he moved to sit down on Meg's other side. "See?" he murmured. "Old married couple."

Meg chuckled and turned to Brian, who sat with his hands wrapped around a massive takeout cup of coffee. "Hanging in?" She glanced at the digital clock on the wall, did the calculation. "It's ten PM your time. Long day for you, especially considering how early your morning started."

Brian's response was to first pick up his cooling coffee and take several deep gulps. "Second wind is finally hitting. Just in time too."

"We won't make fun of you if you doze off on the flight to the Big Island. And Todd will drive the half hour to the resort, so you only need to be conscious for this meeting. After that, we'll get you where you need to go. I know you sleep like the dead. Between the flight back and a good night at the resort, you'll be ready to hit the ground running tomorrow morning."

"Lacey too." Brian smiled in the direction of his dog. "In fact, she's already out."

"Smart girl."

The door to the conference room opened and Hale walked in, followed by Byrne, who closed the door behind them. Both were dressed more formally in dark business suits, and Hale carried two black boxes, each about eight by twelve by three inches.

Gun safes. Hale brought us weapons.

Meg stood and introduced Brian to the newcomers as they settled in chairs across the table.

Hale's gaze shot between the two men. "Where's . . . McCord, is it?"

Meg froze in surprise. Convincing Bureau personnel to trust McCord was always a challenge, and she and Brian were prepared to talk the reporter's way into the case. "You know about McCord?"

"Beaumont mentioned him. Said that he was with *The Washington Post* but not to let that hold us back on letting him help on the case. That he's become an unofficial dependable team member, just like Todd."

"Yeah. We're a little unconventional."

Hale's laugh came quick and sharp. "I'll say. But Beaumont assured me that I wouldn't regret including him. That I'd likely regret it if I didn't. I thought you'd bring him with you."

"He's waiting in the SUV," Brian said. "Knowing McCord, he's already hot-spotted his phone and is deep into research on his laptop, but would one hundred percent rather be here."

"I can text him," Meg offered. "Have him come up?"

"If he's really going to be an amazing resource, he might as well be here from the beginning," said Hale. "You're sure we can trust him?"

"I'd trust my life to the information he can dig up. And have."

"Ditto," Brian confirmed.

"I'm just the rescue and resource guy," Todd added, "but his information has literally allowed me to save multiple lives. He's an asset."

"Then get him in here. I'll get someone to bring him up."

Meg pulled out her phone and shot a text to McCord— **They want you in here. Come now. Front door, someone will bring you up.**

McCord's answer was nearly instantaneous. **SERIOUSLY?** Meg nearly smiled at the implied surprise in his single-word response. **Yes. Now.**

OMW

"He's coming," Meg reported.

"Now that's done, how's the arm?" Byrne asked.

"Still hurts," Meg admitted. "But it's clean and there's no sign of infection."

"Good news."

"Todd has cleared me to work searches. I'll just have to be a little more careful of it, but it shouldn't impede us as a team."

"Even better."

Hale swiveled in his chair to face Todd. "I want to thank you both, but especially you, Todd, for giving up your personal time for this case. Beaumont made it clear you'd only be an asset to the team."

He also made it clear there was no team without him. "We appreciate your understanding on this," said Meg.

"We appreciate your willingness to pitch in."

"You're welcome. Just so you know, Brian is up to speed with everything we know so far, so you won't have to backtrack for him."

"We appreciate you coming all this way, Brian."

"Happy to help." Brian's gaze dropped to the boxes. "Those for us?"

"Yes. Beaumont asked me to get you sidearms. There have already been shots fired in this case, and he doesn't want you unarmed. Nor do we. He said you both prefer a Glock 19."

"That's right," said Brian. "I brought my concealed shoulder holster with me, but Meg will need one."

"Beaumont told us which style you use when you're armed during an active search. We have that available for you. The gun safes are for use in transit and for safety at the resort."

"That works for us," Meg said.

"Great. We'll get the safes programmed for your fingerprints and get you that holster, Meg, when we're done with this meeting."

"Sounds good. Any updates on the birds?"

"They seem to be recovering well so far. The 'I'iwi lacerated by the net will likely only need a week or so to heal. The 'Alawī with the broken wing will need about four weeks. Luckily, it's just a radial break with minimal displacement and the ulna is intact, so they can simply wing wrap the bird with the bone in place and it will knit fairly quickly. They're confident both will survive and are hopeful of returning them to their natural environment as soon as the birds are stable and able to survive on their own. They know where they came from and plan to return them to the same location."

Meg and Todd exchanged relieved glances.

"That's great news," Meg said. "What's your plan? You wanted dogs here to help, but we're not sure what you have in mind."

"You interrupted the members of a wildlife trafficking ring in the act of trapping birds for export out of Hawaii. Being burned once is not going to stop them. They have a quota to make and will be back to try again."

"In that exact spot?" Todd asked. "Wouldn't that be asking to be caught?"

"It would," Byrne said. "So they're going to pick another location. That's where things get tricky. I talked to the rehab experts about this, and they agreed that area was chosen not just because it's occupied by the endangered birds, but because it's their nesting grounds. Currently, it's the end of nesting season and the beginning of fledgling season."

"How long does that last?"

"Oddly enough, the area around Volcanoes National Park tends to be a little on the early side for both. In some areas, nesting is April to June, occasionally stretching out to July, but in that southern area, it's March to May for nesting, sometimes even beginning as early as February. By May to June, we're looking at the young starting to emerge from the nest."

"Are the traffickers going to try for the nests?" Brian asked.

"No, they don't care about nests or fledglings that could die if their parents are removed." Byrne's tone was flat. "They want their prize and don't care who or what gets hurt in the meantime. But parents stay close to nests during breeding season, to protect or incubate the eggs or to feed nestlings and fledglings as they grow."

"You anticipate they'll select breeding grounds to set up their mist nets because they don't wander too far from home," Todd stated.

"Yes."

"Do we assume this is a two-day process?" Brian asked. "I saw the pictures of the clearing you sent to our SAC. Do you think they came in one day to prepare the area and hang the net and then returned the next day for their spoils?"

"Close," said Hale. "They couldn't chance a perfectly good bird flying into an unattended net and dying before they got back. I'm sure they also appreciate these are rare specimens." He glanced at the wall clock, his brow furrowed, but then continued. "Our hypothesis is they clear-cut the area one day and came back the next to put up the mist net and then stayed out of sight waiting for birds to be trapped by it. They won't use the same area now we know about it. They'll have to clear at least one new area."

"Unless they've already done it," Todd stated. "Then they might move faster than expected."

Hale spun in his chair to look at Byrne. "That's a damned good point. They may have selected spots ahead of time and razed the space to hang the mist netting and for the birds to fly through the new clearing. They're not going to want to hold on to those birds for any longer than they need to, so it would make sense to catch them all over the shortest period of time."

"If that's true, we've arrived just in time," said Brian. "But how to find those areas? It's a big island."

"There are limited ranges where the birds will be found," Byrne said. "Many of the most endangered are only found above forty-five hundred feet."

"Which explains Puʻu Makaʻala," Meg said. "I think we started below that altitude but hiked into it."

"A large portion of the nature reserve is above forty-five hundred feet. Which still creates an issue. But we can narrow things down."

As if on cue, the conference room door opened behind them. Hawk and Lacey shot from relaxed to alert and then were instantly on their feet.

"Hawk, stay."

Brian gave an identical command to Lacey as both he and Meg swiveled in their chairs to face the newcomer, and it was quickly evident why the dogs snapped to attention so quickly.

A tall, lean man with deeply tanned skin, brown eyes, and a lined face that spoke of a life outdoors stood in the doorway, dressed in hiking boots, cargo pants, and a long-sleeved athletic shirt. At his side stood one of the most striking Australian shepherds Meg had ever seen, its coat a swirl of brown, white, black, and gray, with shockingly clear ice-blue eyes. Meeting the dog's eyes, Meg swore she could see intelligence in their depths.

"Kai, you made it." Hale stood, rounded the table, and offered his hand to the man. "Come on in. Meg, Brian, Todd, this is Kai Akana and his dog, Makoa. Kai, this is Meg Jennings and Brian Foster, handlers with the Human Scent Evidence Team, and Meg's husband, Lieutenant Todd Webb of DC Fire and Emergency Services."

"*Aloha 'auinalā.*" Kai's voice was surprisingly rich and deep, sounding like it belonged in a much larger man.

Meg offered her hand, and they shook. "And those are our search-and-rescue K-9s at the end of the table. The black Lab is my Hawk; the German shepherd is Brian's Lacey. Are they okay to greet Makoa?"

Kai released Brian's hand. " '*Ae*. Yes. He's excellent with other dogs."

"Ours too. Hawk, Lacey, doggie greet."

The two dogs immediately trotted over, and Meg gave the three animals thirty seconds to sniff each other before ordering Hawk back to the far end of the room, the other two dogs following. The handlers waited until the dogs settled, then Meg and Brian took their seats as Kai shook hands with Todd and circled the table to greet Byrne before taking the chair beside her.

The door opened again to the same junior agent and McCord. McCord stepped into the room, his laptop bag over his shoulder and a look of caution on his face.

Meg stood. "You'll have to excuse McCord's disbelief. It's usually a battle to bring him into a case. We've never had an invitation this early."

"We've never had an invitation, period," McCord mumbled, only loud enough for Meg to hear. He smiled across the table at the three strangers. "Clay McCord, *The Washington Post.*" He dropped his laptop bag into the empty chair beside Todd and circled around to shake hands with everyone he hadn't met, before returning to sit in his chair. "I appreciate joining the team at this early juncture."

"It's not often we work with a journalist on a case," Hale stated.

"Not often? Try never." Byrne's sotto voce comment was still loud enough to reach the far side of the table.

"I'm aware my presence might make things a little awkward for you. To be crystal clear, the deal I have with SAC Craig Beaumont holds for you as well. You share information with me, I do the research legwork and share everything I have with you. I'm not law enforcement, so I can make contact with people you can't. And I sit on anything I find until the case is wrapped. Then I get the exclusive story on the investigation."

"And the *Post* is okay with this arrangement?" Hale asked.

"My editor is, and that's really all that matters. He sent me out here." McCord couldn't help a little preening and sat up taller. "One of my stories from a case last year recently won the Pulitzer Prize in investigative reporting, so I have a little leverage currently. These cases have paid off for the paper and given them access they'd never have otherwise. They're satisfied to wait for a big story."

"And if the case is never solved?"

"Then I got a trip to Hawaii." McCord shrugged. "Hasn't happened yet, but it's bound to at some point. No one's case resolution rate is one hundred percent." He bent down and unzipped his bag, pulling out his laptop and setting it in front of him. "You're okay with me taking notes? Saves me time to do it this way, time I can then spend working on research aspects for you."

Hale and Byrne exchanged a glance, then both nodded.

"Great, thanks." McCord brought his laptop out of hibernation and opened a new document in his word processor.

"Now that we're all here, let's get to it," Hale said. "Meg, Brian, you might be wondering why we pulled in another dog when we already have two at our disposal."

Brian shook his head. "Not if Makoa has skills other than a live-find dog. Let me guess . . . Conservation dog?"

Kai's surprised grin answered before his verbal confirmation. "That's right. What gave us away?"

"It was the specialty that made the most sense. No use for an explosives, decomp, drug, or therapy dog in this situation." Brian looked sideways at Meg. "Ever worked with a conservation dog before?"

"No. I've heard of them, but in our line of work, there's never been a need. Up until now."

"Humor me," McCord interjected. "What's a conservation dog? I've never heard of that kind of K-9 before."

Meg motioned with an open palm to Kai to make the explanation.

"You obviously know a lot about K-9 work if you've worked with handler and dog teams before," Kai said. "You likely know how dogs are trained on specific scents—only explosives, or drugs, or human decomposition, and so on. In this case, our dogs are trained on specific scents related to animal and bird conservation. Mostly they're trained to scent invasive species—invasive rats, for example, which destroy fragile ecosystems or consume endangered seabird eggs, further endangering the species. Or our dogs do biosecurity inspections on incoming vessels to make sure there are no rats, yellow crazy ants, or fire ants onboard that could transfer to the island. Some dogs can sniff out invasive plants like devil weed, allowing conservationists to pull the plants and remove them from the environment. Or some dogs detect coconut rhinoceros beetles—two-inch-long, hard-shelled beetles with what looks like a rhinoceros horn on their noses—which can burrow into coconut and oil palms, as well as banana trees, sugar cane, and pineapple trees. Once the dog detects an infestation, the tree can be treated before it's too late to be saved. However, Makoa's a bird dog. The majority of his work is finding seabird nests."

McCord's fingers flew over the keys as he made notes.

"They're so invisible they need a dog to find them?" Brian asked.

"A lot of seabirds only spend significant time on land to nest. They build their nests in a crevice in the ground and only emerge at night to find food. If we can find those nests, we can protect them from predators who will decimate the nest and kill the parent bird. The predators are all invasive species, so the seabirds never evolved to escape them. Cats, rats, mongooses, dogs, and goats are all predators. We can help these endangered birds by protecting their nesting grounds, but we have to find them first." Kai looked over to where his dog lay next to Lacey. "Makoa is a champ there."

"As important as that work is, we're not looking at seabirds," Meg said.

"He's also trained on forest birds. They have a different scent, but there's enough overlap that he's trained on both. For instance, whereas seabirds have a musky, fishy scent, a bird like the 'Apapane has a musky, sweet scent."

"Where are the birds nesting?" Todd asked. "Where we were in Pu'u Maka'ala, there were some pretty tall trees. If the nests are up top, would he detect them?"

"Part of the detection is the excrement left by the birds. Or the fecal sacs of the young."

"Fecal sacs?" There was a note of caution in Brian's voice. "Is that what I think it is?"

"It is if you think it's a membranous sac around nestling feces." Kai's tone was instructive, as if a discussion on bird excrement was a typical topic of conversation for him. "It's all part of nest sanitation for many birds. When the young defecate, it's via this sac that the parents can then pick up with their beak and remove from the nest. Different birds dispose of the fecal sacs differently, but many never go too far from the nest. And then when the young grow, but before they fledge, they start to defecate over the edge of the nest, which is then detected directly under it. Or some, like the Ākepa fledglings, defecate on the rim of the nest, and the parents let the sacs accumulate there. A concentration of fecal sacs, on the ground or above, becomes a scent target for a conservation dog to identify the nesting area. Then it's up to the handler to identify the nest."

"That would certainly narrow down the area," Meg said. "Impressive."

"*Mahalo.*"

"Can Makoa zero in on a tree, or a couple of trees at most, for identification?"

"Usually just down to one tree, though, as I said, depending on the birds, some of them could take the sacs over one hundred feet away and then drop them from the air to keep the nest hidden."

"But then there won't be a concentration of that scent," Brian said.

"That's correct. That dilute scent won't pull at Makoa. Nests with fledglings are always easier to find once the excrement accumulates on the ground below, especially if there are multiple fledglings in the nest. At this time of year, that's exactly what I'd expect."

"That's a huge advantage. One the poachers won't have. Once you get us on-site, then it's up to us to find the nest. They're usually toward the top of the trees, I assume?"

"Not necessarily," said Byrne. "Take the Ākepa, for example, which nests in tree cavities. That will simply depend on where the best nesting spot is. Or the 'Elapaio, which builds a cuplike nest out of grasses, mosses, and leaves. In areas with rats, they tend to place those nests higher. In areas without predation, the nests might be lower. And while rats cover the island, there are some locations where they're less pervasive."

"When we get Makoa into a search sector, he'll find the nesting areas you're looking for, if they exist." Kai leaned forward to look around Byrne at Hale. "You didn't say why we're looking, just that you needed Makoa. It's wildlife trafficking, then?"

"I didn't want to read anyone in until we were sure that's what we're looking at," Hale responded.

Hale gave a short and succinct synopsis of the scene Meg had interrupted and what she and Todd had found afterward. McCord kept making detailed notes, even though Meg knew most, if not all, of the content wasn't new to him. McCord would always hedge his bets on the side of too much information rather than too little.

"Being discouraged once won't stop them," said Byrne when Hale finished his background sketch. "With this kind of trade, they take orders ahead of time and then collect their prizes. If they collected the prizes first, then tried to sell them, they may lose their investment to sickness or injury, making it a loss for them. They're here and actively collecting because they've already received payment and now have to fulfill that order. They lost yesterday's birds, so we're of the opinion they're going to continue."

"And you want to track them?"

"Essentially, yes," Meg said. "But our dogs, great as they are at human-scent detection, aren't trained for wildlife detection. Now, if you and Makoa can get us to where the traffickers are, we can track them from there. But finding them is our issue. It's a big island."

"It's not as big as you think, if we look at this logically." Byrne pushed back her chair and rose. She circled the table to the end opposite the dogs, where a cluster of maps hung, moving directly to the map of the Big Island of Hawai'i. "Let's start with the likely birds we could be looking at—the Ākepa, 'Elepaio, 'I'iwi, 'Akiapōlō'au, and 'Alawī, among others. Those are the IUCN Red Listed birds we talked about yesterday."

"You're assuming these are large-dollar purchases?" Kai interrupted.

"Yes."

"I hate to suggest it, but what about the 'Alalā? There are thirty birds in the wild right now. In Pu'u Maka'ala, no less. The forest birds you mentioned still number in the thousands. The 'Alalā is somewhere in the low hundreds. Surely that would be a prize beyond measure."

"And a disaster for the species," Meg said. "But Kai's right. If scarcity is the key, wouldn't that make the 'Alalā the more likely target?"

"I actually think the 'Alalā is less likely," said Byrne. "The number one reason is the released birds are being closely watched as part of the 'Alalā Project. The birds are banded and tracked by the research team." Byrne turned to Hale. "Kai raises a good point. We're focusing on small forest birds because we found a mist net appropriate for that size. It's an entirely different process to catch an eighteen-inch bird than a four-inch bird, but we should warn the 'Alalā Project. They'll step up their surveillance while we're working this case."

"Agreed. You'll take care of that?"

"Yes. The other aspect with the 'Alalā is that the entire project is publicized, and the media is all over it. If they tried to take one of those birds at this point in the project, there would be hell to pay. It's doubtful, but I'll warn those who are already in contact with these birds about the potential risks. Back to forest birds, then. They have different natural ranges, but there are some overlaps, and I think that's where we should concentrate. They're going to pick areas where they have the best chance of catching multiple species, to minimize their risk of detection. Puʻu Makaʻala is one such area. That's here." She drew a circle on the map with her finger. "If you look at the endangered birds on this island, the Ākepa and the ʻAlawī will be the most desirable, both with an estimated population under ten thousand birds each, both only found on Hawaiʻi. When you look at overlapping areas of those two birds only, all of which also encompass the others, you have Puʻu Makaʻala, this area in the Upper Waiākea Forest Reserve"—Byrne circled an area just north of Puʻu Makaʻala—"and the Kaʻū Forest Reserve to the southwest of Puʻu Makaʻala. The other birds overlap into those areas as well, so my recommendation is to stick with those areas only to increase our chances of success."

"Seems reasonable." Kai rose to his feet and moved to stand in front of the map.

Byrne watched him thoughtfully for a few seconds before she spoke. "Do you have any insight on this? You and Makoa have likely worked some of these areas."

"We have. I'm just wondering if you're leaving out an important target."

"Which is?"

"The ʻIo." He spun around to the mainlanders on the left side of the table. "The Hawaiian Hawk."

"It's endangered?" McCord asked.

"Yes," Byrne answered for Kai. "In better shape than the ʻAlalā, but with lower numbers than the smaller birds. An estimated max count of twenty-five hundred. I discounted the ʻIo because of the size and ferocity. You're not going to use mist netting to capture an ʻIo. And, as a much larger bird, it's going to be harder to secrete out of the country."

"I guess that depends on how they're moving it," Kai said. "But think of the meaning of the ʻIo. We Pacific Islanders revere the 'Io. Some consider the 'Io to be an *'aumakua*. A family god. One who watches over the Hawaiian people." He turned back to the map. "The 'Io overlaps every area you outlined, so it also could be on their list."

"That would require a much larger kind of humane trap," Hale stated.

"Yes," said Byrne, "but there are several ways to do it, from a bal-chatri, to a goshawk, to a bow net trap. All doable. And if they're already catching birds, if they needed bait, they'd use something common that got caught in the mist net to catch an 'Io, saving the birds that make them money for the trade." She stared at the map, folds of consternation forming between her eyebrows. "I didn't consider something this large, but it could be a possibility."

"The forest birds we're looking at are beautiful and rare, but the 'Io is not only rare, it's large, impressive, and a fighter," said Hale. "The kind of person who sends someone out to find a creature that's nearly extinct would revel in one with all those characteristics. It would command an extremely high price."

"It's going to be more trouble to move that kind of larger trap into an area where they'll be collecting." Todd met Meg's eyes. "Think of what we hiked through yesterday. Now imagine moving through that with anything big enough to trap a hawk. And then back out again with it and the bird."

Meg had a flash of narrow, muddy paths, overhanging branches, and steep inclines. "Depending on whether the trap could be constructed in place, it would be nearly impossible to transport it into an area with the distance we hiked yesterday. Now, granted, our way out was a shorter distance, so that would play to their advantage, but even so, a large or bulky trap would severely complicate things."

"If they were going to try something like that, then

they'd have to pick a location closer to some sort of roadway," Brian stated. "I only saw the pictures you sent yesterday, Meg, but it would have been hard to navigate that density of greenery."

"A bird the size of an 'Io could be caught using mist netting, though it's really at the upper boundary," said Byrne. "But you'd have to use an entirely different size of mesh than that used for the smaller birds. It would be easier for them to use a dedicated trap for a bird that size."

"We'll keep that possibility on the table," said Hale. "We're agreed we need to move on this tomorrow because they won't stick around. We need to look at the map and figure out the more likely areas that they'll try for, based on the areas of the endangered birds."

"You mean like this?" McCord turned his laptop around and pushed it back a foot or two so everyone could see it.

Meg's attention had been on Kai and Byrne at the map, so she hadn't watched what McCord had been doing. On his laptop monitor was a picture of the Big Island with areas of red stripes and yellow . . . but were they overlapping?

"What are we looking at?" Hale asked, leaning in and squinting.

"This is the layered habitats of the birds Special Agent Byrne mentioned. I used an online photo site to overlay transparent versions of the island into a single image."

"Where did you draw the information about the habitats?" Byrne asked.

"You mentioned the IUCN Red List. While you guys were discussing how to catch birds, I was looking them up, capturing their habitat maps, and making a combined image." McCord indicated the screen. "There are several defined shared habitats. I think that's where you need to start. We can cross-reference with road maps and population centers to figure out what areas would be the most likely for them to hit. From there we can make a list. Makoa can get you to the nesting grounds. If they're disturbed, Hawk and Lacey can hit the scent trail."

Meg patted McCord on the shoulder. "Nicely done. I knew there was a reason we keep you around." She looked across the table at Hale with an expression that said, *See? This is just the beginning of how he can help us.*

"I like it. Can we overlay this with a road map and then get it up on the screen?"

"I can do the road map if you can find me a connection to a projector," McCord said.

"We can do that. This is excellent." Hale rubbed his hands together in anticipation. "Let's figure out the details so we have a plan in place for first thing tomorrow."

CHAPTER 11

Lava Tube: A natural tunnel that forms to carry lava as it moves under a hardened lava flow.

May 30, 8:24 PM
Waikōloa Beach Marriott Resort
Waikōloa, Hawaiʻi

Standing in the kitchenette, Meg turned at the sound of the door to the suite opening. Todd and Brian came in, their arms loaded with bags.

"Dinner is served," Brian announced as Todd nudged the door closed with his boot.

McCord looked up from where he sat on the couch in the living room, his feet on the edge of the coffee table and his laptop propped on his thighs. What had to be his sixth cup of coffee for the day sat on the table, just out of reach of his feet. "Excellent. I need food if I'm going to power through a few more hours."

"Then you're going to crash," Meg suggested. "Big-time."

"Like the dead. I'm glad you called Cara from the airport to tell her about your arm, so that covered my check in, as well. It's too late to call her in DC now."

"I'm just glad you were there as exhausted comic relief

after she heard about the shooting. The way you were having trouble constructing logical sentences definitely helped distract her from me."

McCord sat up, his feet dropping to the floor, and beckoned the men forward with one hand, keeping the other on his keyboard. "Explains why that half-hour nap on the flight to Hawai'i was crucial. But it's only going to last so long. Gimme." He eyed the bags. "Our order went through okay?"

"They had it ready for us as we walked in the door," Brian said. "Your ribs smell amazing. I'm regretting not going for that."

"I almost got the rib eye you ordered. I'll split my order in half if you will. We can swap."

"Deal."

Meg brought a tray of drinks over from their now fully stocked fridge and set it down next to the takeout bags on the coffee table. "That does smell good."

"You updating us over dinner, McCord?" Brian asked. "I feel like I'm behind the group."

"No more so than us on what McCord has been digging into."

"You'll all be up to speed within the hour." McCord closed his laptop and angled it against the side of the couch, leaving the table free. "Food first—the topic of this case makes me lose my appetite."

"I'll drink to that," murmured Todd as he snagged an open bottle of Gold Cliff IPA from a local brewery.

They settled in to eat, Meg and McCord on the couch and Brian and Todd in flanking chairs pulled up to the table. They kept the conversation light and focused on anything but the case. There would be time enough for that.

"Then Craig asked, 'What coordinates?' and no one had the heart to tell him that we'd pulled a fast one." Brian chuckled at the memory as he wiped barbecue sauce off his lips with a paper napkin.

"Craig still doesn't know to this day." Meg pushed her takeout container—empty except for a few fries—away from her and sat back against the couch cushions. "Someday we'll have to tell him."

"Someday being in at least a few years."

Todd leaned over and snuck two of Meg's discarded fries, his own New York strip, mashed potatoes, and a side scoop of Hawai'i's legendary mac salad long gone. "What he doesn't know won't hurt him."

"Or get him into trouble." Meg studied McCord's takeout container, which was practically licked clean. "You *were* hungry."

"Part hunger, part desire to power through for a few more hours." He flipped his container closed and pushed it off to the side with one hand as he reached for his laptop with the other. "We ready to jump in?"

Brian waited as Todd snagged the last three fries out of Meg's container, then flipped it shut and stacked all four containers. He rose and carried them to the kitchenette. "Meg? Where do you want these?"

"Just on the counter for now. We'll take care of it later."

"Works for me. Anyone else want anything while I'm in here?"

"I'm on vacation, so why not? I'll take a Coconut Hiwa Porter," Todd said. "McCord, you should try one. It's a dark beer with hints of coconut, coffee, and chocolate."

"That sounds right up my alley. Hit me."

"Make it two," Todd called to Brian. "White and black can with gold accents."

"Got 'em." Brian's voice was muffled from behind the fridge door as he bent low to examine the contents. "Meg, you want anything?"

"I'm still on pain meds, so no fun drinks for me. There

are a couple of cans of Island Ginger Beer. I'll take one of those."

"That sounds interesting. I'll join you." Brian returned with the four cans, handed them out, and then took his seat again.

"Just be warned, it's pretty—"

But Brian had already opened his can and was in the middle of a long series of swallows. His eyes snapped open, and he swallowed before coughing violently, one hand pressed to his sternum as Lacey shot to her feet to push her nose against his cheek in concern.

"Spicy," Meg finished too late. She opened her own can as Brian continued to splutter and took a sip, the bright snap of local ginger dancing on her tongue before she swallowed. "I'd advise small sips."

Brian ruffled Lacey's fur. "It's okay, girl." His voice sounded like he was half under water. "Meg was being crafty, but she can't kill me that easily."

"Hey, don't blame me. You chugged it before I could warn you." Meg couldn't help the smile that curved her lips.

"Funny girl." Brian raised the can again, this time sipping delicately, swishing the liquid in his mouth like he was at a wine tasting, and then swallowing. "That's really good, now that I can actually taste it." He inhaled sharply through his nose. "Clears out the sinuses, though."

"An added bonus." Meg winked at him. "Okay, McCord, rest time is over. We want to hear what you've dug up so far while you're still conscious and have a few functioning brain cells left."

"Good thing we're only in the next wing," Brian said. "We won't have far to stagger to our rooms."

"And Lacey can take care of business here in our private space so you don't have to take her for a walk down into the public areas with grass." Meg curled her legs under her, rotating slightly to carefully rest her left arm along the top of the couch so she was looking directly at McCord. "Whatcha got for us, McCord?"

McCord angled his laptop monitor back a little farther and scrolled up a long document. "Going to give you the *Reader's Digest* version, but I'll make sure to hit the highlights. Now, Brian and I discussed this during the flight, and I assume you also know the wildlife-trafficking basics, right? Elephant tusks, tiger skins, shark fins, pangolins, et cetera?"

"Yes, we know that much."

"Then let's get into what you might not know, just so you can better understand what we're looking at here. And I admit, much of this was new to me, so it's been a learning experience all around." He scrolled down a few lines. "Let's see here . . . Asia tends to be blamed for the majority of wildlife trafficking, but it's not that simple. Yes, Eastern medicine and delicacies involve a lot of trafficked materials, but the US and Europe are huge wildlife-trafficking targets. Not even a decade ago, the feds grabbed nearly two million dollars' worth of ivory from New York City jewelers. New York State itself is a huge market in illegally trafficked wildlife goods."

"Disgusting," Brian muttered.

"Amen to that. But it's a big business. For a long time, people assumed the poaching that led to a flow of materials into the wildlife-trafficking streams was because poor people were trying to survive in any way they could. Not to say there isn't a thread of truth in that, but that's not the majority of it."

"Let me guess," Todd said. "Organized crime? We learned too much about the kinds of businesses they stick their fingers into in the blood diamonds case. This sounds right up their alley."

"You bet it does." McCord flexed his hands, an unconscious response to the memories Todd's point raised. "When it comes to illegal trade, it goes narcotics"—McCord ticked items off on his fingers—"weapons, humans, and wildlife. Wildlife is number four, and often the same people who trade in blood diamonds trade in the wildlife commodities, as well. Depending on the kind of commodity, some of these groups are already set up across the African subcontinent."

"I remember the details around the blood diamond case." The can in Brian's hand crumpled slightly under the pressure of his grip. "The Democratic Republic of the Congo is rife with gem traffickers, so the local transport system is already in place. Bet they handled more than just blood diamonds."

"In the Congo? Absolutely. They're not just a site of slaughter by armed units; they're also a hub. They warehouse and ship illegal wildlife goods to both Europe and Asia. They not only handle animal products like horns and tusks, they also handle live animals."

"So the ones we're trying to protect could go through there," Todd stated.

"Yes. I'm only starting to dig into transportation chains, so we'll cover that more later when I have a better handle on it. Needless to say, like our goal with the blood diamond trade, we're not trying to just nail down the local individuals. We're trying to burn down the whole network, which means the more comprehensive our view of the entire chain, the better. For now, what you want to know about is who's at the end of the chain."

"These birds aren't going to a public zoo," Meg said. "They could only go somewhere where no one would question their presence. Anywhere official would want paperwork about provenance."

"Not to mention," Todd interjected, "if you're looking at an ornithologist who knows their stuff—and you should at a facility like that—they'll know those birds shouldn't be removed from their natural habitat because of their status. Even if there were extraordinary circumstances, like injury, they'd stay on Hawai'i, not be sent halfway round the planet to a public zoo."

"All correct." McCord used an index finger to push his glasses farther up his nose as he scanned his notes. "I've also knocked *private zoos open to the public* off the list for the same reason. Which leaves us with personal collections."

"The most private of private zoos," Brian specified.

"I think McCord hit the nail on the head when he used the term 'collections,'" said Meg. "These aren't people who are cobbling together an ordinary group of animals. If you want to see lions and tigers and bears—"

"Oh my," McCord shot back with a grin.

Meg rolled her eyes but kept going. "—you'll go to your local zoo. But that's not what these collections entail. The creatures within are so precious, very few can be allowed to view them."

Brian nodded in agreement. "Because then they'd risk word getting out."

"You know what this means, right?" McCord asked.

"Follow the money," Meg suggested. "The only way to put together this kind of collection is by paying top dollar to ensure receipt of the bird or animal, and that everyone involved stays quiet about it."

"Exactly. But first we need to find the traffickers so FinCEN at the Department of the Treasury can find out who made financial transactions with them." McCord scrolled down a little further to a bullet point list. "I have a contact at the *Post* who has worked on a number of wildlife-trafficking stories over the years. Elsa Monteith. Heard of her?"

Negative head shakes all around.

"I won't tell Elsa. Actually, considering the case, I'm sure it occurred to Sykes that she might have been the better journalist to send, as she's already experienced in the field."

"But she doesn't have the FBI contacts," Brian pointed out. "That's more important. Having the background doesn't matter if you're locked out of the investigation."

"Pretty sure Sykes circled around to that, which is why I'm here. Anyway, I reached out to Elsa earlier today." He glanced at the clock in his laptop's system tray. "I think that's yesterday, DC time. I explained what we were looking for. She gave me some of her contacts, none of whom are in the trafficking system but are adjacent to it, with knowledge of it. Remember the Democratic Republic of Congo being a hub? One of her contacts is there. One is in Europe." He paused. "And one is in the US."

"And here I was, thinking we were looking at Saudi princes," Brian said. "It could be a homegrown collection?"

"Without a doubt. As we said, top dollar. And who can afford top dollar?"

"The obscenely rich."

"The grossly obscenely rich. And on the *Forbes* list of the richest people in the world last year, just looking at the top ten, seven were Americans."

"The tech bros." Todd's tone wasn't complimentary.

"Overwhelmingly so, yes."

"You're suggesting one or more of the CEOs of the country's biggest technological companies could be collecting endangered animals like they were Beanie Babies?" Meg asked.

McCord held up both hands, palm out. "Whoa, not doing that. Wouldn't do that without a roomful of the *Post*'s lawyers on retainer making sure every word in my article was legally sound. What I'm saying is we like to think we're better than that. That we think a Saudi prince does this kind of thing because he's so obscenely rich, and we might—rightly or wrongly—label him with that kind of cruelty. The truth of the matter is money corrupts. People with that amount of money... change. Most, I'd say, don't change for the better. The richest people in the world have more money than they'll ever be able to spend in their lifetime. And with the exceptions of Bill Gates and Warren Buffet, who are legitimately giving away massive amounts of their wealth to philanthropic causes and are literally changing the world in doing so, the rest are mostly holding on to their wealth. Sure, they have their pet causes, but with the exception of using their fortunes in an attempt to buy the government they feel will be most favorable to them, they intend to hoard the majority of their wealth for themselves or their beneficiaries."

"Which leaves a lot of money to spend on wherever their preferences lie." Brian's voice was flat. "Like a unique collection of living things. They might contribute to an extinction event, but they likely don't care."

"These are the same people who don't care about environmental causes or climate change because it's all about the love of capitalism and the almighty dollar *right now*," said Todd. "Meanwhile, those currently on the other end of the income inequality scale slowly sink and future generations are screwed."

"It's definitely an issue," McCord agreed. "And maybe it's easy for us to point accusatory fingers. We're just the little guys, earning decent salaries but nothing spectacular. We live comfortably, but we pay our monthly car payments and our biweekly mortgages. The thought of buying a big-ticket item outright is unthinkable for us. In fact, they might pay several times more for a single 'item' for their collection than we paid for our houses, without blinking."

"Definitely how the other ha—" Brian cut himself off. "One percent lives."

"Now you have it. I have feelers out with Elsa's contacts. They, in turn, have feelers out. *Carefully.* These aren't people to mess with." He scrolled down to the next page in the document. "The other area I'm working on is transport. This is a major issue. You can't just load cages in your car and drive across country from here. You're on an island, so you have two choices to get off the island— boat or plane. But a boat is slow to get to the mainland— the fastest catamaran is five to seven days, and the slowest sailboat is about three weeks. All too long to risk the life of your delicate prize. Air travel makes much more sense, but then you have the issue of security and sneaking your prizes onboard."

A thought jolted through Meg with the shock of a lightning bolt. She grabbed McCord's forearm. "No, you don't. Brian . . ." She could see from the gleam in Brian's eye he was right there with her.

"The Barron Pharma jet," he said.

Meg jabbed an index finger at him triumphantly. "The Barron Pharma jet," she confirmed. "They let a killer on the plane because private jets manage their own security at . . . what did they call it?"

"FBOs," McCord said. "Fixed-base operations. An airstrip where private jets can pay to land away from the public crowds. Away from the security you find at larger airports."

"That has to be part of the price of doing business, right?" Todd asked. "If you have some superrich patron who is willing to pay through the nose for his illegal prize, you're going to build the price of private jet transportation into the fee. Partly because the deal can't be done without it."

"You'd be an idiot not to build it in. Now, each island has at least one major airport. Hawai'i has two."

"Surely that's not where you're going with this." Disbelief rode heavy in Meg's tone.

"Definitely not. I'm looking for smaller airports of the single airstrip variety, where charter planes land. There are lots of charter planes between the islands, even some paid for by ritzy resort hotels for their 'special' guests. There are private airstrips on every island, but I'm concentrating on Hawai'i to start, as that's where the birds are being captured. I assume they'd like to make transportation as direct as possible."

"What about travel to Asia?" Brian asked. "We're all thinking about the US, but what about that Saudi prince? Think of all the wealth in a place like Abu Dhabi or Dubai. In fact, the whole United Arab Emirates and its concentration of wealth is something to keep in mind."

"We definitely need to remember this isn't an America-centric issue." McCord's tone was thoughtful. "As far as a Saudi prince goes, keep in mind the type of plane Barron used—a Gulfstream G800. While it might not be able to fly the whole distance without refueling, it would probably only need to touch down once on the way. Just as an example of how it could be done. I'm not saying that particular type of private jet was used—it's just one we're familiar with. I'll keep the worldwide reach in mind. The airstrips won't care where the plane is coming from, or leaving for, as long as they accept private flights, and all the paperwork is in order. And there will be a paper trail. No one is landing without having applied for permission and paying the fees upfront, unless it's a true emergency. But some of these private airstrips can have anywhere between two to four thousand takeoffs a year and just as many landings, so you have to plan ahead if you have twenty or twenty-five planes flying in and out each day."

Todd tipped back his head to drain his beer, then set the empty can on the table. "That actually sounds smart. A small enough airport you can avoid the hassle of security, but one busy enough no one's looking at the only plane to land that day with any kind of discerning eye."

"My thought exactly." McCord stifled a yawn behind one hand. "Anyway, that's in progress, and I should have more for you on it tomorrow evening."

"I think we should call it a night," Meg said, looking between McCord and Brian. Brian's color was going slightly gray with exhaustion and McCord was drooping. "You're both starting to fade, and Brian, you're going to have an active day with us tomorrow. You need rest."

"You don't have to tell me twice. Let me take Lacey outside, and then we'll call it a night."

"Wait." McCord held up a hand, freezing Brian in place as he braced his hands on the chair arms to rise. "There's one other thing we need to cover now. Have you guys been getting alerts about the tremors?"

"You mean like the one we experienced yesterday?" Meg asked. "No alerts. We just lived it."

"Interesting. Well, professional hazard, I guess. I'm more plugged into the news, so I've been getting alerts. And an advisory is up."

"An earthquake advisory?"

"No, a volcano alert." McCord opened a browser, then a search page, typed in a search term, and hit enter. "Yeah, this isn't great. The alert is for Mauna Loa, exactly where you're headed tomorrow."

Meg met Todd's eyes. "Definitely sounds like Kainalu wasn't exaggerating."

"Possibly downplaying, even," Todd said. "Is there an actual risk of an eruption, McCord?"

"Hang on." McCord's fingers were flying again. "Volcanoes aren't in my wheelhouse, living in DC. Let me . . ." His voice trailed off as he scanned an open web page. "An advisory is one step up from normal."

The tension in Meg's shoulders released. "That's not too bad."

"It's not great either. Watch is the next step up, but that includes an eruption, though only if it poses limited hazards. After that, it maxes out at a warning. The area is on level two of four, so be aware. The bigger issue is that Mauna Loa is *way* overdue for an eruption. Last one was in 1984, thirty-five years ago."

"That's not *that* long ago in geologic terms," Brian said.

"Maybe not, but for a volcano that historically erupts about every five years, it's well overdue. I mean, not a century overdue like a San Andreas Fault earthquake, but overdue enough." He was silent for a moment as he scanned the text. "And now I kind of feel like I need to bone up on volcanic eruptions too. I don't know enough about this stuff."

"Sounds like one of us better," Brian said, "because we certainly don't either. But that's not a problem for us tonight in this area of the island." Brian pushed out of his chair. "Lacey, come." He opened the screened lanai door and stepped through it into the dark night beyond, the German shepherd at his heels.

Meg felt Hawk's eyes on her and looked down into his intense gaze. She waved a hand in the direction of the open door. "Go ahead. We wouldn't want you to miss a moment of Lacey time."

Hawk scrambled to his feet and bolted into the night.

McCord closed his document and shut down his laptop. "While you're having your active day, I'll have more than enough to keep me busy."

"Why don't you work here in our larger space instead of in your little room or in any of the public spaces?" Todd suggested, looking over at Meg. "Any objections to giving him one of our key cards?"

"None. We'll be out hiking the far side of the island, so

he might as well sit out on our lanai and enjoy it while we're not. You can have my card. I can still access the room through the virtual key card on the resort app."

McCord's exhaustion slid away for a moment as his expression brightened. "Thanks! This space is definitely nicer than ours."

"No need for nicer if you're going to be hanging out here and mostly just sleeping and showering there. But what if you need to leave the resort to do something?" Meg asked. "We'll have the SUV."

"I'll grab an Uber. Or, if I really need to get around, and I might, I'll talk to the front desk about renting a vehicle. This is what expense accounts are for, am I right?" His tired smile was all teeth.

They had their paths laid out for the next day. McCord would have his nose to the ground on his research. Makoa, Hawk, and Lacey would be similarly nose down in their chosen wilderness, followed by the rest of the team.

Hopefully someone would make progress. And if they were very lucky, they'd take their first steps in ripping this case wide-open.

CHAPTER 12

Lava Flow: A stream of molten rock from a volcanic vent onto the Earth's surface.

May 31, 8:17 AM
Ka'ū Forest Reserve
Nā'ālehu, Hawai'i

There had been mutual agreement between the agents and handlers that Pu'u Maka'ala was likely too hot for the wildlife traffickers to return to, at least right away, seeing as they'd been caught in the act. They were of one mind that the area Meg and Todd had stumbled upon would never be used again. Just in case, Byrne and Hale had started their day hiking back to that spot—using the short route Meg and Hale had used to exit the reserve—to install a motion-activated trail camera that captured the entire clearing. They had the luxury of being able to use a camera powered by a small built-in solar panel and with an installed SIM card that could reach the local network, so it was able to transmit pictures and video to Hale's phone.

That just left the remaining 18,999.9 acres in the natural area reserve to worry about.

It had been a coin flip between the Ka'ū Forest Reserve

and the Upper Waiākea Forest Reserve, but in the end, they'd selected Ka'ū for several reasons—not only was it a greater distance from Pu'u Maka'ala in general when they thought the traffickers might be spooked on that location, but it was also not under a rainfall warning for the entire day. If it was raining that hard, the birds themselves would be sheltering and would be less likely to be in flight and able to be caught.

It was a welcome reprieve in everyone's eyes. One less area to worry about.

For now.

There were multiple roads into the Ka'ū Forest Reserve they had considered, but had shied away from some of them: 'Āinapō Road at the northeast end because it led to both a rented cabin and one of the established local hiking trails. Lorenzo and Kiolaka'a Roads at the southwest end were too close to the town of Nā'ālehu. Honanui Road was out as it stood behind a locked gate that required permission from a local ranch whose land would only be open for access between 7:30 AM and 8:30 PM; they all agreed there was no way the traffickers would allow their entry into the forest to be recorded in any way.

In the end, they chose to use the midway village of Pahala as their southern focal point and then drove as far into coffee-farm country as they could, following the gentle incline of the lower slopes of Mauna Loa toward the Ka'ū Forest Reserve. The theory was that the traffickers would aim to find a way to enter the forest without using a public artery, so they'd rely on one of the smaller dirt roads truly only meant for local farmers. Yes, it would be less traveled, so they might attract attention, but the entire area uphill of Pahala comprised a combination of ranch land dotted with cattle and farmers' fields of both coffee and macadamia nut trees as far as the eye could see. Due to the lack of sight lines because of the neatly planted rows of trees, combined with the low population of only local residents and their farm hands, it actually felt like the safest way to clandestinely travel the area. The only question was—where along Ka'ū's southern border would the traffickers enter the forest?

Assuming they'd be dropped off again and would have a meetup location, the team was confident the traffickers' approach would only come up the southern slopes of Mauna Loa. No one would be insane enough to drive partway up and then ascend the 13,680-foot summit of Mauna Loa to descend along the 'Āinapō Trail with the goal of approaching the forest from the northern side. It was going to be a southern entry; they just weren't sure where. After a long time examining detailed maps of the area, they thought Pahala gave them a good chance to be in the approximate vicinity the traffickers would target. These roads took them farthest into the area to save transportation time in and pack-out time with the birds.

Could they be off by a mile or two? Of course, but that was where the dogs came in.

They split up into two four-wheel-drive vehicles, so when they went off the paved roads and onto dirt, the vehicles could handle the exertion. Hale and Byrne were in the first vehicle with Kai and Makoa; Todd drove the second SUV with Meg in the passenger seat and Brian in the back with both dogs.

The SUV lurched, leaving both dogs scrambling for purchase on the rubber-matted floor of the SUV as the double-rut track they were following through the thick trees and brush dipped sharply.

"Sorry," Todd said, white-knuckling the wheel. "Doing my best to keep us as level as possible. I think this supposed road is really only for ATVs."

Meg had one hand on the dash and the other clamped

onto the curved door trim. "Not your fault. If this is the way they came, whoever is driving them in and out is going to love making this trip four times."

"They might have dropped them off farther back," Brian said from where he swayed on the back seat. "But that would mean more uphill hiking, so they might push it as far as they could go. Can't blame them for that."

"Hale's stopping up ahead." Todd indicated out the front windshield, where Hale had pulled his SUV over into a small grassy section just off the double rut. "I think they're calling it here."

"Makes sense." Meg scanned the area. "Up to now, there hasn't been enough room to three-point turn any vehicle around, and you don't want to do that trip down in reverse. He's probably cutting his losses."

"That may be, but this is still going to be a six-point turn at the very least," Brian said. "Still, better than going backward."

"Remember, I occasionally drive a fire truck." Webb cut the engine and drew out the keys. "This is child's play next to that."

"Excellent point." Brian reached down and leashed both dogs, then waited while Meg unlocked her gun safe, removed the Glock, and seated it securely in her concealment shoulder holster. Then she got out and circled the vehicle to open the door, took both leashes, and called the dogs out of the SUV, allowing Brian to similarly weapon up.

They met as a group beside Hale's SUV.

"Everyone make sure their phone is on vibrate," Hale said. "The last thing we want is for someone to text or call, and a ringing phone to clue the traffickers in to our presence. Otherwise, are we all set?"

"Yes," Meg answered for the group. "So we're solid on

the plan to let Hawk and Lacey search for human scent, assuming there will be few hikers away from the established trails to the west and this far away from real drivable roads? And at the same time, have Makoa work on scenting the birds? Whoever hits first, that's who we'll follow, and the dogs will continue to work the area so all angles are covered." Meg turned to Kai. "You're confident he'll be able to map the nesting sites in an area this large? I don't doubt his nose, but isn't there a risk the birds are too spread out at this time of year with nesting? Don't birds tend to be territorial when nesting and space themselves out?"

"They do," Byrne interjected. "But that all ends when the fledglings leave the nest and start to forage with their parents. Then you can have family groupings staying together as well as interacting with other family groupings. The most important thing currently is that the fledglings can't survive on their own yet. It's crucial no adults are removed from this environment."

"Makoa won't need a large concentration of birds to scent them," said Kai. "If they're remaining in the same area, he'll be able to scent the fecal sacs. It's my hope he'll find multiple nesting areas."

Hale shifted his shoulders, settling his backpack, which was jammed full of trail cameras. "If so, that'll give us locations to set up cameras, so if they return to the area, we'll hopefully be able to send someone in if we're too far away. If not, we'll get video footage, and hopefully be able to identify them later."

"We're looking for two things," Byrne stated. "Areas where there are concentrations of birds tied to their nesting areas, as well as areas the traffickers have destroyed so they can set up their mist nets, and possibly 'Io traps."

"Let's get started, then." Meg looked down at her dog. "Hawk, find. We're looking for humans. Find, Hawk."

"Lacey, find."

Kai bent over Makoa, stroking his soft fur. "Makoa, loaʻa. Manu nahele."

The group hiked up a steady incline, the twin tire tracks cutting through the thick forest. This area was different from Puʻu Makaʻala, having considerably fewer ferns, with the foliage leaning toward more trees; though, to Meg's uninformed eye, the variety of trees in the two areas appeared relatively similar, which made sense as the two forested areas were so close to each other. Rather than mainly terrestrial ferns, more thick-leaved tropical plants filled in the understory here.

Deep in the forest, various bird calls sounded.

Makoa moved steadily, keeping up a good pace for a dog who was considerably smaller than both Hawk and Lacey. All three dogs were leashed, but Meg and Brian were ready to let their dogs work solo as soon as the terrain became difficult.

Meg kept an eye on Hawk, and while he seemed alert and interested, he was missing the intensity that came with being on the scent. Lacey looked similarly relaxed and happy.

Meg sped up a bit to fall into step with Kai, leaving Todd hiking beside Brian while Hale and Byrne brought up the rear. "Makoa's trained in Hawaiian commands?" She was always interested to see how other dog and handler pairs made their working relationship work.

"I could have trained him in English, but I thought there might be less confusion this way. Ordinary skills, we use English. Hawaiian is the language of our work with nature."

"Interesting distinction. If we're not keeping a low profile, we use the dogs' work vests to signify the same thing. It's like a mental shift for them."

"It's the same for Makoa. In this case, I told him to find forest birds, so he'll know what scent to identify."

Meg grinned down at the Australian shepherd, at his bright eyes and energetic movements, vitality snapping. "He clearly loves his work. So does Hawk, but Makoa exudes pure joy."

"He's a high-energy boy. He was well behaved the whole time we were driving up here, but I could tell he wanted to get out and get to work."

"Hawk is the same way. A little lower on the energy scale, but I love being out here with him. He's so happy whenever he gets to hit the trail. And this is such a different environment for both Hawk and Lacey. A true feast for the senses."

"Well, you know what they say about dogs—they smell like we see. An area like this is a true smorgasbord of scents for them."

The sound of rushing water came from ahead as the tracks they followed turned left heading straight uphill, while a second, smaller path continued on ahead through an area of low grass. The dogs paused briefly, heads up, scenting the air.

"Lacey isn't picking anything up," Brian said. "Likely no one's been through here in a while."

Meg studied her dog, noting his interest but lack of intensity. "Same for Hawk."

Kai was silent for a moment, watching Makoa, still quivering with anticipation but now leaning forward slightly, making a series of short inhalations as he scented the breeze, his eyes locked ahead toward the running water. "Makoa has something. It's not something strong from his stance, but I think scent is washing down the stream."

"Then that's where we go," Meg said easily.

"There won't be a path."

"We didn't expect one." Meg unleashed Hawk, noting

that Brian had the same thought at the same time. "Lead the way."

"Makoa, *loaʻa*."

Makoa happily broke for the path in the direction of the water, Kai loosening the leash to give him the freedom to follow his nose but keeping them connected.

Meg coiled the leash and stuck it in her jacket pocket. "Hawk, find."

"Lacey, find."

As a group, they went off what little remained of the overgrown path when they came to the rushing stream. Only about fifteen feet wide, the water level was high, rushing downhill, tumbling over rocks at a quick clip.

Meg dipped her hand into the stream, the chilled water swirling around her fingers as they impeded the downward flow. "It's pretty cold." She pulled her fingers out, flicking the moisture off, then following the stream uphill with her gaze. "This must be runoff."

"If you mean snow runoff, not likely at this time of year," Byrne said. "Mauna Loa certainly sees snow, but unlike Mauna Kea, which is higher, snow doesn't tend to stick around for more than a few days—a week at most at the peak of winter—and then it all melts. But whether it's snowy up there or not, it's cold at over thirteen thousand feet, and much of this is rain running downhill from that alititude. Kaʻū is a major watershed for this part of the island, with its water going to domestic use, as well as agricultural and commercial. There are a lot of river and creek beds throughout the reserve."

"All flowing straight downhill, along with the scent of everything above us. Anyone know how high we are?"

"Hang on." Brian fished his satellite phone out of a zippered pocket of his windbreaker and opened an app. "We're . . . just over three thousand feet."

"Then we have a way to go," said Byrne. "Some of these species live at altitudes over thirty-five hundred feet, but most live over forty-five hundred feet." She looked up the long stretch of creek bed. "Think that's our most direct route?"

Kai nodded. "Water tends to flow in as straight a path as possible, and will have for centuries, if not millennia, in this creek bed. If our first task is to get fifteen hundred feet higher, then this is our most strategic pathway."

A chill ran down Meg's spine before she could guard against it, accompanied by a mental slideshow of fields of scree, near vertical cliffs, and long drop-offs into unending blackness. This wasn't Colorado, but her brain wasn't quite grasping that fact.

Meg slid a sideways glance at Brian. "Oh, goodie, more mountain climbing," she murmured. "Like we didn't have enough of that two weeks ago."

"You did it before, you can do it now," he replied. "At least you can feel your fingers here."

"There is that."

"And this is, what? Maybe class two climbing down here? At most? It might be class three above, but we're not going that high."

"Everything okay?" Todd whispered.

Meg shrugged. "You know me. Never met a mountain I didn't love."

Todd rubbed a hand up Meg's back. "You'll be great. This isn't a quarter of the challenge of Pyramid Peak."

"So Brian reminds me. I'm just waiting for my brain to get the memo." She squared her shoulders. "Let's get the show on the road."

They threaded up the bank of the stream in single file. The dirt was long washed away from much of the sides of the stream, leaving exposed rock for the hikers and dogs to climb over, but occasionally, they had to wind their way inland for short distances if the foliage was too thick at the bank. It never failed to amaze Meg that life always found a way, even if it was a seedling taking root in a tiny crevice and then expanding over the decades until a thirty-foot tree towered over the rocks that had once overshadowed the minuscule seedling.

All around were towering trees of different types, a scattering of familiar ferns, and thick, glossy-leaved tropical plants. Green was everywhere, only broken by the occasional tree high above with bursts of red and occasionally yellow.

"What's that red up top?" Meg asked.

"We saw that at Pu'u Maka'ala," Todd said. "Pretty sure it's a flower."

"Of all the trees in here, that's definitely one to notice," Byrne called from behind them. "That's an 'ōhi'a tree, and yes, those are flowers. They're an important tree to note because they're crucial for the birds we're looking for. Honeycreepers like the 'I'iwi feed directly from the 'ōhi'a, but it also attracts the bugs birds like the 'Elepaio feed on. They're all over the Hawaiian Islands, from the shore right up to probably a third of the way up Mauna Loa and Mauna Kea. More than that, they can colonize the lava fields when so many other plant species can't, so they're important after eruptions for helping to turn the barren landscape around."

"They're also important for nesting," Kai said from ahead. "The Ākepa and 'Alawī use them for crevice nesting, while the 'Elepaio and 'Apapane use them to support their woven nests."

"That's one of the issues with biodiversity loss on the island," Byrne added. "Trees are lost due to disease as well as human development and sprawl, and that cuts back on where the birds can eat and breed. It's why the reserves we're searching are so important."

Meg drew breath to respond when Hawk suddenly froze in front of her, his stance stiff and his head cocked. Before she could call out to the others, the earth shuddered briefly under her feet, then stilled.

"Was that what I think it was?" Brian asked from just downslope.

Meg turned to face him. "A tremor? Sure was. That wasn't as bad as the one we had two days ago, though."

"Well, that's comforting," Brian muttered to Meg.

"Let's keep at it," Hale said. "We have at least another thousand feet to get to where we need to be to start the real search."

When they came to a spot where two streams came together to form the larger one they were following, they paused to let Makoa scent the air and pick their direction as Hawk and Lacey both reported no detectable human scent on the breeze.

"Makoa's indicating the left fork heading a little farther northeast," Kai directed.

"Then that's the way we go," Byrne said. "We're now approaching four thousand feet in elevation, and birds don't use yardsticks. Anytime in about the next half hour will get us into nesting territory, if we're lucky enough to find local birds."

The forest was closing in now, and getting around the foliage at the edge of the stream became more challenging, forcing them closer to the water. This branch of the stream was slightly narrower than the merged flow they'd followed from farther downslope—only about eight or ten feet of rushing, icy water. Still, it remained the clearest way to climb.

Meg squeezed under the lowest branch of a sturdy tree stretching high overhead. She turned back to Todd, who followed behind. "Watch that branch. Just about beaned myself on it." She jerked in alarm when Hawk made an odd whimpering sound. She spun around to find him only three feet in front of her, directly behind Brian, but his stance had alarm spiking in her chest.

Braced legs. Fur spiked high down his neck and across his upper back. A look of alarm in his eyes.

"Brace yourself!" Meg yelled as she reached for the branch she'd just cleared.

The earth rolled violently, knocking her off-balance before she could anchor herself. She staggered back, desperately trying to catch her balance as water splashed wildly in the stream and trees groaned under the stress twisting their roots. Then the ground shifted under her boots again with a harder shudder.

She reeled sideways, entirely out of control, lurching straight for the fast-running water.

CHAPTER 13

Ejecta: Materials explosively ejected from a volcano during an eruption.

May 31, 11:04 AM
Ka'ū Forest Reserve
Nā'ālehu, Hawai'i

Meg had enough time to draw in a breath as her body swung sideways, knowing that if the soles of her boots made contact with the slick rocks lining the stream, she had no hope of staying out of the water. Then, as her left arm flailed, desperately reaching for anything grounded enough to grasp, a solid hold clamped around her wrist, hard enough for pain to zing up her arm. With a hard yank, her body was jerked away from the edge. Agony exploded in her upper arm, and she couldn't hold back a cry.

"Hang on!" Todd yelled, pulling her in to curl against him where he had one arm wrapped around the trunk of the tree she'd just passed.

Her eyes screwed shut against the waves of pain, Meg clawed with her free hand at the tree trunk just as Brian yelled, followed by a splash. She tried to look over her shoulder, but it was hard to see anything, as every branch and fern frond in the area danced frantically as if battered by a strong wind. "Brian!"

There was no answer.

For another ten seconds, the earth shook. All Meg could think about was that Brian had escaped the killing power of an avalanche only a few weeks ago, just to fall victim to an earthquake.

To say they had the worst luck was putting it mildly.

Then all went quiet. Ignoring the pain radiating from her wound, her heart pounding and her breath coming hard, Meg pushed off the tree, realizing Todd not only didn't still hold her, but he was already moving past her to push through the bushes ahead. She followed and cleared through the foliage in time to find Brian partially submerged in the stream, his back and backpack pressed against the rocky bank and both hands clamped around whatever plant life he could grab at the stream's edge. Todd went down on his knees on one side of Brian with Kai on the other, while both Lacey and Hawk stood braced on the bank—Lacey's teeth were clamped onto the top handle of Brian's knapsack while Hawk had a mouthful of his collar—keeping the current from tugging Brian downstream and down the slope.

"The dogs have you. Give me your hand." Todd held out his and Brian latched on to it.

"Hawk, Lacey, release! Back!" Meg ordered, and the dogs let go of Brian and backed up a few steps, though Lacey stayed close, not wanting to put much space between herself and Brian.

Hale and Byrne broke through the bushes behind them.

"Is everyone okay?" Hale asked, panting.

"Yeah . . . we're good." Brian's voice sounded strained as Todd and Kai levered him out of the water, helping him to stagger onto the bank and beyond the rocks to dirt and matted grasses. Water streamed from his pants as Lacey shot over to him. He buried both hands in her warm fur.

Meg's gaze swept over Brian, from his bare head to his drenched hiking boots. He looked partially soaked—and extremely irritated—but otherwise whole. "You're really okay?"

"Yeah. I mean, I'm bloody freezing, but besides that, I was never in any real danger." Brian looked up at everyone else. "No one was hurt?"

With those words, the pain in her arm, pushed below the surface in her concern for Brian, swelled again, and she winced, but didn't respond.

It was more than enough for Todd. "Damn it. I hurt you when I reeled you in, didn't I?"

Meg cupped her left elbow in her right hand. "It was that or end up in the stream. You didn't have much choice if you were going to keep me dry and not swimming downstream. Give it some time to settle. If it's still aching like this in a half hour, we can stop and you can check it out. Everyone else is fine?"

Meg scanned the group around her as they all answered in the affirmative. She and Todd had held on to the tree, but from their muddy pants, it looked like both Byrne and Hale had gone down on their knees at the first sign of trouble. Kai looked essentially intact, like he'd managed to keep his feet. More importantly, all three dogs appeared to be fine. Four legs to balance on was a definite advantage when the ground beneath your hiking boots was trying to buck you into the nearest body of water.

She grasped Brian's arm, the wrist of his windbreaker sticking to his sodden arm like a second skin up to just over his elbow. *Waterproof jackets don't do much when you submerge their open holes.* He shivered under her hold, but if being wet was the worst of it, they'd gotten off easy as a group. She grinned at him. "If only Ryan could see you now. Let me snap a picture."

"Do that, and the next time I catch you in an embarrassing situation, it's going straight to . . ." He looked up to take in Todd's smirk and raised eyebrow. "Okay, maybe not to Todd, who would just take it in stride. Craig, then."

"I'm not sure a picture to your husband is equivalent to a picture to *our* boss. But fine, be that way." She let sarcasm playfully fill her tone before turning serious. "What do you need?"

"To start, to pour the creek water from my boots and find my spare pair of running pants in my backpack. We need to keep moving. I'm glad I'm the only one who lost their footing."

"I came close to joining you in the stream. I nearly did, except Todd has lightning-fast reflexes." She smiled at her husband. "I didn't say thank you."

"We were a little busy at the time. It was implied." Todd's gaze dropped to her cradled arm. "And if I made that worse, thanks definitely aren't required." He turned to Brian. "Let's get you wrung out and changed into dry pants. Hypothermia isn't a true risk in these conditions, but you'll be warmer and certainly more comfortable."

"Definitely." Brian stripped off his windbreaker to reveal his shirt was mostly dry. "I'm only wet to just above my waist. I tried to keep my balance but lost my footing close to the edge, hit some wet rocks, and slipped sideways. I managed to partially catch myself, so I ended up sitting on the creek bottom on my ass. It's not so deep there, so there was no risk of the current dragging me downhill. But I think the dogs had a flashback to the Ocoee Flume and overreacted. They both leaped in to help, which made it look dire by the time Kai and Todd got there."

Meg had a flashback herself—Brian overbalancing on the wet, slimy wooden boards lining the edge of the swiftly flowing Ocoee Flume, his arms windmilling for precious seconds before his feet went out from under him and he fell into the flume, only barely catching himself on one of the rail tracks before he was dragged under and away from Meg. Lacey had kept ahold of the shoulder of his jacket until Meg had managed to scramble around to him and finally pulled him out by the top handle of his backpack.

That had been a life-and-death struggle. This, apparently, was a dunking.

"You know, if someone's going to have a water-related incident, it's going to be you." Meg pulled the wet windbreaker from Brian's cold fingers and shook it out. "The avalanche in Colorado. The Ocoee Flume. This stream."

"You know it." Brian opened his damp pack, rooted around, and pulled out a sealed bag. "Be prepared. Dry pants and socks to change into. Now, if you ladies wouldn't mind turning around . . ." He drew a circle in the air with his index finger.

Meg and Byrne turned their backs to him while behind them came the sound of rustling as Brian changed clothes.

"Are we in danger?" Meg asked. "That first tremor was nothing compared to that last shake. That was severe."

"This isn't an official guess, but I'd place that at over a magnitude six," Hale said from behind her.

"That sounds right to me," said Byrne. "That wasn't child's play. That might not have been enough to do structural damage to nearby houses, but it certainly was enough to destroy breakable contents."

"It would depend on the age and form of the house," Kai said. "Newer homes use more stable materials, but dwellings built in the traditional style—the *hale*, which is where our esteemed colleague gets his name—are constructed of wood, with open spaces to allow for air circulation in this humid climate. The entire structure is often built on stilts to keep the house clear of floodwaters when there are torrential downpours, as well as to keep the house a little farther from pests. Invasive termites are a big problem here."

"That sounds like a structure that would be susceptible to earthquake damage," Todd stated. "Light internal structure and no solid foundation."

"You'd know better than any of us, except maybe McCord, after all the research he did following the fall of Talbot Terraces," Meg said.

"You can turn around now." Brian's voice this time.

Meg and Byrne turned around to face the men. Brian was folding his wet pants, tucking his saturated socks into their folds, and jamming them into the same bag that originally held the running pants he now wore.

Brian looked up to find Hale watching him with raised eyebrows. "Not my first rodeo."

"Apparently not." Hale looked on with approval as Brian repacked his bag. "Smart. Are we ready to continue? Kai? Is Makoa ready to continue the search?"

"'*Ae*.' Kai bent low to his dog. "Makoa, *mai*."

They continued upslope, and if Kai kept Makoa a little farther from the rocky stream bed than he had before, no one commented on it.

Fifteen minutes later, Meg's satellite phone alerted to an incoming text. She fished it out of the side pocket of her yoga pants, glanced at the screen, and looked up to meet Todd's and then Brian's gazes. "McCord." She opened the message. "Well, there's our answer. He was just alerted to a six-point-six-magnitude earthquake felt from Ka'ū all the way to Puna."

"That district's the easternmost tip of the island," Hale supplied. "Big shake, as we're all aware."

"He knows we're in this area and wanted to make sure we're okay." Meg took a moment to text McCord back, letting him know all was well and they were continuing on with their search. Then, just to be safe, she opened her GPS, copied their exact location, and included that in another text to McCord in case the 6.6 was a warmup to something bigger. "He's updated, and he knows where we currently are . . . just in case."

Brian nodded in approval. "Good idea."

They stopped a half hour later so humans and canines alike could have water as well as some high-energy sustenance in the form of energy bars or kibble. Then they carried on, being sensitive to the fact they were spending so much time getting to the correct area for the bird population that daylight could be slipping past them for the full return trip.

They were well over four thousand feet up when Makoa led them away from the stream.

"Does he have something?" Byrne called from behind them.

"Yes," Kai confirmed. "He's definitely on the scent trail."

Makoa also seemed to have a skill in not only following the scent, but in forging the path of least resistance, which made sense in Meg's mind, as it would be the most accessible scent pathway.

Makoa slowed near the base of an ʻōhiʻa, spending long moments sniffing around the base, before sitting and looking directly at Kai.

"*Maikaʻi ka hana*, Makoa. Good boy." Kai ran a hand over his dog's head and turned to the rest of the group. "He's indicating there's something up this tree. He sits when he identifies a likely nesting site so he doesn't startle the bird population by barking."

Byrne squatted down next to the tree, pushing aside some small ferns at the base. "These are relatively fresh fecal sacs, so it's not an old site. It's in active use." She slowly circled the tree. "Definitely a concentration on this side." With a glance behind her, she stepped farther into the underbrush, crossing behind Kai and Makoa, trying to find enough space in the underbrush to get a little space between herself and the ʻōhiʻa to be able to see into the canopy. She shaded her eyes with her hand to cut the glare.

"Hawk, come." Meg sidestepped a thick-leaved explosion of green to join her. "See anything?"

"Not yet. But that's why I have these." Byrne pulled a compact pair of binoculars in a case from her backpack. She slid it from the case, flipped open the lens caps, and raised the binoculars to her eyes. "I'm not sure what species I'm looking for. Makoa can get us to the nesting grounds, but as Kai explained, because he's trained on a combination of scents from the birds, he can't tell us specifically what we're looking for. I don't know if I'm searching for a cavity or cup nester."

"Cup nesters are what we think of as a woven nest?"

"Yes. Made of twigs, leaves, grass. Mostly brown in color, could be some green. Of course, similar nests are built inside the cavities—we just won't see that. Either way, chances are good it will be thirty feet up or more."

"Thirty feet?"

"It's not like we have raccoons or foxes here, at least not naturally. We have had the odd raccoon show up in a shipping container, but they're not native to our forests. However, wild boars, goats, and, more importantly, rats are a major threat to the nests. These birds nest higher up to increase their odds of safety." Byrne went stock-still.

"Find something?"

There were several seconds of silence. Then, "No. I thought maybe, but I don't think so."

"Let me help." Meg shimmied out of her go bag and set it on the ground beside where Hawk sat, panting, his tongue lolling out one side of his mouth. She ran a hand over his head, feeling the warmth radiating from him—it had been a solid uphill hike, and they'd kept an intense pace for hours. "Good boy, buddy." He thumped his tail on the ground as she opened the front of her pack and found her own binoculars.

"Anything?"

Staring through her binoculars, up the dark, scaly bark and into the bright green, leathery leaves, Meg didn't take her eye off the prize. "I don't see anything, but I really don't know what I'm looking for."

"Want me to grab mine?" Brian asked. "Three pairs of eyes would be better than—"

Meg stilled at a flash of movement above. "I think I have it," she interrupted.

"You see something?" Byrne asked.

"I think so. I saw movement. Pretty sure it was a bird but one that really blends in." Meg didn't want to move her binoculars in any way for fear she'd lose her place. "I'm looking at a spot where two branches come together on the right side of the trunk, with a third branch sprouting off to the left maybe half a foot above? Thank goodness this thing tends to leaf only toward the ends of each branch or we'd see nothing but foliage." Only moving her eyes, she tried to identify another notable landmark. "Kind of blurred as they're in the foreground, there's a cluster of red flowers at about eight o'clock."

"What did the bird look like?"

"It blended in with the tree trunk. Maybe kind of a smoky grayish olive? I didn't get much of a view before it disappeared, and I have nothing for comparison, but maybe smaller than a sparrow? Sorry, I admit to not being up on the bird world."

"That's okay, because I am. What you've described is wrong for the 'Elepaio and 'I'iwi. And where the eastern slope of Mauna Loa and Puʻu Makaʻala was the right area for the ʻAkiapōlāʻau, it's very unlikely here on the southern slope. Not impossible, but unlikely. But it could be either the Ākepa or Alawī."

A streak of orange flashed through Meg's field of vision, accompanied by Byrne's soft laugh. "Was that . . . ?" A small orange bird settled on the front of the two branches and leaned into the trunk, his head disappearing.

"A male Ākepa? Yup. Mom is a lot duller and blends in. I'm impressed you saw her in the first place. Dad is a lot more visible. But both parents feed the young, so we're likely looking at nestlings in a notch just above those two branches. That cavity blends in so well, we didn't spot it from this distance. Just the parents."

"The nest looks undisturbed?" Hale's voice came from Meg's right.

"Yes. Let's mark the tree with GPS as a potential to come back to, noting the species."

"I got that," Hale said.

"At the very least, we're looking at three birds—mom, dad, and a hatchling—but it could be more," Byrne continued. "Average clutch is one to two eggs."

Meg dropped her binoculars to find all four men standing to her right, staring up into the tree. She offered her binoculars to Todd, who took them and quickly found the bright bird high above.

"He's striking." Todd adjusted the focus slightly. "Am I wrong in thinking he'd be the bird the traffickers would want? If the female is drab so she blends in, wouldn't a collector want the most impressive-looking sample of the species?"

"That would be my guess," Hale agreed. "Whether for their own pleasure or to show off, why have the peahen when you can have the peacock and all his impressive plumage? They might even pay more for that."

"It's just as damaging to the population to take only the males." Byrne lowered her binoculars and covered the lenses for storage. "Pairs form the summer before and only nest once the following year, so it's not like fewer males can mate with all available females. As you just saw, the males are part of the pair and are equally responsible for caring for the young, who are born helpless and need around-the-clock care for weeks. Remove one partner and the breeding season is done for the bird that remains. It's one of the reasons trafficking any of these birds is so disastrous for the species overall." She looked up into the branches as the male streaked away. "Off to look for more bugs." Her gaze dropped and she leaned forward, looking to where Kai stood with Makoa. "Great job on getting us to this site. I think we're ready for more." Her gaze shifted to Hale. "You ready to move on?"

"Just about." Hale crouched down to get on Makoa's level. The Australian shepherd wiggled from head to tail in enthusiasm, but all four feet stayed locked on the ground. "What a good boy." His gaze shot to Kai. "Is it okay if I pet him? He's working, so I don't want to touch him if that takes him out of his role."

"Go ahead," said Kai with a nod. "He'll snap back into work mode on command. But thanks for asking."

Hale ran his hands over the dog, giving him a nice scratch. Makoa closed his ice-blue eyes and tipped his snout skyward, clearly in heaven. "Even if we don't find signs of the traffickers, we'll map any sites we find and set up a trail camera there."

"How many did you bring?" Todd asked.

Hale waved an index finger between himself and Byrne. "We're each carrying four."

"That won't be enough," Kai said. "Even birds that flock together get territorial around nesting time."

"True," Byrne said. "But you'll find that birds of other species will get closer, especially if they don't share resources. The Ākepa eats spiders and caterpillars. The ʻAkiapōlāʻau drinks nectar from the ʻōhiʻa tree by drilling holes in the bark and drinking the sap. They're no threat to each other, so will nest in overlapping territories. But we'll set the trail cameras to go as wide as possible."

"Really, all you want is to see if people pass through the area," Brian said with a sidelong look at Meg. "You said you saw two men, but we know there was a driver. Could be a woman. We can't be certain there also isn't a larger team. So we can't limit a definitive alert to only picking up two men."

"Great point." Hale pushed off the ground to stand, leaving Makoa looking slightly disappointed at the lack of attention. "Let's set up the camera here and keep pushing on."

They were on their way ten minutes later, after having installed and tested the first camera. They naturally fell back into their previous order and pushed into the thick rainforest.

They called the search two and a half hours later. They'd hiked hard during that time, only stopping briefly for the light lunches they carried to keep their energy levels high. In total, they found seven nesting sites, all untouched, with a variety of endangered birds and a mix of more common birds, like the ʻAmakihi and the ʻApapane. But as the day ticked toward dusk, they became concerned about being high on the slope of Mauna Loa as darkness fell. Each carried a flashlight, but they all agreed on leaving the area before dark for safety. Besides, even when they descended several thousand feet, there were still miles to walk northeast along Cane Haul Road, back to their vehicles.

Brian let himself drop back a little bit in a section where the trail widened slightly, falling into stride with Meg. "What's wrong?"

"Nothing."

Brian snorted a laugh, then looked over his shoulder. "Hey, Todd. Your wife is trying to put one over on me."

"You think she'd know better than that," came the amused response.

Brian faced forward again, just in time to avoid beaning himself on a low branch. "I'd think you know better than that," he echoed. "Seriously, what?"

Meg knew she could tell Brian anything, knew that he might even share her misgivings. But if he didn't, she didn't want to bring him down. "Hawk, go walk with Lacey." She watched as he trotted ahead of her to walk shoulder-to-shoulder with Lacey, head up, tail waving, though she could see his energy level was waning slightly. They might be hiking downhill, but care still needed to be taken to avoid a fall. And her own muscles were starting to tire after over six hours of hiking, most of it at a significant angle.

Brian elbowed her but stayed quiet.

"Okay, okay." Meg tried to keep the irritation out of her voice, but could hear it nonetheless. "I don't think this is going to work."

"These searches, you mean?"

"Yes." When long seconds stretched and Brian stayed quiet, she continued, "It's too much territory and the birds are endangered, so their numbers are low and their nesting territory is spread out. Sure, they're mostly spread over common areas, but we're probably talking a hundred thousand acres in total."

"Agreed."

"We've been up here for hours. Makoa did a great job and identified the relevant nesting areas."

"While Lacey and Hawk have done nothing."

"*Exactly.*" Meg kept her voice low so it wouldn't filter back to Byrne and Hale. "The traffickers haven't been here. Were they ten miles south of us? Maybe. Are they in Puʻu Makaʻala right now? *Maybe.* Makoa is amazing and his nose is spot-on, but what does it matter if we're not getting to where the traffickers are?" She blew out a breath and stepped behind Brian as the path narrowed and they had to push through a stand of ferns. "Sorry. This is why I didn't want to talk about it. At least up here while we still have a ways to go."

"I'm always up for a discussion about how to better work our searches."

"I think I didn't really understand the size, the scope of what we were taking on. McCord's going to have better luck tracking them if he can figure out how they're getting the birds off the island."

"True. But by that time, they might be dead birds. And then the species count drops, all because someone wants to make a buck." Disgust dripped in Brian's tone.

"That's what Todd said at the beginning of all this. That what we're doing here matters."

"It does."

"We need to figure out a way to make this whole process work better. We're three dogs and a handful of people against thousands of square miles of wilderness."

"A little less than that for what we're looking for." Brian shrugged when Meg sent him a narrowed look. "But I hear you. Work smarter, not harder."

"Yeah, the question is how. We have to come up with a way, or they'll nab the birds they need and be gone within the week. And if they have what they need, they'll never come back to face justice."

They had to figure out a new strategy, or all their efforts would be for nothing. Nestlings would die. Breeding pairs would be severed. And the wildlife traffickers would turn their attention elsewhere to threaten other endangered species.

It wasn't just about the delicate balance of creatures on this one island. It was about the safety of endangered wildlife worldwide, the people who had the resources to find and capture vulnerable species, the greed that allowed those people to act so heinously, and the road once taken that could never be retraced.

They had to act here. Now.

If they lost the traffickers, how many other species might be put at risk?

CHAPTER 14

Hypocenter: The origin of an earthquake below the Earth's surface. It lies directly below the epicenter.

May 31, 7:37 PM
Waikōloa Beach Marriott Resort
Waikōloa, Hawai'i

Meg followed Todd through the door to their suite after he carded it open. She felt exhausted, body and soul, and utterly discouraged.

They had set themselves a gargantuan task with simply too much ground to cover and too little chance of success. She'd cut short her once-in-a-lifetime honeymoon for this?

You need a shower and a hot meal, in that order. Then you'll think more clearly.

Knowing her internal voice was talking sense, she pushed the weight of her doubts aside as best as she could. There would be time later to take them out and examine them in disheartening detail.

"You're back. How did it go?" Relief filled McCord's tone from where he sat on the padded chaise on the lanai, the screen door open to the suite, a luxury of mostly bug-free Hawai'i.

"Not particularly well." Meg bent and unlaced her hiking boots, then toed them off. "It's too much land. Land that's incredibly hard to navigate as well as being thousands of feet above sea level. We found nesting sites, but no sign of the traffickers. They could have been a few miles from us and we'd never have known. Scent can't travel far in that environment. We lost a whole day making essentially no progress."

"Sorry to hear that." McCord closed his laptop, set it aside on one of the seat cushions, and stepped into the suite to take them in. "You're not as filthy as I thought you might be following that earthquake." His gaze shot from Meg, down to Hawk, and back up to Todd. "Where's Brian?"

"He went straight to his room. He was tossed into a stream when the quake hit and then did the rest of the hike in wet boots and never really warmed up."

"It's eighty degrees out there."

"It wasn't that warm almost five thousand feet up Mauna Loa. On top of that, he got chilled, and because he never truly dried out, he stayed that way. He's grabbing a hot shower, dry clothes, and then he's coming here for dinner, because rather than take the time to eat there, we opted to start the two-hour drive back."

"I haven't eaten yet either because I was out and about and had a late lunch. Want me to grab us all something for dinner? You guys probably want to clean up too." His gaze lowered to Hawk, and he dropped to crouch in front of the dog, whose whole body turned into one sinuous and happy undulating wag. "You make me miss my insanity factory back home."

Meg couldn't bear to be separated from Hawk for long, so she totally understood how McCord felt when he was away from his hyperactive golden retriever. "You know he misses you. You also know he's in great hands at home with Cara."

"Possibly even better than mine. I just miss the dumb lug. Granted, even Cody is cleaner than you, Hawk. You're a little dirty, buddy."

"He was worse a few days ago, but every forest we hike on this island is muddy." Meg ran a hand down the warm fur of Hawk's back. "He mostly stayed out of it. What he really needs is his paws and belly wiped down. And a good meal."

"Ditto," Todd said. "McCord, we'll take you up on that offer." He reached into his back pocket and pulled out his wallet.

"Put that away." McCord waved him off. "Consider this one my treat. Thanks to your generosity in sharing your space, I had a very productive day today and have some decidedly useful leads, all while enjoying your lovely space and getting some sun. Least I can do."

"It was hardly an imposition," Meg scoffed. "We weren't here, and I'm glad you enjoyed it. Though I'd love to hear about what you learned."

"Add to that, after the earthquake, I spent some time looking up info on Mauna Loa and what that quake might mean. I definitely want to share *that* with you. You guys could be in the line of fire there."

Alarm shimmered through Meg to tingle at her fingertips. "Not sure I like the sound of that."

"We'll talk about it when Brian is here and with a decent meal to give us a bit of an energy boost, which, I admit, I could use too. What do we want? How about burgers so we can sit out on the lanai and don't need a table to eat? It's really gorgeous out there."

"Red meat always works for me." Todd slung Meg's backpack off his shoulder. "I'd hit the restaurant downstairs. They do a good burger. You know our orders?"

McCord laughed. "It's like you think we haven't eaten a meal together. Yes, I know everyone's orders, including Brian's."

He checked the time on his phone. "I'll tell him to be here at eight fifteen. That will give you time to clean up in peace and quiet before we invade your space again." He ruffled Hawk's fur and rose, looping back out to the lanai to grab his laptop and plug it into an outlet in the kitchen. "So it's powered up and ready to go when we are. See you in a half hour." He whistled his way out the door.

For several seconds, they could hear his whistle fading, then blessed silence.

Meg turned to look up at Todd. "I feel like I need to apologize again." At his questioning look, she elaborated. "You know, for having our peaceful, quiet honeymoon overrun? For . . ." She made a gesture that encompassed all of them. "This."

"I seem to remember agreeing with your assessment that you were needed on this case."

"I'm not saying we aren't needed. I'm just saying we might not be up to the task."

"We're all up to the task. I could hear you talking to Brian, and I agree we need a better plan. But we're tired and frustrated and need to disconnect from it for a bit. And look at us." His tone dropped as a single eyebrow arched. "With a whole thirty minutes all to ourselves."

"Thirty minutes, we'll need to clean up before we're invaded again." She made herself stop, made herself push down the irritation that Brian and McCord would be back shortly. She was letting her sour mood rule her emotions. "Sorry. I'm being snarky, and it's not your fault, or theirs."

"Or yours. So let's get rid of the dark mood."

She gasped in surprise when he grasped her hips with both hands and pulled her in tightly against him. "Oh. Well, now." Her lips curved in a half smile, breaking some of the hold on her mood. "You planning on working fast? We still have to get clean."

"No problem. Firefighters are amazing multitaskers."

He intertwined his fingers through hers and pulled her toward their bedroom. "Sorry, Hawk. We'll clean your feet later."

Meg's last view of her dog as Todd drew her through the doorway showed Hawk wandering into the living room to relax on the rug there. *Perfect.* That allowed her to concentrate on her husband. *Thirty minutes of honeymoon time, starting now.*

A half hour later, Todd opened the door to Brian and Lacey. Lacey's fur was still slightly spiky, indicating she'd showered with Brian.

"Out here!" Meg called from the lanai, where she was wiping down the last of the mud that still stuck tenaciously to Hawk.

"You still cleaning him up?" Brian asked, flopping down on the padded wicker chair next to Meg.

"Yes. Us first, then him."

"You didn't just . . ." Brian's words trailed off as he glanced from Meg's wet hair to Todd's. His grin went wide. "Riiiiight." He drew out the word and stretched out his long legs, crossing them at the ankles. "He's not that dirty anyway. Everything good otherwise?" He gave Meg a pointed look.

"Fantastic."

"That's what I like to hear. No McCord yet?"

As if on cue, a triple knock sounded at the door, then it cracked open. "Am I clear to come in with the food?" McCord called from the hallway.

"All clear!" Brian called back.

Meg gave him a slanted side-eye. "Make yourself at home."

Brian's grin was smug. "Thanks."

Meg rolled her eyes, but rose as McCord came through the lanai door, loaded down with two plastic bags stacked full of takeout containers. "Need a hand?"

"Nope. Got it. Todd offered, too, but I didn't need help. He's grabbing some drinks inside." He carefully set the bags on the table. "There we go." He turned and walked back into the suite and returned seconds later with his laptop and charge cord, which he set on the table. "It's okay to take the other half of the couch? In case I need the outlet later." At her nod, he opened the first bag and pulled out a container. "Fully loaded. Webb, that's you."

Todd stepped onto the lanai with four cans tucked into the crook of his arm. "Thanks. Just set it off to the side for now."

"Can do." McCord pulled out the next container. "No tomato . . . that's you, Brian."

"Thanks." Brian took the container, popped it open, and sampled a fry. "No gravy?"

"Hold your horses. You think by this point I don't know you always drown your fries?" He pulled out the next container. "Tomato, lettuce, pickles, and Dijon. For you, madam."

"Thanks." Meg accepted her container and settled on the couch as Hawk wandered over to snuffle in the direction of food. "Nice try, mister. You inhaled dinner five minutes ago." She pointed a finger across the lanai. "Go hang out with Lacey, who's being a proper lady over there."

"Probably only because she knows I'm so hungry, I could eat two dinners, so she's going to be SOL." Brian picked up his burger and took a huge bite as they watched Hawk join Lacey, then flop down beside her on the woven outdoor mat. "So good. I'm definitely not sharing." His words were garbled behind his full mouth, but years of working with Brian allowed Meg to translate.

She patted his knee. "Enjoy."

"Mmm-hmmm." Brian took another bite before he'd even finished the first.

"Breathe between bites. Yes, you're eating with a paramedic who can revive you after the Heimlich, but let's not add to the day's excitement, okay?"

Brian grumbled low in his throat, but chewed and swallowed before taking his next bite.

"Gravy." McCord set a small covered container next to Brian's burger.

His mouth full again, Brian waved his thanks.

Todd set two identical cans in front of Meg and Brian. "For the wine drinkers in the group now that Meg's on normal painkillers."

"Your arm's better?" McCord asked.

"It wasn't for a while this afternoon when Todd had to haul me away from the stream when the earthquake hit and that was the only arm he could reach. But it's better now. I'm going to try to deal with just ibuprofen instead of your heavy-hitter med."

Brian picked up his can, turning it as he read. "'Sparkling pineapple wine'? Sounds like it will be worth your while, Meg, to splurge on alcohol."

Todd settled into the wicker chair at the far end of the table. "Not your usual dry red, but I thought, when in Rome..."

Brian popped the top on the can, and Meg was hit with a whiff of pineapple... and was that mango?

Brian took a slow sip, swished for a few seconds, swallowed, then smiled. "Different. Interesting. I approve."

"After the day we had, I think we deserve it," Meg said, reaching for her own can.

McCord studied the can Todd extended to him. "What's our selection?"

Todd opened his own can. "We went with dark ale yesterday. Today we're going with Bikini Blonde Lager."

"Now that's an interesting name. Let's give it a try." McCord popped the top and drank deeply.

"Winner?"

"Gold star." He pulled his laptop next to his takeout container and woke it. "I can eat and update at the same time, so let's dive in." He took a bite of his burger while the computer spun up, opening on an active document. "Let's begin with the case. While you guys were out there trying to find the guys doing this with the intent of stopping them in their tracks, I'm taking a different tack. Even if they avoid you guys and collect every endangered bird they need, they still need to get them off the island. More than that, unless they're locals, they had to get here in the first place. And as we said last night, air travel is the only way that makes sense—private air travel, specifically. I spent my day calling around. There are multiple airstrips on the island—and that's about all you could call them, with no tower or paved runway. Most of them are meant for crop dusting. Definitely not a place where you're going to land a seventy-million-dollar jet, if you're fancy. Or even a ten-million-dollar jet, if you're not. You're going to pick a real airport, with a runway that won't wreck your expensive investment, not a backwater airstrip."

Todd laid his burger into the container. "We saw the Mountain View Airstrip when we dropped Hale off after our search two days ago. Hale and Byrne were coming in and out by helicopter and needed an open space, but that open space was next to the airstrip. Which is using the term lightly. It was paved once, but is now broken down to cracked asphalt, gravel, and dirt. No one with a real plane is going to use that strip."

"Illustrating my point. I called around, posing as a harried, frantic underling assistant, and found out quite a bit. Apparently sounding stressed, vulnerable, and like you're a total underdog to the corporate overlords plays on people's sympathy."

"No one likes an overlord," Brian quipped.

"You were just looking for who would accept flights?" Meg asked, ignoring Brian's sass.

"No, I could figure that out partly by doing web searches. For some places that didn't list much info online—and that was mostly airstrips as I was getting started—I just asked about being able to accept flights, knowing I could always come back with another persona and another round of questions later. But those airstrips got knocked out immediately because they didn't accept the kind of longer-distance flights we're focusing on. I found it much more useful to pretend to be panicked because I couldn't find my boss's plane at airports I knew would accept private flights."

Brian nearly choked on his wine. "You pretended to lose a plane?"

"My story was it got borrowed by one of the execs, but we weren't sure where he'd gone. He'd logged a flight plan, but then deviated from it. Which is entirely believable because, contrary to most people's opinions, you aren't legally obligated to stick with any logged flight plan. The FAA doesn't have a law enforcement arm that comes after you if you don't. And anyone involved in the industry knows that weather, mechanical or medical emergencies, or pain-in-the-ass passengers can all cause deviations. So I posed as someone who 'lost'"—McCord made air quotes with both hands—"a plane and whose boss was going to fire his ass if he didn't find said plane. At first, I was worried I was laying it on too thick, but people took pity on me. From those calls, I think I have a lead." McCord turned to Meg and Brian. "You have no idea how long someone has been on the island trafficking these birds, correct?"

"Correct," Meg said. "Though Byrne made it sound like she didn't think it was for long. The idea is to come in, find what they need, and get out again. Keep the birds moving so none of them have time to die in their care. Once they're out of their care, keeping these expensive creatures alive isn't their problem. We spotted them on Wednesday, but we don't know what their activity has been before or since. There was no trace of them today."

"Hmmm..." McCord stuffed three fries in his mouth, chewing as he studied his screen. "I have a couple of potentials for you, but I'm not sure the timing works. Of all the airports on the island of the size we discussed last night, there's only one that really fits—Waimea-Kohala Airport. It's about thirty minutes from here, so not that close to where they're collecting the birds, but it ticks all the boxes. Big enough to service their kind of plane, yet small enough there's no security and only minimal staff to manage the flights that come and go. And they've had three private planes parked there since varying times last week." McCord frowned at his screen. "That's probably too long. You're probably looking at someone who arrived this week, maybe Sunday or Monday, so I may be on the wrong track. But if I am, then maybe I'm looking on the wrong island. Maybe it's a boat to Maui and then a plane to the mainland."

"That seems needlessly complicated," Brian said. "It not only extends the travel time and time where they could get caught, it's an additional stressor on delicate birds."

"You're not on the wrong track when you take their prep time into account," Todd stated. "They have to clear-cut specific areas for collection. If so, they spent days preparing for collection, which is what they're doing now."

McCord brightened. "Good to know. Then these might work. When I went out there, all three planes were on the tarmac, so I got photos."

"Wait a minute," Meg interrupted. "You went to the airport?"

"Yeah. As I said, it's a half hour away. And wouldn't

you know it, there's a car rental desk just off from the resort's main lobby. They keep vehicles here for when someone needs one as a spur-of-the-moment decision. I rented, did my thing, and returned it. Super handy." McCord pulled his cell phone from his back pocket, woke it, scrolled to his gallery, and opened it to a specific photo. "Take a look at these." He passed the phone to Meg.

She held it so Brian could lean in and examine the photos with her. The first picture was taken from within a narrow parking lot, showing a long, low, weathered beige building with a shallow corrugated metal roof backed by a cloudless blue sky. Double glass doors led to a shaded interior. "Did you go in?"

"No, I didn't want to attract that much attention. Besides, what I needed was outside. Keep swiping."

Meg swiped right, to the image of a chain-link fence at the end of the building revealing a blacktop beyond. The images progressed as McCord approached the fence, enlarging the scene until the fence was gone and he was shooting through the mesh. The next picture showed them exactly what he'd sought.

A sleek white jet sat at the end of the asphalt apron beyond the terminal, parked off to the side. The next pictures showed a close-up of the front half of the plane, then the back half, and the third image zoomed in on the tail number, which in this case was emblazoned on the side of the engine rather than the tail itself. Parked behind that plane were two more planes, mostly blocked by the first, but one number was visible on the tail, while the other was completely obstructed. The last photo was a long-distance shot of the airport from what looked like the far side of the runway.

"Three parked planes?"

"Yes." McCord put down the last bit of burger that remained after he'd taken advantage of the time Meg and

Brian spent looking at photos to plow through his dinner. "At the time, I wasn't sure which plane arrived when, but that was before I spent some time on flightradar24.com."

"Is that some kind of aircraft-tracking website?"

"Yes. Hang on. Let me show you." McCord flipped over to his browser, typed in the address, fiddled for a moment, and then turned the laptop so everyone could see.

"These are the Hawaiian Islands." McCord indicated the archipelago. "And all these planes streaming from the US mainland? We're watching those live." He randomly selected one yellow plane from the swarm and clicked it, turning it red and illuminating its flight path in green. The left side of the screen populated with information about the plane, including a picture of the aircraft, the airline, the flight and tail numbers, the altitude, speed, and direction of flight, as well as the scheduled and actual takeoff and scheduled landing times.

"Holy smokes." Brian leaned in. "We're watching a Southwest flight from Long Beach flying to Honolulu in real time."

"Yup. Now, if we open up the section on recent flights for that tail number, and then go to more . . ." As McCord talked, he followed his own instructions. "Because I signed up for a one-week free trial, we get the full flight history for this aircraft for the entire previous year."

"That's impressive. Honolulu from Long Beach." Todd read off the list. "Before that, over just the past few days, it was Denver to Las Vegas, to Dallas, to New York, to Houston, before heading to Long Beach." He shook his head at the lack of evident rhyme or reason to the flight patterns. "Who plans these things?"

"No idea, but it must be a nightmare. Anyway, you get the idea of how useful this site is."

"But you only had two of the three tail numbers to look up," Meg pointed out.

"You didn't look close enough at that last photo from a distance. If you zoom *way* in, you can see the last plane. Now, to get that photo, I had to park down the road a ways and do a little off-the-books reconnoitering."

"You mean trespassing," Todd said dryly.

"One man's reconnoitering is another man's trespassing. I got myself onto the land that's on the far side of the runway, on the other side of the security fence. Then all I could do was hope from that distance that any pictures I took would be clear. There was no closer spot that had the correct angle."

Todd picked up McCord's phone from where he'd set it on the table and swiped to the last picture, zooming in on the plane in the background. "Is that a three? Or an eight?" When he realized it was zoomed in as far as it could go, he brought the screen closer to his face. "Or an *S*?"

"It could be any of those. But that's the beauty of these websites. Try any and all combinations, and see if there are any that aren't valid and collect information on those that are. You can also look up tail numbers on the FAA website. They'll report on all sorts of data on the plane—who manufactured it, when, who owns it, where, details specific to that aircraft like its make, model, serial number, make and model of the engines, et cetera. Just a note that all American-owned planes have tail numbers that start with a capital *N*."

"Have you run the tail numbers already?" Brian asked.

McCord's laugh was more of a snort. "Oh, ye of little faith. Of course I have." He flipped back to his document. "The two we could easily see are N4814A and N897VT. Then we have the last one. Which is either N1593M, N1598M, or N159SM. When I looked those up, the last is a Raytheon fixed-wing fighter jet owned by the US Air Force—"

"Pretty good chance that's not our bird," Brian commented.

"Then there's N1598M, which is a four-seater, twin-engine Cessna out of Minnesota with a range of just over one thousand miles."

Todd laughed. "That's not going to get all the way out here. Partway before ditching in the ocean, sure. All the way to Hawaii? Nope."

"That leaves N1593M as the likely number on that plane. And now we have the three possibilities."

"And what have you figured out about them?" Meg asked.

McCord turned back to his screen. "N4814A is a 2017 Bombardier Global 5000, owned by Aviatronics Customs Brokerage in Maryland, which, as the name suggests, is a customs brokerage firm that specializes in aircrafts and aircraft components. The flight arrived on May twenty-third. No flight plans to go out, but as all previous flights for this tail number are short-haul flights around mainland US, it makes me think the CEO or owner is vacationing."

"Actually, that could be someone's story," Meg pointed out. "If someone is using a company plane for this, they could be using a vacation as their cover. Send one person, or that person and their spouse, to take a vacation, send several others as 'staff.' Staff who get busy while the cover person is vacationing." Meg sat back and looked thoughtfully at Todd. "This whole thing could be done in under two weeks, couldn't it?"

"Might be better to ask Byrne and Hale that question, but at a guess, I'd say it could be done in that time period with advance planning," Todd said. "But who's to say this is the first trip to the island? There may have been another trip in the past weeks or months, where they planned out the best locations, complete with escape routes. If it was me, that's what I'd do."

"You're a firefighter." Brian's tone was amused. "You're the very definition of a Boy Scout. Being prepared is what you do."

"True."

"But Todd has a point. The area we stumbled onto on Wednesday was relatively freshly cleared, but that could have happened in the previous few days or week." Meg swiveled in her seat toward McCord. "Can you check those tail numbers and see if any of those planes made a repeat visit. Or visits?"

"Definitely something we should put into the mix. If they did enough remote planning ahead of time, they might not have needed an expensive exploratory trip, but you never know. Let me run the other two planes with you, then I'll circle around to those searches. The next one is N897VT, a Gulfstream IV. It's owned by DiamondJet, one of the big players in the US luxury jet rental market."

"There's a market for that?" Brian rolled his eyes. "What am I saying? Of course there's a market for that. People with too much money love to toss it around."

"There's definitely a market for that. Businesses hire private jets for corporate retreats. Cheaper than owning your own, but you still get that luxury experience. Families hire private jets for vacations. Or they're contracted for exclusive experiences, like weddings or anniversaries."

"Surely if you were going to rent a plane like that, it wouldn't just sit on the tarmac waiting for takeoff. It would come back for you."

"I guess that depends on how much you were willing to pay. Most companies would be fine with you keeping their jet if you weren't sure how long your trip would take, as long as you pay for the flights that plane could be making. Let's say you were negotiating a contract, and it would take days of meetings, but you want to split as soon as things were settled. So you pay for the luxury of having the plane there at your fingertips.

"The last plane is N1593M, a Cessna 700 Citation Longitude, owned by Conaghan Partners, LLC. But when I look into Conaghan Partners, LLC, I find what appears to be a shell corporation based out of Ireland."

"Because offshore shell corporations aren't suspicious at all," muttered Brian.

"Yeah, I'm going to need to do more research there. It's a well-known fact that organized crime loves to use offshore shell corporations as covers, so that could be the story here. Now, let me look at those three tail numbers for repeat flights over the past year." McCord copied the first number, then went back to the flight tracker web page and searched it. "Aviatronics Customs Brokerage's N4814A. Flights around mainland US, but nothing to Hawai'i in . . ." He scrolled down the list. "Nothing in the last year. None of the Hawaiian Islands, in fact. Next is DiamondJet's N897VT." He paused, scanning down a much longer list. "Not really a surprise, but this plane has seen a lot of airtime. And some of it has been to Hawai'i, O'ahu, and Maui. Last trip to the Big Island was . . ." He scrolled further. "Last November. Though it landed in O'ahu in February, but returned to San Diego the same day. No long stopovers on that trip."

"Have there been long stopovers?" Todd asked. "Or is this trip an anomaly?"

McCord ran an index finger down the dates. "No, there have been stopovers. Some for a few days. This one is a week."

"If someone is willing to pay through the nose, they can arrange for the plane for however long they want it," Brian stated.

"That's what it looks like. Likely any initial quote on the rental would include time and mileage. Hmmm . . ."

"What are you thinking?" Meg asked.

"That it might be time for me to play the same frantic assistant and see about renting from DiamondJet. Get an idea of the cost and availability. How fast could a trip like this get set up?"

"I'm just spitballing, but it probably depends on how long you'd want the plane," Todd said. "But it would be good info to have."

"Agreed. Okay, the last plane, Conaghan Partners' N1593M. Now, this is interesting. It has been to the islands a few times in the last two months. Twice to Hawai'i, once to Kaua'i. Makes you wonder if some of the birds are on both islands."

"Or if there are different birds on different islands. It was a fifty-minute flight from Hawai'i to O'ahu. Kaua'i is even farther. Flight between islands could be a deadly endeavor for the birds."

Meg picked up her phone. "Byrne likely knows. I'll shoot her a text. She may not catch it until later or even tomorrow, but I'll see what she can tell us about crossover with Kaua'i."

"Good plan. So, if those are the three planes we're looking for, our most likely chances are Aviatronics and Conaghan if we think an advance trip was made. Otherwise, we still need to consider all three."

"Also consider that if they're using DiamondJet to rent for this little project, they likely aren't renting the same plane each time," Todd said. "That would mean different tail numbers, so we may not be looking at the whole picture. Can you look up all the tail numbers of a certain owner?"

"Hang on. Let me circle back to the FAA search page." A few clicks, then a low whistle. "Apparently you can, but this will take some serious work. Seventeen pages and over sixteen hundred results. Now, I'm sure these aren't all current entries—some may be decommissioned aircraft—but considering each tail number has a complete history of every plane that ever used that particular number, this is a *long* list. And depending on how tail numbers are recycled, they might even reuse some of the numbers on their own planes. I need to look into that."

"Wonderful." Brian's tone was dour. "This could be Russian nesting dolls of tail numbers."

"Welcome to the sexy life of investigative reporting. It's not all breaking into condemned buildings, posing as someone buying an engagement ring, or saving the damsel in distress. Sometimes, it's just hours of slogging through records." His shrug was easy. "Sometimes that slogging pays off."

Meg patted McCord on the shoulder. "As we've seen many times," said Meg. "What do you think the chances are that they flew in and are going to meet their plane on a selected date? In which case, none of these planes would be the one?"

McCord stroked his jaw, staring into the middle distance, his eyes unfocused. "They could have done that. But wouldn't that be risky in the end?"

"It would be too risky for me, if this was my plan," Todd said. "I'd want an escape hatch available to me at all times if things got too hot. They might have a plane standing by in case of emergency, but at best it's somewhere else on the island. It could be on another island, but that could take up to a couple of hours to get here once the alarm goes up. Or worse, it's on the mainland, and you're talking six or seven hours, at best. Their clients are spending big bucks for these birds. I think they'll build the safety measure of keeping a plane handy into what they're charging them."

"Agreed. There's one other thing to keep in mind, though."

The caution in McCord's eyes was reflected in his tone. "I may have gone down a rabbit hole with this. We all think using one of the busy major airports on the island would be too risky, but we don't know that for sure. There's a chance I'm steering us wrong."

"What's your gut instinct say?" Meg asked.

"That I'm right." McCord's answer was instantaneous, reflecting his certainty. "That they'd be insane to use a busier facility for multiple reasons. This is a federal, felonious crime. If they can't keep it off law enforcement's radar, they're done."

"I've learned to trust your gut over the last few years. That's good enough for me."

"Thanks." A gust of wind from over the warm blue waters of 'Anaeho'omalu Bay swept through the lanai. McCord pushed back from his chair to stand at the stone wall, looking out at the moon and the surrounding starscape. "God, I wish Cara was here to see this."

Meg rose to join him at the wall, the lava rock rough under her fingers, but still warm from the day's heat. "Me too. She'd love this. You need to bring her here. Or somewhere tropical. Leave your dogs with us and go."

McCord's gaze shot from Meg to Todd. "Really? You'd do that?"

"Don't see why not," Todd said. "We're literally on the other side of your wall. They could live in our space, or yours, and hang out with whoever's home."

"Not to mention, Hawk would love it," Meg added. "I don't think he really minds being an only dog, but when Cara and I split up, bringing our dogs to our respective sides, he was confused. They all shared the backyard, but Saki and Blink didn't live in his space, and now Cody was there too? It was all very weird for him. He'd welcome spending more time with them. And we could manage it. Think about it."

"I will."

"Anything else you need to update us on?"

"Just the other angle I'm following up on, but I don't have a true update." McCord returned to his chair.

Meg sank into the couch cushions. "What's that?"

"The trafficking angle. I reached out to Elsa's contacts and there might be something there, but I need more time. I also put out feelers with my *Post* colleagues for local contacts, and one of them put me in touch with a reporter from the *Honolulu Star-Advertiser*, Ori Palakiko. I'm picking his brain about local crime syndicates and black markets."

"Is that a good idea? You're bound by your promise to hold the story, but another reporter isn't."

"True. But I set the whole thing as a long-term historical investigation, so he doesn't see the story as anything current. I promised him credit in the article for his help, but told him it would be a while coming out, as I'm just in the beginning stages."

"He bought that?"

"Seems to have. Helps he doesn't know I'm actually here; he just saw my DC area code and assumed I was calling from the *Post* offices."

"Smart." Brian braced his hands on his knees. "If that's it, I'm going to head back to my room. I promised Ryan an email update when I talked to him this morning. He knew we'd be finishing our day long after he went to bed."

McCord held out a hand, freezing Brian in place. "That's the case update. But you guys may have a bigger problem."

"Bigger than illegal wildlife trafficking?" Todd asked.

"From what you experienced today, as well as everything I've read and from the real-time updates I'm seeing, there are serious concerns about Mauna Loa. I'm afraid you're going to be out there and things will go to hell."

Brian squirmed like McCord's unusual intensity was making him uncomfortable. "You know us. We're prepared for anything."

"Not for this. If things go sideways, you can't be prepared for it. And that could put you and the dogs in deadly danger."

CHAPTER 15

Rift zone: Areas of weakness radiating outward along the flank of a volcano; a frequent location of non-caldera eruptions.

May 31, 8:51 PM
Waikōloa Beach Marriott Resort
Waikōloa, Hawai'i

McCord's words sent a shiver down Meg's spine. She looked first to Todd, then to Brian, seeing the same apprehension that curled in her gut.

"I think you'd better tell us everything you've learned so we know how to mitigate the risk as best as possible."

"There's risk mitigation, and then there's knowing when you're beat. You're used to being able to control your environment much of the time. You may not pick the area to search, but you choose what teams need to go in, how you'll communicate, what kind of backup you'll have, how you'll be armed. Nothing like that counts here. If Mauna Loa erupts, there's no mitigation strategy except escape. Lava is two thousand degrees Fahrenheit. You can't reason with it, divert or redirect it, and you certainly can't stop it. If you come into contact with it, it will boil all the fluids in your body and cook you to death in seconds."

"Jesus..." Brian muttered. "Okay, we've got it. It's dangerous."

"Beyond dangerous."

"But it's slow, right?"

"It can be." McCord's expression was grim as he flipped over to a second open document on his laptop. "The lava flow speed at Kīlauea's Fissure 8 last year clocked as high as thirty-eight miles per hour. And while the average human can run five or six miles per hour— faster for you guys because you're in shape, so maybe twelve miles per hour under pressure for short periods of time—that's still not something you can outrun." He turned to Todd. "You're the most knowledgeable here. You're used to intense danger and heat on a regular basis."

"The situations are hardly comparable. We're in turn-out gear specially treated to be flame resistant and to withstand up to sixteen hundred degrees Fahrenheit. As well as wearing full SCBA respirator masks while we carry compressed air."

"Good point. The gases are another deadly hazard."

"Okay, McCord, you have our attention, and it sounds like we need to know what we're getting into. Lay it on us." Meg took a long swallow of her pineapple wine, bracing herself. When McCord dove into a subject, he dove *deep*. He was about to open the research fire hose on them, even though they'd likely only need a fraction of the detail he was about to drench them in. Granted, that fraction could save all their lives, so it was worth hearing the whole thing just to get to the kernel of information their survival might depend on.

"Let's go back to basic fifth grade science when they taught us about volcanoes. Tell me I wasn't the only one to build a working volcano for the science fair." Silence and raised eyebrows from everyone else, and McCord's smile faltered. "Well, you all missed out on some serious fun. And a hell of a mess. Anyway . . . the Hawaiian archipelago is actually part of the Hawaiian-Emperor seamount, a nearly four-thousand-mile chain of undersea mountains formed by a magma hot spot from the molten core of the planet. Now, think back to what you learned about tectonic plates and how they're always moving, even if it's just an inch a year. The visible Hawaiian Islands were formed from eruptions through the Pacific plate that piled up as undersea mountains. But here's the thing about volcanoes: They're constantly expanding the land mass they create, and in time, those mountains cleared sea level and became volcanic islands. All the islands are in a chain because the plate is constantly moving in one direction, so each new island formed by repeated volcanic eruptions is younger than the previous in line. Kaua'i is the oldest Hawaiian island, at about four million years old. Hawai'i is less than a half million years old. And the newest island, Lō'ihi, is still being created."

"Did I miss something?" Brian asked. "Lō'ihi?"

"You didn't miss anything. Lō'ihi is about twenty miles from Hawai'i and is still about a half mile underwater. Come back in fifty thousand years and you'll be able to spot it."

"I'll put that in my calendar."

"Not to be missed. But as new islands are born, the older islands slide into the ocean and disappear as the plate submerges. That's why most of the islands in the seamount chain can't be seen above water. Back to volcanoes. The only active volcanoes are those near the hot spot. Haleakalā on Maui's east side is still considered active, though it hasn't erupted in between four and six hundred years. Other than that, the Big Island of Hawai'i has the four other active volcanoes above water—Kīlauea, Mauna Loa, Mauna Kea, and Hualālai. And while Mauna Loa hasn't erupted since 1984, it's looking like its time has come."

"Thus the earthquakes," Todd said. "How are they connected?"

"My fifth grade science project had a single tube that pumped red fluid out the top of my papier mâché volcano, but that's not how the geology of some volcanoes work, especially shield volcanoes like these. Some volcanoes only erupt at the caldera—the main volcanic crater—but rifts can add to the problem. Rifts are areas of weakness that radiate out from the caldera. I guess you guys haven't hit Volcanoes National Park yet?"

"It was on our list, but somehow we haven't made it there so far."

"You may be volcanoed out by the time you leave this island, but it's supposed to be amazing. Anyway, the worst of the Kīlauea eruption last year didn't take place at the caldera in Volcanoes National Park. There was activity at the caldera, but the worst of the eruption took place almost twenty-five miles away, along Kīlauea's east rift zone. In fact, just before the eruption, the level of liquid lava in the caldera dropped because it was moving along the rift into the eruption area. Similarly, Mauna Loa has rift zones—one that stretches from the caldera down the southwest flank, and another that runs northeast from the caldera. Where you were today, that ground was right in between those two rift zones. But where you were Wednesday was *on* the northeast rift zones."

"The earthquakes are coming from these weakened rift zones?" Meg asked.

"They don't help, but the earthquakes are coming from the magma below. If the magma just took a straight path up to the caldera, you'd likely have fewer earthquakes. But instead, the magma is finding weaknesses in the rock, and as its pressure builds, it's fracturing the rock and essentially cleaving its way through laterally a hundred feet down, making its own new pathways that could then break through anywhere along those weakened rift zones. Does the intensity of an earthquake like the one that hit today mean a true eruption is coming closer? Possibly, but not necessarily. Apparently, a seismic swarm—a cluster of earthquakes all in one area—is a bigger sign of trouble."

Meg exchanged dark looks with Brian and then Todd. "Uh . . . we didn't tell you that we had two earthquakes today. And I could have sworn I felt a smaller tremor later on."

"That's not good. A lot of the earthquakes that make up a swarm may not always be felt by someone standing on the mountain, but they'd be picked up by the sensors laid out by the Hawaiian Volcano Observatory research teams. You guys need to watch it up there."

"Well, so far it's just earthquakes. As long as there's no other signs—"

"Except there are. There's liquid lava running in the caldera, raising the level, though no pressurized explosions yet."

"Comforting." Todd's tone was anything but impressed. "What do we need to watch for? Swarms of earthquakes, but what else?"

"In a lot of ways, there won't be any warning. Obviously, the National Volcano Warning System is out there doing its thing and monitoring all the country's volcanoes, with Kīlauea and Mauna Loa their highest priority in Hawaii. You can sign up for updates from them as warning levels change, so I've already done that. You won't be on your phones while you're out trying to catch wildlife traffickers, so leave that part to me. If anything changes while you're out in the field, I'll let you know. You'll continue to use your satellite phones?"

"Yes," said Meg. "We got lucky in Pu'u Maka'ala because it was so close to Volcano, so there was a signal. But the other forest reserves are too remote."

"Good to know. Another thing to watch for when you're out in the rift zone is natural steam vents. Essentially those are cracks in the earth, but they leak steam and often smell like hydrogen sulfide or rotten eggs. However, a little steam from an old vent may just mean the volcano is still active, which we already knew, not that it's about to erupt. Still, would be good to keep your eyes peeled for that. If the earthquakes continue, watch for gas rising from any new cracks in the earth or in paved areas. The gases are a real problem. Hot steam, carbon dioxide, carbon monoxide, sulfur dioxide. Less commonly but still possible, hydrochloric acid, hydrogen fluoride, mercury, arsenic." McCord exhaled heavily, his cheeks briefly puffing outward. "If this thing takes off, it's going to be bad."

"I guess I'm glad we're having this conversation." Meg shifted uneasily on the couch. Going after men who shot first and asked questions later was bad enough, but being up against them and one of the most vicious natural threats on earth was a bit overwhelming. "I'm sure it's all going to be nothing for us to worry about, but we need to be prepared."

"Not so fast. There's one other thing. If Mauna Loa blows, there's always a risk of pyroclastic flow."

"Everyone knows pyro means fire," stated Brian. "What's 'clastic' mean?"

"I looked that up. Clastic is a geological term, often referring to sedimentary rock, broken and ejected over significant distances by great force."

"Broken by fire. Ejected by a volcano. So watch out for ejected rocks?"

"Yes, but it's worse than that. Pyroclastic flow is a cloud of ash, pulverized rocks, and a mixture of toxic gases, all bad enough. But ejected as part of the initial volcanic eruption in front of the lava? It would have temps of about eighteen hundred degrees Fahrenheit. And as it rolls downhill, it can travel anywhere from sixty to four hundred miles per hour. There is no escaping it."

Shock froze Meg in place—her muscles locked as she tried to imagine the threat of a roiling, boiling, toxic cloud of death she wouldn't be able to escape in a Formula 1 race car as it thundered toward her.

"Remember Pompeii? It wasn't the ash that killed the majority of the residents. In fact, they survived the first day of the eruption and the ash that buried the city. Approximately two thousand of them died instantly on the second day when Vesuvius collapsed and a pyroclastic flow raced down the mountain and covered the city."

McCord paused, meeting the gazes of each of them in turn, making sure they understood the risk they were potentially undertaking.

"You're possibly not going to be on the far side of the island in case of an eruption. You're going to be in the shadow of the volcano itself. If Mauna Loa erupts and spews out a pyroclastic flow in your direction, there's no way to survive it."

CHAPTER 16

Intrusion: The influx of molten magma into older, surrounding rock where it solidifies rather than erupting.

June 1, 6:46 AM
Waikōloa Beach Marriott Resort
Waikōloa, Hawai'i

Three sharp raps sounded on the door to the suite.
"McCord, can you get that?" Meg called from the bedroom.
"Got it!" McCord's reply was followed by the sound of footsteps, then the front door opening. "Come on in."
Meg jammed two more energy bars into her go bag and zipped it shut. She picked up the neatly folded concealment shoulder holster from on top of the gun safe, which lay on the bed, and slipped it on, making sure the band was comfortably snug under her breasts before closing the hook and loop fasteners. She set her go bag down next to the gun safe so she could grab them as soon as they were ready to leave.
She strode out into the front foyer to where Hale and Byrne stood as McCord closed the door behind them. "Morning."

"Morning." Hale's smile was a little sleepy as he dumped his bag onto the floor. "Sorry this is so early."

"We were originally on East Coast time. Keeping that in mind, it's going to be lunch soon, though I admit to floating somewhere in time between there and here at this point."

"And here we are, not even having had breakfast." Byrne bent over and unlaced her hiking boots, toeing them off and nudging them with one foot out of the way of the door and against the wall.

"Brian and Todd went out to get breakfast," said Meg. "We thought about eating at the restaurant downstairs, but it's open-air, and we didn't like the lack of privacy while discussing the case." She indicated the living room with one extended arm. "Come on in. We can either eat here around the coffee table or outside on the lanai." Her gaze traveled out through the open lanai door, where Hawk and Lacey lay together on the mat by the lava rock wall, enjoying the sea breezes. "The lanai is pretty private, but if you want to make sure we're not overheard, here is better."

"Here it is, then," Hale said. He also removed his boots, then padded to the couch in his socks. He dropped onto the cushions, tipped his head back, and then rolled it to look out the open lanai door to the bright new morning. Facing west, the lanai was shaded from the sun, but the riot of greenery beyond popped bright in the morning light, and the scent of blooms—bougainvillea, hibiscus, and plumeria—floated inside on the gentle ocean breeze. "Being here isn't a hardship. In fact, maybe they can take their time getting breakfast."

"Did you fly in from Honolulu this morning?" Meg asked.

"No, we grabbed hotel rooms in Waimea last night, so we're only about twenty minutes away. We got a good six hours in the rack before having to get up and get ready to drive to the other side of the island again." Hale stifled a yawn behind a cupped palm. "You sure you don't want to stay over there?"

"Is it as nice as here?"

"It's nice, but it definitely doesn't have the same beaches."

"And it rains a lot of the time," Byrne added.

"We're good here, then," Meg said. "You planned to stay and brought a change of clothes?"

Byrne huffed a laugh as she dropped into a chair. "We're right beside a local shopping center. We both cobbled together another outfit, and we're carrying our IDs." She pulled at the collar of her blue cotton T-shirt emblazoned with the silhouette of palm trees against a background of multicolored surfboards with ALOHA written in flowing script above. "I look like a damned tourist."

"This damned tourist can do better for you than that." Meg's smile showed she wasn't insulted by the epithet. "I have a clean athletic shirt that looks to be about your size." Meg studied the rest of her outfit. "The pants look fine."

"Standard yoga gear. Athleisure wear is everywhere now, so that wasn't a problem. But the T-shirt is definitely for the tourist trade." Byrne winced. "Sorry."

"Nothing to be sorry about. Follow me."

They were back in three minutes, Byrne now wearing one of Meg's long-sleeved, wicking athletic shirts.

"Better?" Hale asked.

Byrne sat down again. "*So* much better." She glanced at her watch. "Do you expect them back soon? We should be on the road by no later than seven thirty."

As if on cue, the door to the suite opened and Todd entered, bearing an overstuffed paper bag in one arm and his key card in the other hand.

Brian followed behind, carrying a paper bag and a tray

of juices and coffees, and nudged the door shut behind him. "I swear all we do is eat and plan in this suite."

"That wasn't our original intent," Todd said dryly. "Though that's certainly what it's turned into."

"Don't forget drink," McCord quipped. "We've tried some fine new Hawaiian beers and wines in this suite."

Brian set down the tray of drinks, then the bag. "True."

"I have to say, it's nicer than the Kona FBI satellite office," said Hale. "Which was our other best option."

"I'm all in favor of the beachside resort," Byrne said, leaning forward to peek into one of the bags. "I'm ready to gnaw on this table. Let's get that food moving."

Within minutes, they were settled and diving into breakfast.

"Now that my stomach isn't going to digest itself," Byrne said after a few minutes of dedicated eating and small talk, "let's get our ducks in a row. Meg, you said you guys wanted to discuss strategy."

Meg wiped her mouth with a napkin, then set it down. "Search strategy, yes. Yesterday was a lot of work. Yes, we tracked some nesting sites and set up trail cameras to detect any movement—"

"Like it did at one thirty this morning," Hale muttered. "And again at four."

Meg stared at him in surprise. "By hikers?"

"No, wild boars. They sleep during the day when it's warm and forage at night when it's cooler. You can find them even higher up Mauna Loa than we were. But they set off the motion detector just like a human would."

"Can you mute notifications for overnight?" McCord asked. "And then check in the morning for them? I mean, if you're on this side of the island and trackers are cutting through the forest at night, they'll be long gone by the time you get up, drive to the far side of the island, and get to the spot."

"I could be staying at a bed-and-breakfast in Volcano, and if they're out there, on the move in the dark, I'm never going to find them." Hale took another bite of his toast, then washed it down with some coffee. "And there aren't going to be birds flying at one thirty in the morning, so I think I'd be safe muting notifications overnight. Good idea, thanks."

McCord's mouth was full of eggs, so he saluted Hale with his coffee cup.

"Back to the trail camera, then, at least in daylight," Meg continued. "What we did yesterday was useful, but the thing I came away with was that's not an area they're going to use to capture birds unless they have no other hunting grounds. It's simply too isolated and is too far inset from the nearest roads. Having to hike in for two hours and then back out again for two hours means a good chunk of your daylight hours are simply spent getting there and back, severely limiting the amount of time you can spend actually acquiring your targets. And then you have to carry those targets out for hours in bags or boxes, where they could be hurt if you fall."

"Or if they're just struggling to get out," Todd added. "Also to think about, we're all in shape, but we don't know they are. If they aren't in decent shape, that's a long, difficult hike. Maybe too long and difficult."

"I agree," Brian chimed in. "On paper, Ka'ū seems like a logical search area—it's a concentration of the birds we're concerned about and isolated enough for them to work unseen. But in practice, it's too hard on the traffickers and the birds, and the isolation is too extreme. I'm not sure they ever tried it, but if they did, I'd bet they abandoned that area after the first attempt."

"It sounds like strategy is exactly what you need." McCord got up and walked back to the door of the suite.

Meg sent Brian a sidelong look. "I think you nailed it yesterday. 'Work smarter, not harder.' "

"If what you're saying is true," Byrne said, "that leaves us with Puʻu Makaʻala and the Upper Waiākea Forest Reserve."

"Northeast rift zone," McCord singsonged under his breath as he sat down with his laptop bag in hand.

"What?"

"We spent some time last night with McCord schooling us on the other danger we're facing on this case besides the guys with the guns—Mauna Loa. It may be getting ready to blow, and both of those areas are in the northeast rift zone of the volcano."

"I've had half an eye on that." Hale pulled up his phone and started a search. "When you live here, you're always attuned to the volcanoes, but because they become commonplace, you don't pay real attention until HVO and USGS send out the serious alerts." He paused for a moment, reading, the creases across his brow deepening. "It seems Tūtū Pele is angry."

"Tūtū Pele?" Brian asked.

"In Hawaiian mythology, Pele is the mother of fire and volcanoes and is the creator of the islands. They say she lives in Halemaʻumaʻu, the active fire pit in the Kīlauea caldera. Legend has it she has a fiery temper, and when she's angry, her volcanoes erupt." He set his phone down on the table. "We'll have to be aware of our surroundings at all times."

"I have the alerts coming in on my phone." McCord waggled his handset. "If anything happens, I'll raise the alarm. You may be busy and may not know there's a problem until it's too late, otherwise."

"Appreciate that."

McCord picked up his empty takeout container, closed it, and set it on the ground at his feet. His coffee followed.

"Can we make some room on the coffee table? I think this might help." He bent and pulled a large, folded map from his laptop bag.

Meg moved her container, making space for him. "Where on earth did you get the massive paper map? Straight out of the nineteen nineties?"

"Believe it or not, the car rental place in the lobby has them for sale. Older people come to the island, and some of them aren't so tech savvy, so they keep a few full-island maps on hand. I figured this was the easiest low-tech way to plan, so I picked one up." McCord laid the map out over the whole table.

"This is great." Todd studied the map. "Here's Puʻu Makaʻala." He circled the area on the east flank of Mauna Loa with his index finger.

"And this is where we were yesterday." Meg tapped the southern slope. She leaned in for a better look. "This map is pretty good. It even has smaller roads."

"Triple-A map," said McCord. "They know their roads. They also know it's a tourist area, so the more complete the map, the better to avoid people getting lost."

"Yesterday we went from about here to here." Meg planted her index fingers on their rough start and finish positions once they hit altitude on the slope of Mauna Loa. "That really was a long way from any transportation."

"Which is the point," Brian said.

"Let's think about this logically," Todd suggested. "You guys know hiking through all sorts of terrains. If we're going to set boundaries on how far in we think the traffickers would go, I think we should think about it in terms of time. They're unlikely to pick a spot that takes too long to get to and from without endangering the lives of their prizes or risking being caught out in the wilderness in the dark. What do we think—an hour max in each direction?"

"Leave it to a firefighter . . ." Brian muttered, and Todd flashed him a grin.

"I think that's a fair call," said Byrne. "These birds may seem inconsequential, but they're real moneymakers for the traffickers because of their endangered status. They'll protect them, because if they don't, they just wasted their time, and time is money, which is the only goal for these people. They won't see it in terms of lives lost, or species in jeopardy, only in terms of profit."

Hale rotated the map slightly, bringing the northeast slope of Mauna Loa into the middle of the table. "So we're only looking at Puʻu Makaʻala Natural Area Reserve and the Upper Waiākea Forest Reserve. One of the reasons we chose Kaʻū yesterday was because of the bad weather, but that gets taken out of the equation."

"A ticking clock is going to be what matters here," said McCord. "You guys got my email last night about the stationary planes at the Waimea-Kohala Airport and why I think they may be relevant?"

"We did, thanks."

"Your reasoning made sense to me," Byrne said. "We can't definitively say one of those planes is the one they're keeping on-site, but considering the lack of privacy at the only two other airports on the island that would accept a plane like that, as well as the need for a quick exit, I think you're on to something."

"Everyone understands the time crunch. They've been here for a week. Every day that passes is a day they could get caught. If they do get caught, we're talking . . . what?"

"For the federal felony of wildlife trafficking? Which, by the way, involves both civil and criminal charges." Byrne's smile was feral. "This is criminal all the way. Let's start with the Endangered Species Act. As a criminal violation, they could each be fined up to twenty thousand dollars and could get a year in prison. For each bird."

"I like it," said McCord. "Throw the book at them."

Byrne held up a hand to stop him. "That's not all though. Then we have the Lacey Act that protects against the illegal taking of any wildlife, as well as the import, export, and trade of that wildlife. Those charges also apply, so now there's an additional fine of a half million dollars and five years in prison."

"Really starting to add up now," Todd said. "We wondered why they took one look at you, fired blindly after you in the forest, and ran. They were trying to avoid this kind of sentence at all costs, and couldn't afford to be seen or caught. Do the birds we released in Puʻu Makaʻala count?"

"They absolutely do. Thanks for filming those, by the way. Really strengthens the case."

"So they're each looking at bankrupting fines and decades in jail," McCord said. "Now I'm even more certain they're not going to have a plane waiting somewhere off island to get them in case of an emergency. They're going to want to run right for the airport and get gone."

"Agreed," Meg said. "That's the other thing about staying closer to Hilo on the east coast, rather than Pahala toward the south coast—there are more opportunities for escape. Leaving Kaʻū, you have two choices—southwest or northeast. But the other two reserves are much closer to Hilo, which allows for three paths of egress—north, to circle the island from the northern end; west, straight across Saddle Road; or south, to circle the other way along the southern edge of the island."

"That's the thing about this island." Brian tapped a fingertip first to Mauna Kea, then to Mauna Loa. "With two massive mountains running north to south, there are extremely limited main thoroughfares. Basically, one road to circle the outer perimeter of the island and one to cut through the middle. The other advantage to staying closer to Hilo and the east side is that it puts them closer to the Waimea-Kohala Airport. When every moment counts, that would save them probably an hour on the roads where law enforcement could be watching every vehicle."

"Even starting from closer to Hilo, it's likely an hour to the airport," Todd said. "But every minute not on the open road is a minute of safety." He picked up his coffee cup and took a sip. "East side, then. And we're looking at an hour max hiking time in each direction. How far will you get in that time?"

Meg met Brian's eyes, saw the complexity of the question reflected in his expression. "It's not really that easy," she said. "Who's doing the hiking? A couch potato or someone fit like the group of us? What's the terrain? Is it a jungle like Puʻu Makaʻala or an open, unobstructed trail? Is there an incline? How steep?"

"I guess that question was a little too simple." Todd stared at the map for a long moment. "And this is a great road map, but it tells us nothing about the terrain. Even something as simple as elevation, or if there are any footpaths into the reserve."

"That's what hiking apps are for." McCord pulled out his phone, opened an app, typed in a location, and brought up a colorfully graduated map, using two fingers to zoom into his area of interest before glancing back at the map. "It depends on how you're entering the area, but there are basically three ways. Puʻu Makaʻala lies in the south, reaching north to the border of the Upper Waiākea Forest Reserve, the lower Waiākea Forest Reserve to the east being too far downslope for the birds we're looking for. When you guys hiked Puʻu Makaʻala, you drove north out of Volcano, correct?"

"Correct," said Meg.

"Our suspects used the restricted Stainback Highway to head south into Puʻu Makaʻala. However, they could use the same road to go north into Upper Waiākea. Conversely, to the north of Upper Waiākea is Saddle Road and the Puʻu Oʻo volcano trail and the Emesine Cave nature trails, which both come south toward Mauna Loa." McCord paused for a minute, staring at the app. "About three miles to get into Upper Waiākea from Saddle Road. It looks like this is across a lava desert." He looked up to meet Todd's eyes. "I haven't driven Saddle Road. Are there sections like that?"

"Many. Lava stretching for as far as the eye can see. Huge flows coming down from Mauna Loa."

"Northeast rift zone, thus the Puʻu Oʻo volcano trail. Which, by the way, cuts pretty much straight south from Saddle Road to run behind the Kulani Correctional Facility. Assuming they might come in from Saddle Road, how hard would that lava be to cross to enter the reserve?"

"Three miles? If there was an established trail, Brian and I and the dogs could do that in forty-five minutes or an hour tops. If there's no trail?" Meg met Brian's eyes. "What do you think?"

Brian sat back, drumming the fingers of one hand on his knee. "From the SUV, it looked like miles of uneven rocks piled one on the other. Like rubble. You'd think a lava flow would be smooth because of the molten rock, but it's not."

"It's like the miles of lava rock we saw on the way from the Kona airport?" McCord clarified. "Rough black rock for miles, studded with the odd tree or shock of grass?"

"Just like that," Meg said.

"That's because of the way the basalt lava forms," Byrne said. "We have two kinds of lava flows here—ʻaʻā or pāhoehoe. Pāhoehoe is formed by hot flowing lava, often with a low silica content, and has a rippled texture, like you'd see in any fluid, except it then solidifies like that. Go to Kīlauea and hike the Kīlauea Iki crater—you'll see miles of pāhoehoe lava. 'A'ā lava, though, is what you see on much of the island, the stuff that looks like piled chunky rubble that comes from high eruption rate volcanoes. It forms because the top of the molten lava cools first and hardens into rock, but the flow underneath is still moving, and that motion rips up the solidified rock above. They say 'a'ā lava is called that because that's the sound you make if you cross it in bare feet." She chuckled. "Take my advice, do *not* do that. It's bad enough that the rocks are so loose and jumbled, but because basalt lava rock is so porous, it's an even rougher surface. I've hiked some of those areas before. It's not quick. If you hurry, you'll wipe out and likely scrape off the top two dozen layers of skin. And possibly break a few bones. It's porous, but it's rock. It will break you."

"So, doable, but less likely," McCord said. "And time-consuming."

Brian nodded. "Extremely. Probably triple or quadruple the time."

"Unless they can get to Upper Waiākea from an established trail or only have to break from the path for a short period of time, I'd guess they're using Stainback Highway as their entryway."

"Is there any reason for them to assume they were followed after the shooting?" Todd asked.

"I wouldn't think so," Meg said. "I didn't announce myself as FBI. They never saw Hawk. Even if they had, they wouldn't know he's a tracking dog. For all they know, I was alone and they killed me and my body is still lying there, undiscovered."

"Not to mention, we went off the trail to let Hawk track the scent. They might assume that even if someone has reported you missing by now, unless they're sending out search dogs to Pu'u Maka'ala, chances of you being found off-trail in that jungle are extremely small. That would be if someone knew where you were hiking in the first place. All in all, there's no reason for them to think law enforcement followed their trail. They may still consider that a safe route."

Meg followed Stainback Highway with her index finger. "Where does the road shut down for only authorized vehicles?"

Todd tapped the map about a quarter of the distance to the Kulani Correctional Facility from the junction with N Kūlani Road. "About here."

"Can we get some sort of law enforcement to oversee that road?"

"We could," Hale replied. "The problem is that road is legitimately used by a lot of people. Prison staff, Department of Corrections and Rehabilitation personnel, inmate visitors, people who run the development programs on-site, delivery drivers. We could pull over and question every vehicle. They'd be trespassing if they were on the restricted part of the road, so we'd have cause to search the vehicle. There won't be many who would be carrying transport bags and mist netting. Of course, that's not a crime, but it could give us cause to arrest them. Then we'd depend on Meg for an identification to actually hold them."

"I didn't see them for long, but it still was long enough," Meg said. "And you have my descriptions of the two I saw, though we know there could be others. I guess the only issue I can see is if they enter either reserve before the restricted section of the road. Then there's no cause to search the car."

"Here's an idea," Todd said. "Have you thought about using drones?"

Hale looked at him sharply. "They're not clear-cutting up to the canopy. That's likely on purpose so there's nothing for anything flying above the forest to see."

"But drones could be useful with the right equipment. DCFEMS sometimes uses drones when we're attacking a fire. The drone has both a high-res thermal camera and a 4K color camera mounted on it, so you can see both images in real time. In our hands, it allows us to see the location of the fire from the outside, evaluate roof integrity, locate hot spots, identify the location of hidden victims, and track our firefighters during the blaze. In this situation, depending on positioning, it would not only allow you to track all incoming and outgoing traffic, it would allow you to see inside the forest. You walked that jungle, so you know how dense it is. With the thermal cam, you'd see their heat signatures under the canopy. There's no way for them to hide."

"Not trying to douse the idea with cold water," McCord said, "but won't any hiker look the same? It will pick up any warm person."

"Any kind of heat signature. Goats and boars are blocked from part of the area, but where they're allowed, they'd be detected as a heat signature. You can tell from body shape what you're looking at, but yes, it could pick up anyone who chose to hike the area at that time. However, let me tell you, it's a challenging area and extremely low traffic. When we parked, we were the only vehicle. Minus the traffickers, we didn't see another soul."

"Likely why they were in that area in the first place," Byrne said. "I bet you were a hell of a shock to them. I think the drone is a solid idea." Byrne studied the road that separated the two nature reserves. "These are big areas. How far away could it detect a signature?"

"Ours is a midrange camera that picks up signals up to about four hundred feet. Which is fine for us when it's hovering forty feet above a structure fire. But there are industrial models that can detect signals one to two thousand feet away."

Interest and hope lit Hale's expression. "That could be a game changer."

Unease crept up Meg's spine. She still wasn't entirely over the first case they'd worked with McCord when an East Coast bomber had used drones to deliver his killing blow to far too many victims. Especially far too many children. The sound of those whirring blades had followed her into sleep for months following the attacks. "One thing to keep in mind—drones aren't quiet. As we learned during a case two years ago, you can usually hear them coming from a distance, and you definitely know when they're directly overhead. That one- or two-thousand-foot distance might be what's needed to keep them unaware."

"You raise a good point." Todd nodded in agreement. "We wouldn't necessarily need them directly overhead. The strategy would be for them to alert us as to where to go to track them. It would narrow the field when we're dealing with this." He drew a large circle in the air over the areas of the map in question.

"I'm going to make both a search of anyone on that road as well as the drone happen." Hale pulled out his phone, opened an app, and started making notes. "The search I can set up for today, but I'm not sure I can get the equipment we'll need for overhead visuals in place as quickly. This is the issue of having people and equipment spread across a number of islands. Still, I'll try." He turned to Byrne. "You drive today. I'll make calls. What's our plan in the meantime? Where do we want to start? You guys are the experts. What does your gut say?"

Meg met Brian's eyes, and they leaned into the map together, considering.

"They're not going to get near the correctional facility," Brian stated. "Too big a risk of being seen coming in."

"Too big a risk of being heard clear-cutting a big enough area to string the mist net," said Meg. "You only saw pictures of the area we found, but that would be impossible to clear quietly."

"Nothing was done with power tools," Todd said, then shrugged when Meg fixed him with a raised-eyebrow stare. "Professional interest. I tend to notice how things go up and how they come down. I took a look at how they'd clear-cut the space they needed. I'm guessing they used an axe and saw for the trees and bigger stuff, and a scythe for the smaller stuff."

"Using manual tools makes sense," Brian said, his eyes still locked on the map. "They wouldn't want to do anything to attract attention. And the sound of a chain saw would do just that. Still, even with a saw or axe, you'd hear stuff coming down if you were close enough."

"How much space would you need to not be heard?" Meg glanced at Todd. "What do you think?"

"In a normal forest with that airspace between underbrush and leaf canopy? I'd say probably half a mile, if not a full mile. But in the fern forests, that thick, tall underbrush will deaden the sound. Maybe a quarter mile, tops."

Brian snapped upright. "We're missing an important aspect here. McCord, your laptop's in that bag?"

McCord reached down and pulled out the slim black laptop. "What do you have in mind?"

"Is Google Earth on it?"

Meg suddenly realized Brian's intent. Google Earth: for elevation. For satellite imagery. For the ability to make plans by setting pins and making measurements. "Damn it, why didn't we think of this sooner?"

"I got us." Brian laid a hand on the map. "Old-fashioned paper actually works well for this initial planning. We can't close in on selections until we consider the whole space."

"What are we missing?" Hale asked.

"This will tell us elevation so we can cut out anything that's too low for the birds themselves. Add in the satellite imagery that will show us roads or paths that might be taken and we'll have a better idea."

"Here. Put it at the end of the table where everyone can see." McCord passed his open laptop that already displayed the area in question in Google Earth to Meg.

She angled it so everyone could see the map, but so she could also use the touch screen to move around. "Here's Stainback Highway." She dragged Pegman—the little yellow man that allowed for street view—out onto the map. All mapped roads glowed blue. "This shows us where the end of the road is." She dropped Pegman as far along Stainback Highway as was mapped. The map rushed up, and then they were looking at the road from street level.

"There's the sign." Todd pointed at the white sign on the edge of the road that read NOTICE—USE OF THIS ROAD WITHOUT AUTHORIZATION IS TRESPASSING.

"To hell with the sign," said Brian, excitement lacing his tone. "Did you see what I saw as we dropped onto the road?"

"I guess not. What was it?" Meg asked.

"Take us out of street view. There's something in the satellite view that's not reflected on the paper map."

Meg pulled them out of street view, and their perspective sprang into the air. This time she spotted it. "Wait, you mean those paths?" She leaned in closer to the screen. "Dirt roads? Twin tracks? I'm not sure what I'm looking at."

"I'm not either, but pull back a bit and look at it."

Meg zoomed out a bit, then realized what Brian indicated and zoomed out farther. "I'll be damned."

Running parallel to Stainback Highway was a break in the trees. And from it, several trails branched off to enter Upper Waiākea.

Meg slid the map toward the east, following the extra track. "This runs for most of the length of Stainback Highway. Probably ten or twelve miles. This would be the way to get into Upper Waiākea unseen. And there are numerous entrances from the highway onto this back road."

"I think you just found our plan for the day," Hale said. "I bet that dirt road, or track, or whatever it is, is going to be like what we followed out of Puʻu Makaʻala a few days ago. It may not even be gated."

"Is there a place where that track intersects with a road with street view?" McCord asked.

"Hang on." Meg pulled Pegman out onto the map again and then dragged him along until she found a place near the eastern end of the highway where it intersected with W Mamaki Street, and dropped him there. Then she rotated the view.

"There it is," said Todd as they all stared at the twin dirt ruts in the grass that led directly off the highway and into the thick trees flanking it on both sides. "As you said, it's likely twelve or so miles away from the correctional facility. From satellite view, it looks like it travels the entire distance. In fact, when we interrupted them on Wednesday and they ran, maybe they didn't use Stainback Highway for their escape. And maybe they weren't picked up."

"You're thinking they might have left a vehicle on one of these backwater trails."

"Maybe. Only one way to find out."

"Let's get there, get the lay of the land, and then decide on a search area based on what we find. Kai and Makoa will meet us there. They stayed in Hilo last night, so I'll call from the SUV on the way there and give him time and place."

"And while you're doing that," McCord said, "I'm going to be spending some time trying to crack the offshore shell company, because I still think that's the perfect way to hide an organization's real ambitions. Then my contact at the *Honolulu Star-Advertiser* gave me some tips to get started on my research into the local black-market trade, so I'll have my head down on that too. Figuring out who they are might also give us some advantages."

"I can help there," said Hale. "One of our agents at the Honolulu field office has his finger on that pulse in this area. Special Agent Harry Lawrie. I'll ask him to get in touch with you."

"That would be great, thanks. Hopefully by the time you're back, I'll be on the trail of something."

"I think we have a plan," said Byrne, glancing at the time. "It's seven twenty. If you haven't finished eating, bring it on the road." Her gaze moved around the room, touching on each of them. "Let's end this."

CHAPTER 17

Seismic Storm: A series of earthquakes occurring during a short time period in a specific location.

June 1, 9:42 AM
Upper Waiākea Forest Reserve
Hilo, Hawai'i

"I'm going to need a chiropractic adjustment when this case is over," Brian muttered, his arms braced to steady himself as the SUV lurched over a hunk of rock. "The dogs might too."

Meg looked around from the front seat, peering down into the footwell where Lacey lay near Brian, crowding his boots off to the side. Hawk lay behind Lacey, with only his head in sight from her current perspective. "Are the dogs okay?"

"I'm fine, thanks for asking. They are too. But we're getting tossed around back here."

They'd arrived at the intersection of W Mamaki Street and Stainback Highway fifteen minutes earlier. After a quick discussion, they'd decided that Byrne, driving with Hale, Kai, and Makoa, would take Stainback Highway, while Todd—with Meg, Brian, Hawk, and Lacey—would follow the alternate route. They'd paused only long enough to get their sidearms out of their gun safes and into their holsters in case of an encounter with the armed traffickers and then headed onto the rough road.

Even though Byrne couldn't see their vehicle due to a thick dividing wall of vibrant green foliage, she'd attempted to run parallel to them. Each time they passed a cross track that led toward the highway, they'd find Byrne pulled off to the side, ready to pull back onto the highway as soon as they became visible, to keep pace with them as best she could when they had no impediment to the thirty-mile-per-hour speed limit.

"You can see why they'd use this supposed road," Todd said as they bumped along the twin tracks. "Except for those few cross paths, we're completely invisible here."

Meg scanned the dense greenery to either side of them. Todd was correct—there was likely only a few hundred feet between them at this point as they made their way west, but the forest protected them. Towering evergreens with drooping needle-like branchlets, thick bushes with foot-long, thick, multilobed leaves, wide fans of ferns, and a profusion of tall grasses lined the gap, making them essentially invisible.

The rain they'd avoided in this area yesterday must have arrived in buckets because the dirt track below their tires was churned into thick mud. The four-wheel drive handled the difficult terrain and slippage, but Meg had a bad feeling about what they'd be hiking through.

"How far do you think we've gone?" Brian asked. "Are we running parallel to the restricted section of the highway at this point?"

Meg opened the map app on her phone, let it locate them based on their GPS signal—driving through the forest as far as the app was concerned—and then zoomed out to estimate. "Well past it." She dropped the phone into her lap to turn her gaze out to the road. "Still nothing to say they came this way, though."

"It's too muddy." Brian turned around, lifting partway off the seat to stare out the back window. "We're hardly leaving marks because of how wet it is. The water is flowing into our tracks. It would have been worse yesterday. How much rain did they get?"

"Not sure what they actually received, but the forecast was for six inches."

"Yikes."

"Seems like a lot to us, but apparently, it's not uncommon on this side of the island. The day we landed on Hawai'i, they had another four or five inches."

"Even worse, with the combined amount. We'll definitely be dealing with the remnants today when we're on foot."

"What's that?" Todd eased off the accelerator, and they coasted for a few seconds. He pointed quickly through the windshield, then grabbed the wheel again as the SUV veered to the left. "That clearing up ahead. There's enough room to turn a vehicle around."

Meg leaned forward to peer through the windshield. "That's something we haven't seen up to now. This whole way, minus the few cross paths we've come across, it's been single car width only. If you ran into another vehicle on this path, one of you would have to back up until they hit the next cross path, or no one would go anywhere."

Todd pulled forward slowly. "I'm not going to leave the road, but it opens out on both sides here. Roll down your windows and look for any traces of a vehicle."

Meg lowered the front passenger window, while Brian did the same on the opposite side in the back.

"It would be a tight fit on this side," Brian called, his head right out of the vehicle, both hands gripping the bottom of the window frame. "And I don't see any sign of tire tracks. The ground looks pretty soft, so I think there would at least be depressions."

"I need to get a little closer," Meg said. "Keep it slow . . . a little more . . . more. Stop." She unlatched her seat belt and got on her knees, leaning out the window. "Yeah, I think you nailed it. The whole area is filled with ground cover—some green, some pink, like we saw lining the edge of Saddle Road. But there are definite depressions. No tracks, but it might be enough to at least get some idea around chassis size. That could help narrow the list of possible models."

"The biggest issue around a vehicle is whether they're renting like we are," Todd stated. "I think half the vehicles on this island are short-term rentals. Even if you can track down the exact vehicle—which would be hard, if not impossible, to do through impressions in damp grass—there's no guarantee they didn't use a fake identity for the rental agreement."

"Todd has a point." Brian's voice floated out from the back seat. "I think the most important thing it tells us is that someone has been here."

Meg leaned out even farther, trying to get a better look, then felt fingers slip under the back of her shirt and into the waistband of her yoga pants to grasp the material. "That better be you, Todd."

Brian's responding crack of laughter made her smile.

She turned her head to find Todd stretched over from the driver's seat, keeping a hold on her. "I'm not going to fall out."

"Just making sure. You wouldn't really hurt yourself, but the mud facial you'd get isn't how you'd like to begin this search. Brian did the wet search last time—let's not have it be you today."

"Yeah, yeah." She turned back around, looking carefully for a moment, and then pulled her upper body in. "I think this is where we need to start." She pulled out her phone and dialed Hale's number, put it on speaker, and began talking as soon as he answered. "It's Meg, you're on speaker. We have something."

"A vehicle?"

"We're not that lucky. But traces of a vehicle in the first spot we've found so far on this narrow track where you could turn around."

"So they wouldn't need to come back via the authorized access road where they might get caught trespassing."

"Exactly. Where are you?"

"Waiting at the side of the road at the next cross path."

Todd tapped her on the arm and then pointed ahead and to the left. "I think that's it there. Hale, come down that road. I think you'll come out just past where we are."

Byrne's voice sounded in the background, then Hale said, "We're moving. According to my map app, it's only about a hundred fifty feet in. Tell me what you see."

Meg gave him a quick sketch of what the road was like up to that point and then what made them slow down and take a closer look. "We haven't left the main track," she finished, "so we haven't disturbed the area." Movement drew her gaze forward as a black SUV pulled into view. "And there you are. Check that area out in front of you and see if it's clear. If it is and there's room for us, too, we'll park there and get out."

"Hang on."

In the background, Byrne's voice was followed by muffled discussion.

Hale's door opened and he climbed out, walked over to the grassy space in front of the SUV, gave it a careful once-over, waved Byrne forward, and then put his phone back to his ear. "You're good to come over here." He ended the call.

Todd parked so their SUVs were side-by-side, and they climbed out, leaving the dogs in the vehicles for now. The clearing was about forty feet across from tree line to tree line and only slightly longer, bisected by the muddy double track they'd been following.

Meg led them back to the depressions. "Looks like they pulled off here."

Hale squatted down for a better look. "Pulled off or parked. Not sure which, but I agree."

"This is why."

Meg looked up from the depressions to find Brian hadn't followed them, but had instead walked to the edge of the clearing. "What's there?"

"Come see."

Meg, Todd, Kai, Byrne, and Hale crossed over to where Brian stood at the tree line. Except it wasn't the tree line—it was a narrow path leading straight into Upper Waiākea Forest Reserve. A narrow, muddy foot path, with distinct, soft boot prints in the mud.

"Nice going." Meg clapped Brian on the back. "I didn't spot that."

"The way it's angled, unless you were looking in the right direction, you'd miss it entirely," said Brian. "You and Todd got out and headed toward the road. Kai had his door open still, so I went to circle the front of our SUV to join you. I had to be in front of the SUV to see this. My guess is this is their entry to Upper Waiākea."

"I agree." Meg turned to Kai. "This may end up being a dual search. Makoa will search for the nesting sites; Hawk and Lacey will follow the scent of whoever went through here last."

Kai nodded in agreement. "And the paths may lead to the same location."

"At least to start," said Brian. "But they don't have

Makoa's great nose, so they may be searching by sight. Let's get the dogs and get going."

Hale held up a hand to stop the handlers as they turned toward their vehicles. "One more thing. I got lucky with the drone request. We have a real tech whiz in the Honolulu field office, Greg Austin, and he said he has a drone with an infrared sensor that would work for us. He's on his way here with it now, putting down in Hilo. I expect he'll be on-site within an hour and a half to two hours. I knew we had drones in-house for investigations; I didn't expect they'd have a heat sensor, but it makes sense."

"Especially in an environment with so much open terrain so heavily covered in tropical forest," said Todd.

"That's essentially what Austin said. He's going to contact me when he gets here. Which reminds me. Everyone make sure your phone is on vibrate."

While Meg, Brian, and Kai got the dogs down and leashed, Hale took photos of the boot prints in the mud. As they entered the forest reserve, they took care to not disturb the boot prints, in case they needed to be cast. Digital capture of boot and shoe prints to re-create the sole was the new normal, but old-fashioned forensics sometimes still worked better, depending on the substrate.

Even though they were only half a dozen miles from the site in Pu'u Maka'ala where the traffickers had set up their mist nets, the terrain was already quite different. Instead of thick rainforest foliage and a heavy soil base packed with tree ferns, this area had considerably less undergrowth and was more heavily forested by tall trees, their pale, naked trunks and branches reaching for the sky in an explosion of green leaves. The ground beneath their boots was broken down and packed into a fine powder, now turned into a soggy silt with the rains, but the ground on either side was studded with black lava rock, filled in between with spongy mosses and clusters of pili grasses and smaller fiddlehead ferns.

They were passing into an area where the underbrush grew a little thicker when the sound of a startled cry came from behind them.

Meg whipped around to find Hale hauling Byrne upright as she clutched his forearm. "Did you trip?"

"Slipped. Sorry, we need to keep our voices down in here in case the sound travels and the suspects hear us, and I was entirely too loud." Steady again, Byrne dragged the toe of her boot through a slurry of small lava rocks and water. "Watch this path . . . It's not as stable as we think. Some of the rocks have been ground into tiny pieces, and they're acting like ball bearings when they're in soggy areas with just enough water to suspend them." She released Hale's arm. "Thanks for keeping my ass out of the puddle."

"You're welcome. Onward and upward." Hale nodded at Kai and the group continued.

The first time the ground swayed under their feet and the leaves shivered overhead, Meg exchanged a sidelong look with Todd, but no one commented on it. She scanned the area on both sides of the path, but as the tremor passed and the leaves settled, it seemed like nothing more than the breeze had disturbed them. The fact that the tremor was more of a ripple than the strong shake of the day before didn't serve to quiet Meg's unease.

Makoa was in the lead with Kai, but Meg kept an eye on Hawk as he and Lacey followed, unleashed and free to follow the scent.

"Pretty sure Hawk has something," she said quietly to Brian, who walked alongside her, Todd following between them and the two agents.

"Lacey too. Something human, though there's no guarantee it's our guys. And in here, protected from air currents, the scent is likely holding strong, even if it was days ago." Brian was quiet for a minute as he scanned the landscape. "There's something I don't get."

"What?"

"How they're finding the nesting grounds. They're parking out there, or they're being dropped off, and they're hitting the trail. How do they know where to go?"

"Keep it simple, stupid," Todd said from behind them. "And I'm not calling you stupid, but it's the thought that counts."

"Meaning?"

"They paid someone. Cost is no object on a mission like this. They found someone who could supply the information."

"You mean they paid a conservationist bird nerd to give up the goods to put the birds in jeopardy?" Meg asked. "That's not the kind of thing they'd do."

"It's not unless there are obscene amounts of money in play, which there could be, so we shouldn't discount the idea. But that's not what I meant. Look at the research tool we have at our disposal."

With a jolt, Meg realized what Todd was saying. "You mean McCord. We have him onboard, working with us, digging up all the details we need, making contacts."

"Pretending to be someone he isn't to befriend some poor schmuck who takes pity on him," Brian interjected.

"While we're out here, hiking the trails and interacting with suspects, he's sitting on our lanai or driving around the island digging up facts."

"And McCord can dig," Todd agreed. "But what if they also had a McCord, who had joined them on the dark side? What could Dark McCord dig up?"

"A lot, possibly." Meg thought back to the meeting in the Honolulu field office, how McCord had come up with a combined map of a number of the birds in question in only minutes while their attention was focused elsewhere. "Especially if given some time. We've given McCord only a matter of days, and he's already found the likely transportation route, and possibly the plane. He hasn't had to spend time on the birds because we had Byrne, and then Kai came onboard, but I bet he could have identified more specific areas for us if we'd needed him to."

"What is it that McCord says?" Brian asked. "That research is his superpower? He's right. Take someone with that same superpower, someone who is willing to pay for access to records and scientific papers, someone who is willing to reach out to talk to people about their particular passions, and they could get the same information as a bird nerd."

"Especially for endangered populations," Meg said. "Anything that's in trouble like that is being studied so we can assess how to better help them. Is their territory disappearing? Is it a disease? Invasive predators? And people like that don't keep that information to themselves. It's in a government database or it's published in a journal so others can springboard off that information to continue the work." She turned to look back over her shoulder at Todd. "You think they're being directed to certain sites."

"Yeah. We don't have time to do that kind of research, but we don't need to. We have Byrne, Kai, and Makoa to get us to where you and the dogs need to be. I think when all this is said and done, you may find an information network that allowed them to put this package together for their buyer. In fact—"

Meg's attention snapped down to the dogs when both Hawk and Lacey suddenly stopped, heads cocked, on alert, their hackles rising. "Here we go again," she called, stepping forward to straddle her dog.

The tremor passed through with more sway than the previous, though still not as bad as the day before.

The severity wasn't what had Meg pulling her phone from her pocket to type out a message to McCord. **We just had two quakes in short order. Any Mauna Loa alerts?**

McCord's reply came quickly. **Still on advisory level. Will let you know if that changes. Be careful. That may be the beginning of a swarm.**

Thanks

Meg slid her phone into her pocket. "McCord says the advisory level is unchanged. If anything changes, he'll raise the alarm."

"Good to know," Brian said.

Up ahead, Makoa veered off the path, climbing a rocky slope and slipping into the underbrush. Brian grabbed Meg's wrist, and they both stopped.

Kai stepped onto the first chunk of lava rock, then stopped. "Makoa, *kali. Kū.*"

The dog stopped and turned around to look back at Kai. Kai in turn looked back at Hawk and Lacey—they'd finally reached the moment where the paths might diverge.

"Let's see what the dogs say," said Brian. "Lacey, find."

"Hawk, find."

Meg and Brian didn't move, but watched as Hawk and Lacey both put their noses to the ground, breathing in the shallow inhalations that meant the air was diverted to their olfactory cells instead of their lungs. Together, and without hesitation, they walked past the spot where Makoa had turned off the path.

"Hawk, Lacey, stop!" Brian called out. He turned on the path to face Hale and Byrne. "What do you want to do now?"

Hale's gaze flicked first to Makoa, then to Hawk and Lacey. "We knew this could happen—Hawk and Lacey could be following the exact path of the suspects, while Makoa could be following the scent of a nesting sight. If that nesting site is their final destination, Makoa could in fact get to the site faster because he's not following a circuitous route followed by a couple of guys."

"The two paths might converge," Meg said, "or Makoa could be leading us to the nearest nesting site, which might not be the one the men went to."

Hale turned to Byrne. "Kai raised the issue of the 'Io. Could one of their nests be in play?"

Byrne nodded. "Possibly. They nest high in the canopy, usually in 'ōhi'a trees. The same search strategy will work here as the young defecate over the edge of the nest. But even if the traffickers found the nest, catching one would be a much larger task."

"With a bigger payoff," Todd stated.

"Definitely. The 'Io would be harder to catch, contain, and transport. You don't worry about injury from an Ākepa. But the 'Io? With those talons? That's a different story. That kind of risk requires that larger payoff." One hand shading her eyes, Byrne studied the canopy overhead. "Though this is an area where they could do it."

"Capture an 'Io?" Brian asked.

"Yes. They range over the area of Pu'u Maka'ala, but that's not easy hunting grounds for them, and the jungle-like forest structure makes it hard for a large bird of prey to easily penetrate. They'll consume small rodents, amphibians, or even larger insects, but birds are the main part of its diet. Remember the 'Alalā Project? The main risk to those birds is the 'Io. But it makes me wonder if this area with more trees and a considerably less dense understory would be a better range in which to catch an 'Io, as it would allow for easier movement inside the forest structure itself. Conversely, it would mean less clear-cutting for mist netting."

"Why didn't they come here directly instead of bothering with the difficulty of Puʻu Makaʻala?" Meg asked.

"What makes Puʻu Makaʻala harder for the ʻIo makes it safer for the other forest birds. Simply put, they had a better chance of catching the other types of birds in Puʻu Makaʻala."

"Which makes me think they might be going after the bigger prize here," Hale stated. "Bottom line, I think we need to split up. Both paths could be important."

"How about I go with Kai and Makoa?" Byrne offered. "You stick with the rest of the group. We'll stay in touch via text if anyone finds anything. Then, if the other is clear, we can call so the entire team is on the same page."

"Sounds good. Stay safe."

"You too."

Kai ran a hand down Makoa's back, where he sat patiently waiting. "Makoa, *loaʻa*." They disappeared up the rocks and into the green.

"Hawk, find."

"Lacey, find."

Hawk and Lacey trotted off down the path, heads low, noses scenting, and their tails high and waving.

"They have the scent." Meg power walked after her dog, Brian beside her as Todd and Hale followed close behind.

If discomfort crawled up Meg's spine as another tremor rippled under the surface, this time without the dogs even pausing as they acclimatized to the small disruptions, she didn't comment on it.

Nearly twenty minutes later, Hale stopped walking. "Hang on. Getting a text." He pulled out his phone. "Makoa found something." He speed-dialed a number and put the phone on speaker, dialing down the volume so the sound didn't travel.

"Makoa found a nest on the ground," Byrne said as soon as she picked up.

"Knocked out of a tree?"

"No, it's a ground nest. A Kalij pheasant nest. One adult bird dead, four eggs crushed, one rolled under some foliage. Fetuses all dead. I'd assume some type of predator attack except for the intact adult and the boot print nearby."

"What are your coordinates?" Hale opened his map app and typed them in as Byrne recited them. "As I thought, the paths might converge at some point. We're only forty or fifty feet from you. Stay there. We'll let Hawk and Lacey follow the trail. I bet it leads to you."

Several minutes later, Hale's guess proved true as Hawk and Lacey led the group off the main path to find Byrne, Kai, and Makoa standing at the base of a towering ʻōhiʻa tree.

"Makoa was right on the money," Meg said, stroking a hand over the dog's soft fur. "Good boy." The dog's tail beat a happy tattoo on the mossy ground. She scanned the area. "Where's the nest?"

"In a hollow under that cluster of bushes. Makoa led us straight to it. I can't be sure, but I'd guess they got too close to a nest and the parent defended it. The chicks in the eggs would have died without the parent, but crushing the eggs was an asshole move of retribution." Byrne's voice was flat, as if she'd spent the previous few minutes reining in her temper.

"Model members of society." Hale's tone made it clear they were anything but. "If they've done their research, they'll know the place is lousy with pheasants, so they have no value to them. They could have walked away, but no." He shook his head in disgust. "They were here recently. Today? Or yesterday?"

"We can't tell," Meg said. "The trail is relatively fresh,

but we're sheltered from the winds in here, so their scent could stay strong for days."

"This isn't good."

Meg turned to where Todd stood with his back to them about forty feet away in the trees. "What's wrong?"

"Come and look."

Hawk naturally at her knee, Meg had only gone about fifteen feet when the smell filtered through, rolling her stomach. "Is that . . . ?"

"Rotten eggs? Yes."

With every step, the smell grew stronger, and Meg paused. "Hawk, buddy, if it's bad for me, it's unbelievably bad for you. Stay. Brian, you better leave Lacey here too."

Brian's nose wrinkle only deepened his expression of disgust. "Five by five on that."

Todd stepped back as Meg approached, allowing her to see the narrow cloud of steam puffing from a thin, craggy break between rocks. Alarm streaked through her like a blast of ice. "That's one of the steam vents McCord was talking about."

"Yeah. What we don't know is if it's one of the existing ones he discussed, or a new one formed because of the pressure below in the rift zone."

Hale squatted down for a better look. "That one's probably new. See how clean the surrounding rocks are? Older vents are lined with crystallized minerals. Often sulfur, which leaves them coated in yellowish crystals."

"And produces that nauseating smell," Brian muttered, taking a step backward.

Hale looked up at Meg. "Any news from McCord?"

She pulled out her phone to double-check in case she'd missed her phone vibrate. "No. I know he's on top of it, so if something goes out, we'll know right away."

Hale pushed to his feet. "We should keep moving. Let's

keep the dogs on the scent and see if they try to split up again."

"Agreed."

They moved forward as a group, letting the dogs scent the way. From here, Hawk and Lacey took the lead, staying confidently on the trail while Makoa wasn't picking anything up in this area. They strayed farther and farther from the trail, the difficulty of the topography slowing them down as they maneuvered over the rocky terrain, slippery with moss.

They came to a low-lying area, a dark rocky depression filled with water, with a jagged wall of rock to the right and a thick tangle of ferns and undergrowth to the left. Hawk and Lacey, used to being on outdoor hikes in any kind of weather, weren't fazed. Both immediately leaped over the puddle, Lacey landing on the mostly dry path, and Hawk—with his shorter legs—landing just short, his back paws landing in the shallow edge. He sauntered out to follow Lacey a few feet up the path, then both dogs stopped. Makoa, however, didn't attempt the jump.

"Can Makoa make that?" Brian asked. "He's pretty energetic, but his legs are considerably shorter."

"I don't think so. Makoa, *mai*." The dog came to stand beside his handler. Kai made sure the straps of his backpack were secure, then bent, wrapped his arms around his dog lengthwise, and picked him up, leaving Makoa's legs dangling. Kai waded through, the water rising over the tops of his boots.

"Waterproof hiking boots are only waterproof until the water comes up over the top," Brian said. "I had wet boots on the last hike and it rubbed my feet raw, even after changing socks, because they got wet from the boots. I'm going this way." He veered off to the right, sidling sideways between the edge of the puddle and the rise of lava rock. The rough rock scraped at his backpack, catching at it, slowing his progress and almost setting him off-balance. "This looked easier from over there."

"Should have come this way," Meg said, taking a step to her left. She eyed the underbrush—a few ferns, some tropicals with multilobed leaves, and a scattering of smaller trees. Light came from behind the underbrush. Maybe the dogs were circling around to another clearing.

She stepped around the puddle, giving it a good foot, the small rocks crunching under her boot. "This way looks clearer. It might be better to—"

The rocks shifted under her boot mid-step, as she only had one foot on the ground, jerking her sideways. She got her other boot under her, but she was already sliding, her arms windmilling.

Some of the rocks have been ground into tiny pieces, and they're acting like ball bearings.

Byrne's words echoed in her head as she skidded sideways, grasping for any hand hold to keep her steady.

"Meg!"

Out of the corner of her eye, she saw Todd lunge for her, but she was overbalanced and slipping too quickly, skidding into the underbrush.

The world dropped out from under her feet and then she was falling.

CHAPTER 18

Pali: A cliff or steep slope on a Hawaiian volcano.

June 1, 11:06 AM
Upper Waiākea Forest Reserve
Hilo, Hawai'i

One second, there was a precarious path for her feet—the next, *nothing*.

Her body dropped into thin air. Her hands, madly scrabbling for anything to grasp, grabbed at some slender woody branches, clutching tight. Her body jerked violently, her arm shrieking in agony as muscles shredded by a bullet attempted to help carry her weight.

She couldn't contain the cry of pain as she struggled to hold on, her feet kicking, trying to find anything to stop her fall, having no idea what was below her, how far the drop might be.

Her left hand started to slip just as the branch under her right hand broke with the stress.

She had one lightning-fast glimpse of Hawk shooting through the bushes toward her, and then she was falling again.

It felt like she was falling for no more than a second, but it was enough time for her training to kick in and her body to respond. She instinctively pulled in her knees, leaning into the twist caused by her right hand dropping first to fall on her right side with that arm curved around her head for protection.

She had just enough time to force her muscles to go loose before she crashed through the underbrush, branches scraping and leaves slapping. She slammed into the ground in a bone-jarring crash, the air knocked from her lungs. For a moment, panic rose as she couldn't inhale. *Calm down. Panic and it will get worse.* She gave herself a full ten seconds to lie still before putting her spasming diaphragm to the test, relief flooding her body along with warm moist air.

"*Meg!*" Todd's bellow came from above, and she tried to pull in enough air to answer, but her lungs weren't cooperating and all that came out was a croak.

Stay calm. You'll get your breath back faster.

She concentrated on shallow breaths, slowly deepening them, expanding her lungs. She tried again. "Here..." It came out as a wheeze. *Not enough. Breathe.* In and out, while she imagined the rescue attempt taking place above, Brian ripping his climbing cord from his bag, Todd looking to anchor it and body-rappel down like he had in the Boundary Waters Canoe Area Wilderness.

"Meg!" Brian this time. "Call out if you can hear me. We're getting ready to come down!"

One more breath, filling her lungs normally. *Finally.* "Here! I'm here."

"How badly are you hurt?" Todd again. "Where are you?"

"Don't come down yet. It may not be needed. Give me a minute to assess."

Time to discern the damage. No one could afford to be injured in an area so remote. And if she was suffering from internal bleeding from the fall—

Stop. Figure this out.

She slowly unwrapped her arm from around her head, gradually straightening the joints, rotating her wrist, and flexing her fingers. Every bone, every muscle felt bruised, but nothing hurt so much she thought it was broken. Her left arm came next, and while it burned with the fires of hell where she'd been shot, she didn't think there were any new, serious injuries. Her legs came next, and then she slowly uncurled her spine, straightening as her head tipped back.

Her breath of relief was audible as it became clear there were no spinal injuries.

"I'm okay," she called. "Battered and bruised, but I don't think anything's broken. Let me get up and see where I am."

She pushed her right hand against the ground to push to a semi-seated position. When the world stayed steady, she turned onto her hands and knees before getting one foot, then the other, under her. She pushed off the forest floor with both hands and slowly straightened.

"There you are." Relief rode heavy in Todd's tone.

Meg's gaze tracked up to find Todd and Brian about twenty-five feet above her, with Hawk's head jammed between their knees. "I'm okay. Hawk, buddy, I'm okay. Stay with Todd and Brian. Stay." She raised a hand to the back of her neck and rotated her head, hearing bones crunching as they tried to find the proper alignment.

And Brian thought he'd need a chiropractic adjustment. He can get in line.

"You're really okay?" Brian asked.

"I don't think anything is broken."

"Did you hit your head?" Todd called down.

Of course that would be his first concern. One more concussion could be a real issue. "No, I managed to cushion my head with my arm. And I landed on a pile of greenery."

Meg straightened slowly and turned to look back at

what had broken her fall to find the crushed remains of ferns, small leafy tropical plants, and a thick carpet of moss over soil instead of rock.

It's porous, but it's rock. It will break you. More words from Byrne. She'd been beyond lucky. Had she fallen onto part of an exposed lava flow, she could be suffering from debilitating spinal injuries. Or she could have shattered her skull or broken her neck and been beyond saving.

But where was she? She turned to scan her surroundings.

She stood at the mouth of an inset curve of rock, something that looked like it had once been part of a cave, but had collapsed. Rain and weathering over the decades—or more likely, centuries—had filled this low-lying area with dirt. That was what had saved her life and broken her fall—inches or feet of soft dirt, wet with recent rains, covered with moss and mostly tender green plants.

She looked up to where now five human faces looked down at her. "I'm okay," she said before they could ask. "I landed at the base of some sort of cave. Low-lying area, it's full of moss and greenery. Broke my fall."

"Thank God," Hale said. "And if it's a cave, it may be some sort of remnant of a lava tube from an older eruption. There have been ten thousand years of lava flows on this upper surface of the island."

Meg looked back at the cave, noting the odd horizontal striations that ran along the rear wall, trying to imagine it being carved by two-thousand-degree lava.

If the carving of tubes like this was what was causing the tremors, they could be in real trouble.

Take a breath. No word from McCord.

Her satellite phone. She jammed her left hand into the side pocket of her yoga pants—nearly cursing in pain as her gunshot wound screamed in protest at the movement—

and pulled it out, relieved to see it was undamaged as she'd landed on her right side. Still nothing from McCord. She slid it back into her pocket.

"Do you need me to rope down to bring you up?" Todd called.

"Let me look around. If I can circle around to get back up to you, that will be easier and faster than you coming down to me." She parted what was left of the underbrush that had broken her fall, climbing up an incline that gained her about five feet. She smiled at the group overhead. "See? Up a few feet already."

Brian gave her a thumbs-up, but Todd didn't move, his eyes locked on her, looking for any sign she wasn't being truthful about how much she had to be hurting. And she was—she felt like she'd been hit by an eighteen-wheeler—but bumps and bruises would fade. Though she had no doubt she'd be colorful tomorrow.

As she moved slowly a little farther uphill, the terrain became rocky again, and she watched where she put her boots, not wanting to go down again. Staying parallel with the rise of rock that led to the rest of the group, she hiked forward about twenty feet, then studied the ground ahead before hiking back closer to the cave.

"I think if I keep going in this direction," she called, "I can angle my way up to you! Brian, pull out your GPS and let's test something. Can you send me your coordinates from the map app?"

"Yeah, hang on." Brian dug out his phone and started tapping.

While she waited, Meg looked up at her dog. "Hey, Hawk, buddy." His ears perked, and she smiled at him. "I need you to stay with Todd for now. Stay with Lacey and Brian. I'll see you soon." She knew he'd never understand all that, but he understood her tone, heard her love for him, and that would soothe him during the separation. He would understand she wasn't hurt, wasn't scared.

Her phone buzzed in her pocket, and she found a text from Brian with their coordinates. She copied them, entered them into her map app, and found herself looking at her own blue dot, located near a red pin. She copied her own coordinates and sent them to Brian. "This will work!" she called up. "Brian, enter the coordinates I just sent you in your app, and you'll see me in relative position to where you are."

Brian fiddled with his phone for about twenty seconds, then looked down at her. "Got you. How about we send coordinates to each other every few minutes? If either of us wanders, we'll see it on the map. The dogs are taking us roughly north-northeast, so we'll stay with the dogs, but watch for you as well."

"Sounds good. See you shortly."

"Lacey, come." Brian pulled away from the edge, as did all but Todd and Hawk.

Meg let her phone drop to her side as she looked up. "I'm really okay."

"I find that hard to believe, considering the height you fell from."

"You don't believe me?"

He cast his eyes skyward for a moment, shaking his head, before he looked down again. "I said I found it hard to believe, not that I didn't. I watched you move. It doesn't look like you broke anything."

"It's all about the landing. I won't lie and say nothing hurts. Just nothing terrible." She craned her neck to examine her left arm, found blood seeping into her sleeve over the bandage. "Okay, except my arm. It's on fire. And bleeding."

"It was healing. You likely tore it open between the sliding fall and the landing." Todd looked over his shoulder, back toward where the group must be waiting for him. "I'll see you soon. You send those coordinates every few minutes."

"I promise. Off you go. Hawk, stay with Todd."

Todd bent and said something to Hawk, then they both moved through the bushes and disappeared from sight.

Time to get moving, to get back to them as soon as possible. Todd wasn't going to rest easy until he could touch her and ensure she wasn't hiding an injury.

"Forward ho," she murmured, then started the parallel hike.

Down at this level, the landscape was nearly identical to up above. She pushed through underbrush and wound around trees, stopping every few minutes to send her coordinates to Brian and to track his. They still seemed about the same distance apart, but Meg thought she was gaining altitude, though she still couldn't see them, as the forest was too thick.

She sent off her coordinates again and jammed her phone into her pocket, waiting for Brian's return text. A particularly dense section lay ahead, and she contemplated forging a path farther to the east, but really didn't want to vary from her parallel path for fear she'd drift away. No, better to hold steady.

The scent of sulfur registered and she paused, searching the ground for a steam vent. That she couldn't find one didn't make her feel any better—if a large vent was pumping out that much vapor from the earth's crust that she could smell it from a distance, that could spell one of the worst dangers they'd ever faced.

Time to move faster.

She pushed both hands into the bushes, her palms facing outward, and parted some particularly thick ferns, sliding into their depths and then squeezing around a trio of tall trees growing close together. She stepped into an area where the underbrush thinned out a bit.

Her phone alerted with Brian's next text, and she moved to pull it from her pocket.

Then something cold and solid pressed against her right temple at the same moment a dark shape stepped into her peripheral vision.

"Don't move, or I'll blow your head off."

CHAPTER 19

Fracture: A break in rock in response to stress, often open wide enough to see inside.

June 1, 11:31 AM
Upper Waiākea Forest Reserve
Hilo, Hawai'i

Meg froze, hardly daring to breathe. She recognized the unforgiving pressure against her skull. The muzzle of a handgun.

"That's it." The man's words carried a quiet satisfaction, pressing the gun harder against her temple.

Her heart beat so loud, she was sure he'd be able to hear it. She struggled to keep her breathing slow and steady, not willing to give him the satisfaction of seeing her fear.

Thank God Todd and Hawk aren't here.

She drove their names from her head, not allowing herself to think past that. Despair lay in that direction. If she wanted to keep their anguish of loss at bay, she needed to keep her wits.

She slid her gaze sideways without moving her head, trying to see the man, but all she could see was the horrifying black bulk of the handgun and a flash of the hand holding it.

"Eyes forward," he snapped.

She stayed still, staring at the trunk of an 'ōhi'a tree straight ahead, trying to discern as much as she could from only his voice. "What do you want from me?" She was impressed at the flat control in her own tone.

"I want to know what you're doing here."

"Hiking."

"By yourself?"

Had he heard her fall? Heard Todd and Brian calling for her? They hadn't been quiet. Who knew how far sound would carry?

One wrong answer could mean instant death.

She'd try to feel him out. "Would it be a problem if I did? This is public land."

"Spend much time up here?"

Trick question? She hadn't had enough time to see the figure before the gun at her temple froze her in place. *Is this one of the two men from before?* Neither had talked, just shot at her and ran.

Meg knew very well that if he attempted to search her, between the holstered Glock and the FBI credentials she kept safely zipped into the concealment pocket in the waistband of her yoga pants at the small of her back, she'd be dead in seconds. There would be no more questions. Just... nothing.

Had the gun been damaged in the fall? She hadn't landed on it, but it, too, had experienced the rapid deceleration of the landing. Normally, she wouldn't use it until she'd had a chance to examine it. That wasn't going to be a possibility here. Though, in truth, the bigger issue wasn't her firearm, but his.

Skirt the truth. "I'm here for a few weeks to rest and recharge. For me, that means hiking. I've been in this area a few times this week."

"By yourself?"

This was giving her a bad feeling. He'd now asked about her being alone twice; he had to suspect something. She needed to be careful with her response. *Two voices could be confused for only one.* "I'm here with my husband." She looked down at her clothing, dirty and moss-stained. "I took a fall and am trying to connect with him again." She purposely let fear creep into her voice. "I don't understand. Am I trespassing? I thought this was a public nature reserve." She raised her hands as if in surrender.

"It is. But sometimes you're just in the wrong place at the wrong time."

His words sent a chill down her spine. Even if she was an innocent bystander, and even if he didn't recognize her from their encounter on Wednesday, he was threatening lethal force against a stranger for the crime of hiking through a forest.

And if he did recognize her? She'd be dead either way. She needed to act and act now before she did anything to reveal she was armed and skilled in hand-to-hand from her years with the Richmond Police Department. With a gun pressed against her head, she had no choice but to disarm him as her first step. She'd have a bullet in the brain before she could access her own firearm. She could only pray those above were clear in case any bullets flew.

She moved like lightning, pivoting, jerking her head back so her skull was no longer in the line of fire, while grabbing his wrist with her right hand at the exact moment she locked her left hand over the barrel of the gun to trap the weapon. She torqued his arm outward as she rolled the gun forward. Two uncontrolled shots rang out, booming through the peace of the forest. A cacophony of bird calls and a flurry of wings rose from the canopy.

They'll know I'm in trouble now.

"You bitch!" the man roared, his left fist slamming into her kidney before he tried to reach around her to catch and contain her wrist.

The force of his impact sent pain arcing through her torso, but she took advantage of her body's jolt to throw herself farther forward, using the full force of her weight as she twisted the gun back toward his wrist.

She heard his index finger snap a millisecond before he screamed and released the weapon.

But her own forward motion worked against her as she staggered against his body and the gun spun out of her hands. It soared about ten feet in a blur of black with a streak of blue, then struck a protrusion of lava rock and disappeared into a steam vent as it spewed a stream of vapor.

One gun down.

Her edge of surprise was now gone as the man realized what he was up against, and she knew she had to get free so she had enough space to pull her own gun. Still pressed against him, she snapped her right elbow up and caught him under the chin, hearing his teeth click together with a grunt of pain as his head was thrown backward. His hold loosened, and she spun away from him. One quick glance told her it was one of the men she'd spotted in the clearing who'd tried to kill her as she dove into the underbrush. Bad luck for her it was the blond man, because he was the bigger and heavier of the two and would be more of a challenge to take down.

She stepped several paces, yanking the zipper of her jacket down, her hand darting inside for her Glock.

The man gathered himself to charge, clearly prepared to take her down with his superior size and weight, when suddenly the ground bucked under their feet.

Meg staggered, her empty hand flying out of her jacket and both arms splaying wide as she desperately tried to keep her balance and keep herself upright. If she went down and he got on top of her, things could get ugly fast.

But her attacker was having the same problem and was trying to keep his balance even as he barreled toward her.

"Meg!" The sound of Todd's voice echoed through the trees, coming from the north.

The man's head snapped up, his eyes going wide as realization hit—he was unarmed and injured, so he was at a disadvantage in a fight and on his own with Meg's reinforcement incoming.

With a growl, even as the ground stilled and he found his balance, he struck out sideways, slamming his left fist brutally against her upper left arm, aiming for the bloody spot on her sleeve like it was a bull's-eye. The strike was clumsy, but his aim was dead-on and pain exploded. Staggering backward, her boot slipped on a mossy rock and she went down on one knee. She caught herself with her left hand while her right shot to her shoulder holster, flicked back the band of elastic keeping the Glock in place, and pulled it free.

In the intervening seconds, though, the man had sprinted eastward for the trees as fast as he could over the uneven terrain. Meg had time to pull off one shot—aiming for a nonlethal lower body target—but he ran a zig-zagging path and the bullet missed him. Then he was gone in the trees.

No point in following. She'd be essentially blind in the forest.

But her dog was not.

As if he'd heard her thinking about him, Hawk raced out of the trees as she climbed to her feet, nearly crashing into her as he skidded to a stop on the soft moss and then danced around her.

Meg holstered her Glock and bent to her dog, calming and praising him. "Good boy, you found me. Clever boy. Sit, Hawk. Sit. Good boy."

Todd, Brian, and Lacey burst from the trees next with Byrne and Hale right behind them and Kai and Makoa bringing up the rear. Every eye was fixed on her, looking for bloody gunshot wounds.

Meg straightened. "I'm okay!" she called, then huffed out a breath and grimaced as she laid her palm over her left kidney. "Mostly okay."

"I couldn't hold Hawk by voice command." Todd dropped into a walk only feet from her. "He knew you were in trouble, and there was no slowing him down. He wouldn't listen to Brian either."

"He could probably hear me struggling. You know what he's like when he gets defensive of me." She stroked Hawk's head. "My brave boy."

"What happened?" Todd pulled her hand away, gently letting her arm drop, and discreetly pulled up one edge of her top to examine her side. "We heard shots."

"I walked out of a dense patch of bushes, and suddenly there was a gun pressed to my temple."

Hale's eyes were scanning the forest, watching for any sign of danger. "Where's the shooter?"

"He rabbited when he heard you guys coming. I'd already stripped him of his gun—which is over there. See that steam vent?" Meg pointed to the vent about fifteen feet away. "It's inside."

"Let me look," Brian said to Hale and Byrne. "Keep the area covered in case he comes back."

"Be careful. Don't get burned. It's pumping out a lot of steam," Meg said. "It's unlikely he's coming back. He heard you calling me. Not to mention I took his gun, and broke his trigger finger in the process. I heard it snap."

"Normally I wouldn't condone violence, but good for you." Todd ran gentle fingers over her side and back. "He hit you here? There's the beginning of a contusion."

"Punched me, but good. Granted, I was forcing the gun out of his hand and breaking his index finger at the time, so things were getting a bit rough." Meg met Brian's eyes as he returned with the missing handgun, a stick poked through the trigger guard so he wasn't touching it. "He didn't expect me to have any hand-to-hand skills, so I caught him off guard for a fraction of a second."

"That's my girl," Brian said, extending the pistol so they could all see its compact design with a black body and bright blue pistol grip inserts. "It's a CZ Shadow 2. I fished it out of the vent with a stick so I didn't get burned by the steam. Which stinks to high heaven, by the way. The only thing I touched was the safety, but I did it with my sleeve over my hand to avoid getting burned by hot metal. And I wasn't sure if he was wearing gloves or not."

"He wasn't, so good thinking. There might be prints."

As Hale slid his pack off his shoulders and pulled out an evidence bag and a pair of gloves to disarm and pack the gun, Todd let Meg's shirt drop and turned his attention to her arm. "Is this from the fall?"

"Partly. Then the guy spotted it as an injury and used it to knock me back a step when he slammed his left fist into it." A smile ghosted over her lips. "Couldn't use his right hand with that broken finger." The smile faded. "But I was obviously injured there, and he took advantage to get away. The quake helped, too, as it put me off-balance just as I was reaching for my weapon." Her gaze drifted to the forest where he'd disappeared. "By the time I could pull it and tried to hit him as he escaped—seeing as he was guilty of assault and is clearly a danger—I missed." She turned to Hale and Byrne. "He was one of the guys we interrupted on Wednesday. One of the traffickers."

Hale cursed. "Any chance he thinks you're just a hiker?"

"I think that got blown away when I disarmed him and then tried to stop him from escaping."

"Show, not tell," said Byrne. "You didn't have to announce yourself when your actions clearly stated your status. Do you think he stopped you because he recognized you?"

"If I were him and saw the same person twice while I was in the middle of committing a felony, I'd be suspicious of them too. If I hadn't fallen, he might never have realized we were here, but I wasn't quiet as I fell."

"Not to mention that we were then yelling for you," Todd said.

"That too. I think he came to investigate and saw I was on the move and tracked me, found a place to get the jump, and took it. Bottom line, they know we're here, and it would be reasonable at this point for them to suspect I'm law enforcement and have backup."

"They're going to want to clear out of here."

"And try somewhere else or call the whole thing?"

"I'm not sure."

"They may consider calling it," Brian said. "How many quakes have we felt today?"

"Four," Meg said. "And that's not counting anything that hit before we came into the region or ones too small to feel."

"That last one was a good shake."

"Don't I know it." Her gaze found the spot in the bushes where the man had disappeared. "We have a solid trail for the dogs. He thinks he's out of sight, out of mind, but he's left essentially a visible trail as far as the dogs are concerned. We need to follow it."

"Are you up to it?" Brian asked. "You had a twenty-five-foot fall, and then had to fight for your life. You have to be pretty battered at this point."

"Last trip, it was your turn to be battered; this trip, it's my turn."

"Next time, let's stay home."

"Deal." Meg looked down at Hawk. "He's ready. I'm ready. Let's go." She grasped Todd's forearm, gave it a squeeze. "If I'm not able to manage the search, I'll let you know. Brian and Lacey could handle it solo, but I'd rather not leave it all up to them."

She could see the reticence in his eyes, but he didn't voice it. Just gave her a single nod and stepped back.

"I'm ready when you are," Brian stated.

"Let's do it."

"Lead us to the spot, and let's get them going."

The dogs found the scent trail immediately and started after it in unison. Meg and Brian held the dogs to a moderate pace. Meg had stepped into the wrong situation only moments before; they didn't want it to happen a second time because the dogs were moving too quickly. Everyone holstered their firearm—too big a risk of a slip and fall over the rocky terrain, which could lead to an unintentional firing and someone being injured—but everyone kept their weapon close at hand. They kept the search as silent as possible, not wanting to give away their pursuit in any way.

They'd been on the move for about fifteen minutes when Meg's satellite phone vibrated in her pocket. As she reached for her phone, she noted Brian mimicking her action. Alarm prickled up the back of her neck. Only one person would contact them both at the same time—McCord.

She pulled out her phone to see her intuition was correct—McCord had texted their group chat.

Important! Need to talk to you now!

"Lacey, stop." Brian kept his voice to a whisper.

"Hawk, stop." Meg echoed Brian's tone, then sent a return text to McCord as Brian showed his phone to Byrne and Hale and she shared hers with Todd and Kai. **What's wrong? On trail of suspect. Can't take a call.**

Volcano advisory is now a warning. No eruption yet but HVO *very* concerned. Lava levels in Mauna Loa caldera are dropping.

McCord's words from the night before echoed in her head: *Just before the eruption, the level of liquid lava in the caldera dropped because it was moving along the rift into the eruption area.* Meg's head snapped up, and from the look in Brian's eyes, he was thinking the same thing. She sent a return text: **Got jumped by one of the traffickers. Going after him. Likely our only chance to catch them before they run. Let us know the moment things get worse.**

Will do.

She looked up to meet Brian's gaze. She fixed him with a raised-eyebrow look and pointed farther down the path. *Keep going?*

Brian's single determined nod echoed her own opinion of the search—keep going while they could, as it would likely be their last chance to catch these men. Without them, the entire organization might slip through their fingers.

With the dogs looking to them for instruction, both handlers used hand signals to get the dogs back on the trail, and the group fell into step behind them.

Meg glanced over at Kai, who still kept Makoa on lead, but he shook his head—no indication of scent currently.

The forest started to thin out around them, the sky opening above, the ground more uneven and rocky, with fewer low-lying areas of soil and the resulting underbrush, and more exposed areas of porous lava rock. But the dogs stayed on course, winding through the widely spaced trees.

Meg looked west along the long stretch of sparse flora, so different from the previous thicker forest.

Hale caught her questioning look. "Older lava flow," he said quietly. "Plant life is coming back now, but it usually takes eighty or one hundred years for the forest to start to reestablish itself. Give it another two or three hundred years and you'll never know a lava flow lies underneath."

They hiked back into a thicker stand of trees, the dogs still focused on the trail. They'd traveled over a half mile when Meg noticed the forest seemed backlit about one hundred feet ahead. "Is that a clearing ahead?" she asked Brian in a low tone.

Brian scanned the distance. "Not a man-made clearing, if that's what you're thinking. Way too big. Maybe a natural break in the trees?"

But as they came closer, it became evident this wasn't just a break in the trees. It was a massive interruption.

They'd hit a recent lava flow, so new—in geologic terms—that nothing but the odd tuft of wild pili grass had been able to take root there due to the lack of basalt breakdown to produce Hawaii's infamously fertile soil.

But the trail led right to it, so that was their direction.

They were about fifty feet from the flow when Meg and Brian received simultaneous texts again. They paused to pull out their phones to see McCord's message.

After you said suspects were on to you, I checked the flight schedules of all three planes. Aviatronics Customs Brokerage plane just posted a flight log for a 4:30 pm departure to Montgomery-Gibbs Executive Airport, a small air-

strip outside of San Diego. Likely to refuel. Where they go from there . . . ?
Other two planes? Brian texted.
No flight plans logged.

The plan coalesced in Meg's mind in a rush of details. They'd been distracted by the shell company because they were so often used to hide criminal dealings or at least were used as a tax haven to increase the haul for company investors. But what better way to move illegal items through the border than by a group making customs brokerage their business? Transport enough airplane parts on a regular basis, and no one notices a few extra boxes moving through the chain. They'd have agreements with transportation companies as well as common dealings with different countries' customs bureaus worldwide. They could easily hide animal parts in among genuine aviation shipments and would likely know how to move the odd box with air holes in it to avoid detection. Or who to pay off to look in the other direction.

Meg waved Byrne and Hale over to read McCord's messages. Hale's expression darkened, and he pulled out his own phone and sent a text to someone in his chain.

Starting the investigation, as well as dispatching someone to Waimea-Kohala in case we can't get there in time.

Meg sent back her reply: **Excellent work! Have to keep moving. Keep us in the loop if you learn anything more.**

Stay safe. Run for high ground if things start moving.

God help them if they actually needed that advice . . .

"Makoa has something."

Meg turned at Kai's quiet words. The Australian shepherd stood stock-still except for his nose, which was furiously scenting the air in his head-up stance. "Coming from the edge of the forest?"

"From beyond it would be my guess."

"And Hawk and Lacey are still indicating this way. I bet those scent trails will collide."

Everyone tucked their phones away, and they continued toward the edge of the forest.

"Lacey, slow." Brian slowed his own steps as they approached the tree line. "We need to stay inside the forest until we know what's going on."

"Agreed. Hawk, stop. Stay." Meg peered between the trees. Beyond, the landscape was one of uneven devastation and what looked like miles of black lava flow in both directions. She stepped forward, staying mostly behind a tree as she stared out at the barren landscape. "Is that . . . ?"

Todd stepped behind her, his superior height giving him a slightly better angle on the uneven terrain. "Someone moving out there? I think so."

Meg, Brian, and Byrne all scrambled to pull out their binoculars.

"I see him," Byrne said, speaking at a normal level. "He's headed straight across the lava flow. He has to be about three hundred yards out. Too far out to hear us." She handed her binoculars to Hale so he could see.

"Why is he heading out there?" Kai asked. "He has to think he's been identified in some way or his activity has been. I expected him to circle around to where they could be picked up, especially considering those flight plans."

"Maybe he needs to meet with his colleague," Brian suggested.

"Or they have one more prize in mind," Hale said.

Meg turned around to find Hale standing a little closer to the tree line, perched on a fallen log to give him a better view. "What do you see?"

"The other guy. He's right at the tree line of the kīpuka on the far side. That's an upland area in the middle of a lava flow that wasn't overrun and remains green. An oasis in a desert of rock." He dropped his glasses and turned to Byrne. "If they're going to go after an 'Io, they're not going to do that deep in the forest, are they?"

"They could, but depending on the growth environment on the kīpuka, it might be too dense." Byrne stared out over the lava flow. "It might be easier to bait a trap on the outskirts."

"Would they bring the trap already baited or use birds they found here?" Brian tested the stability of a higher rock and stepped up, trying to see better.

"Time is of the essence, so I bet they'd have already caught something common. Rock pigeons were introduced to the islands, so they sometimes use them, or they could use native birds like a zebra dove. The trap will have two compartments—one filled with the bait and a second with a pressure mechanism that swings shut and traps the raptor when it tries to swoop down to make the kill. Depending on the type of trap, that upper compartment can then be removed for transport with the captured raptor inside. Can I get the binoculars back?"

Hale stepped down and offered her the binoculars. "Take a look."

Byrne stepped up on the fallen tree, taking a moment to get her balance, and then raised her binoculars. She adjusted the zoom and then the focus. "That's a goshawk trap. That's what I was describing. And their positioning makes sense. The jury is out whether hawks sense prey by smell, but it's well established that they use sight and hearing."

"Leave a trap like that deep in the forest, and it could take a very long time to be found by the target bird," Todd said.

"Too long," Meg agreed. "These guys are on a timeline. And if we think they were likely out yesterday in a different area than we were, and that they were successful with small birds—"

"Not to mention we don't know if they'd been successful in the days leading up to you running into them," Brian interjected.

"Then this might be their last goal." Meg pulled out her phone and opened her map app.

"From what McCord says, it's definitely their last goal now," said Hale. "And if Kai is correct that this is a valuable bird not only for its endangered status, but because of its spiritual status, something the other birds are lacking, that would explain why he didn't try to immediately escape via the road. This is one last chance for them to fill their order."

"Good luck to them," Kai said. "If they're not experienced with large birds, especially with raptors, this could be a rude awakening for them. They could get torn apart."

"They can't kill the bird or they've lost their expensive payoff," said Brian. He turned around and looked out across the lava flow. "What's our next move? The dogs have shown us where they are, but if we follow the direct trail, we'll announce ourselves and be sitting ducks. At the same time, we can't take this to committee without possibly losing them or getting caught in an imminent eruption."

Meg zeroed in on her satellite map, finding their exact position. They were just south of a ragged flow of lava labeled "1984 Waiākea Lava Flow Forest Reserve" and directly opposite a ragged streak of green completely surrounded by more arms of the flow.

"What's that?" Todd's voice came from her left as he leaned in close to look over her shoulder.

"This is where we are." She zoomed in so he could see

both the lava flow and the kīpuka in detail. "They're here." She held a long tap on the screen and a red pin appeared in what looked like a small bay in the lava flow.

"We need to go west and cross the lava flow here." Todd indicated a section just to the west of them where the lava flow was at its narrowest. "If we try to go farther in either direction to remain out of sight, we might lose them entirely because it will take too long to circle around. If we cross here, stay low, and move fast, that's likely only . . ." He looked through the trees to the area he indicated. "Maybe three hundred yards? Three-fifty?"

"I agree. I don't think any other way is feasible. Guys." She raised her voice slightly. "Take a look at this." Once everyone gathered around, Meg showed them the satellite view and Todd's suggested route.

"That makes sense to me." Byrne said.

Hale nodded in the affirmative. "And if they run before we get there, Hawk and Lacey will track them."

"I have a suggestion," Kai said. "This is about to become a law enforcement action. Makoa isn't a trained law enforcement K-9, and that's not my wheelhouse either. We wouldn't be any kind of addition to the team at this point if we go with you. But if we stay here with one of the pairs of binoculars, I can keep an eye on them and advise you if they've changed position. Or if they outright leave, I can give you a heads-up to move faster and can give details about how they escaped to assist the team."

"I think that's a good idea," Hale said. "And while I disagree that you wouldn't be an asset to the team, I agree you'd do more for us this way."

Brian offered his binoculars. "Take mine. Meg has hers, and we'll share if needed."

"I have your contact numbers. I'll text the moment anything changes. *Pōmaikaʻi*. Stay safe."

"*Mahalo*," said Hale. He turned to the rest of the team. "Is everyone ready?" After affirmative answers all around, he turned to look out over the barren landscape to the lush green life—and the contribution to the potential extinction of a species—that lay a quarter of a mile away. "Time to end this once and for all. Let these guys be the first dominos in the organization to fall."

CHAPTER 20

Volcanic Bomb: A viscous, partially molten lava fragment, 2.5 inches in diameter or greater, ejected during a volcanic eruption.

June 1, 12:53 PM
Upper Waiākea Forest Reserve
Hilo, Hawai'i

They only paused at the edge of the lava flow long enough to confirm their order and the plan, as well as to let Brian and Meg quickly outfit their dogs. One close look at the rough rock told them their dogs' feet would be sliced to ribbons by the time they made it across the lava flow, so they'd pulled out the boots they always carried in their go bags—nylon uppers with sturdy rubber soles that Velcroed snugly around the dogs' pasterns on each leg. The dogs stood patiently as their boots were put on, took a few steps to settle into them, and then were ready to go.

As a group, they stepped out onto the lava rock, the humans bending into a half crouch, and started across at a light jog.

The terrain made the crossing extremely difficult, especially as they were trying to stay out of sight of the curve of the kīpuka, or else they risked the men bolting and likely splitting up, increasing the chances of one or both of them getting away. The tumbled landscape was their main challenge, the rubbly 'a'ā lava rock often loose at the surface of the flow and ready to roll at the slightest pressure, risking taking an ankle with it. Some of the smaller rocks simply collapsed under significant weight. Meg had already slipped once and caught herself with one hand—it had been like bracing herself on pieces of broken glass that shattered under pressure, driving tiny shards into her skin.

She'd picked herself up and kept going, not giving anyone time to question how she was. But it had taken a full minute for her to brush the tiny pieces of basalt out of the heel of her hand.

She was glad no one asked her status because it was a question she didn't want to answer. Or more to the point, she didn't want to lie because she was beginning to struggle. Normally, this would be a challenging but entirely manageable hike, as it seemed to be for everyone else. But the rest of the group hadn't fallen twenty-five feet and suffered a rough landing, then followed that with a life-and-death struggle with a suspect whom she knew would have killed her without a second thought and then walked away, leaving her corpse for her husband, best friend, and colleagues to find. And her dog . . . She didn't want to think about how Hawk would have reacted, how he'd have had to live with her loss for the rest of his life.

Having a heart dog carried the reverse rules as having children. As a parent, the unwritten rule was that you should pass before your children and no parent should ever have to bury their child. As far as Meg was concerned, the rule when you had a heart dog—and she'd been lucky enough to have two—was that you should never die first so they had to live with your loss. Hawk might be a fraction of Meg's life, but she was all of his. As it should be. Thank God she'd survived the day.

So far.

Right now, it was with considerable pain. Running in an awkward position along the viciously uneven lava field meant each step jolted pain through every bone, every muscle. But that just made her push harder. She could rest in the SUV on the way back to Waikōloa. She could rest on the lanai when they got back to the resort. She could rest on the plane back home.

For now, there was no rest. But it was something to look forward to.

They were three-quarters of the way across when the tremor hit.

Meg nearly went down but managed to find a stable place to stop, her legs bowed, knees bent, arms extended as if she were standing on a surfboard, eyes fixed on Hawk as he scrambled for a moment then found his footing without falling. From behind came a grunt she was sure was from Hale, and in front of her, Brian went down on one knee with a sharp "Son of a . . ." A quick glance back showed Todd on his feet successfully riding the tremor upright, as did Byrne behind him.

The earth stilled again. Meg cast a cautious look around the lava field and back in the direction of the obscured peak of Mauna Loa. But there were no signs of impending doom, certainly no pyroclastic cloud as McCord had warned. Maybe they still had time.

She looked forward—only about one hundred fifty feet to go, and they'd be back on more forgiving ground.

They made it to the kīpuka, and both Byrne and Hale checked their satellite phones, but there was no word from Kai—the men must still be trying to catch their hawk.

They moved along the edge of the high ground, where the grass grew thick at the border, the trees and their deeper roots staying inland by a few feet. As they had previously agreed, Brian went first with Lacey beside him, so worst-case scenario, if they burst into view, it would look like nothing more than a man and his dog taking a walk. What they wouldn't immediately see was the unholstered Glock in Brian's hand, pointed at the ground, his finger resting along the trigger guard, but ready to snap into shooting stance at any moment.

Byrne and Hale followed Brian, with Todd and Meg bringing up the rear—Todd because he was the only one unarmed, and Meg because she was not only recognizable, but injured, even though she tried to downplay it. Everyone knew there was no way to fall that distance without the landing causing at least minor injury, and she'd been overruled when she'd protested.

Meg's attention was drawn upward as a high-pitched, descending, keening cry pierced the air.

Keeer... Keeer...

A large bird with a dark brown body and shoulders, with white flight feathers crossed by dark bars, soared overhead.

Byrne turned around and pointed.

An 'Io was circling. They needed to interrupt this before the traffickers managed to catch it and possibly hurt it.

Brian was clearly on the same page, because he broke into a run, Lacey picking up the pace to match his stride, with everyone else joining them.

Above, the 'Io gave another cry and suddenly dived. Meg had a flash of a short, curved beak and razor-sharp talons stretched out along fanned tailfeathers, and then the bird disappeared below the canopy. A second later, a shout echoed, the sound a combination of surprise and fury, and then the bird soared skyward again.

The bird was attacking?

The situation became clear when the cry of another bird sounded, but this time from ground level. Byrne turned around and mouthed, *Mated pair*, then kept going.

That bird was going to work in their favor. If Byrne was correct and the men had already trapped an 'Io with its mate dive-bombing them, then the men were going to be distracted.

They came to the edge of the curve of the kīpuka and pulled farther into the forest to stay hidden. Peering out through the underbrush, Meg could see two men about forty feet ahead at the edge of the kīpuka with a trap made of wood and chicken wire. Several beige birds called frantically from the bottom half of the cage, while an 'Io was trapped in the upper, triangular portion of the cage.

The 'Io circling overhead dove again, coming in at a breathtaking speed, banking at the last second, but coming close enough to rake a talon over the face of the dark-haired man. Blood welled across his forehead from a slash that disappeared into his hairline, and he screamed in pain. Then he pulled out a matte black handgun and shot three times in the bird's direction. Meg wasn't surprised when the bird simply soared away; rage-shooting like that without actually aiming did nothing more than waste bullets.

The blond man—the one she'd fought—grabbed the other man's hand, jerking it down. "What are you doing? Trying to get us caught? They're already here. Why don't you just fucking send up a flare? Put that away. Let's get this goddamned bird and get out of here."

Trouble in paradise.

It was time to finish this now. They were starting to panic, were distracted by a bird who could do them significant harm, and the clock was ticking.

Time to move.

Hale clearly thought that, too, because he had a quick whispered discussion with Byrne, and then he indicated to Brian to follow him. The two men and Lacey melted into the forest.

"Come this way," Byrne whispered to Meg and Todd. "We're going to get a little closer and wait for the signal. Then step out, gun raised, and announce your designation," she said to Meg.

They moved closer to the edge of the forest, Byrne selecting an area where they were hidden but could easily step through and would end up about twenty-five feet from the men and the trap.

"I need you to stay here with Hawk," Meg whispered to Todd, pulling back about five feet to stay more hidden and pulling the leash from her pocket. She snapped it onto Hawk's collar and handed it to Todd, ensuring that Hawk wouldn't get away from him again. "I don't want either of you in the line of fire. If shots are fired, get down."

Todd nodded, but grabbed her hand, squeezing tight. "Be careful."

She returned the pressure of his grip. "Promise." Then she stepped away, moving closer to Byrne.

They waited about three minutes, listening to the men argue as they tried to figure out how to disengage the two sections of the trap so they could transport the 'Io out of the forest reserve. They were dive-bombed again by the 'Io, who missed both men this time. From inside the crate, the trapped 'Io called to its mate.

Byrne didn't take her eyes off a section of forest near to where the men stood. "He's there," she murmured to Meg. "I'll cover the one with dark hair. You take the blond. Here we go."

Hale emerged from the forest. "FBI! Hands in the air!"

Brian appeared to his left, shouting his own designation.

Byrne stepped out of the trees. "US Fish and Wildlife! Freeze!"

Meg followed, her Glock extended in two hands, her

sights on the blond man who'd threatened her. "FBI! Hands where we can see them!"

"We have you covered!" Byrne called to Hale and Brian.

Not wanting to risk tripping on the uneven terrain, Meg and Byrne stayed locked on their targets as Hale and Brian approached, ordering the men to their knees, their hands on the back of their heads. Brian covered Hale, and he dragged first one man's hands behind his back to cuff him, then the other, once having to duck as the 'Io swooped low again. The dark-haired man, blood dripping over his temple and down his left cheek, swore viciously at the bird as Hale patted him down, quickly finding his handgun in a holster on his belt. Hale removed the clip and the bullet in the chamber and bagged it as evidence.

"They're contained," Hale yelled. "Can we get this hawk freed so its mate leaves us alone?"

"Coming!" Byrne called, holstering her weapon and hurrying down the grassy edge.

"Todd, all clear!" Meg called into the forest, and a minute later, Todd and Hawk appeared and followed her toward the trap and the kneeling men.

Byrne was already busy, first snapping several photos of the trap from different angles with her cell phone, then freeing the bait birds from the bottom of the trap. Chattering, they flapped away, winging their way over the lava field and into the safety of the thick forest on the far side. From above, the circling 'Io screamed, drawing her gaze. "Patience! I'm working on it!" she called back. But she continued to struggle with the latch on the upper cage as the bird inside screeched and flapped its wings. She looked up and spotted the only person on the team who didn't have their hands full guarding the traffickers. "Todd, can you give me a hand?"

Todd handed Hawk's leash to Meg and jogged over. Upon quick inspection of the workings of the spring-loaded aspects of the pressure trigger, he unlatched it. "Pull back a bit," he advised, still holding the gates shut. "You don't want to get close to it as it takes off." Byrne took a few steps back, and then Todd released his hold on the gates, instantly dropping into a crouch.

With a scream, the 'Io launched itself skyward with powerful strokes of its wings. An answering call came from its mate, who swooped down to meet it, then they soared away to the north, instantly lost behind the kīpuka's tree canopy.

Byrne's smile was wide as she turned to the two men on their knees as Hale finished reading them their Miranda rights. "That's better. So, who do we have here?"

Hale reached in the back pocket of one, then the other, pulling out two wallets. He opened the first and gestured to the blond man. "This is Jude Griggs. Maryland driver's license."

"Funny," said Brian. "I could swear we were just discussing a Maryland corporation."

"Imagine that." Hale looked at Meg. "Want to send this info to McCord? I don't know where he is in his investigation, but this could be the beginning of the thread to pull to unwind it all."

"For sure." Meg unleashed Hawk, coiling and jamming the leash into her jacket pocket as she crossed to Hale, Hawk at her side. She drew her phone out of her pocket and snapped a picture of the driver's license.

Hale pulled out an evidence bag and dropped the wallet into it, then flipped open the second and held it out to Meg to photograph. "And this is Miles Hinton. Pennsylvania driver's license this time." The second wallet joined the first. Hale tucked them into his backpack and slung the bag onto his shoulders before pulling out his phone. "Cover them for a minute. I'm going to call in local support from the Hawai'i Police Department for a pickup. We need to arrange the closest point." He stepped back from the group, already placing his call.

"FBI, huh?"

At Griggs's words, Meg looked over at him as she finished texting the photos to McCord. "Yes."

"How did you find us?"

"We figured out your goal and where you'd go to fill your 'order.' Oh, wait, do you mean the first time?" She couldn't keep the triumph out of her smile as she dropped her hand down to rest on Hawk's head. "That was just plain bad luck. We were hiking and my K-9 scented you. I went to investigate and stumbled right into you."

"Fuck . . . you're K-9? We were brought down by a dog?"

"Two dogs, actually." Brian stepped up beside Meg, Lacey at his knee. "Never count out the dogs."

Griggs's gaze dropped to the blood on her left sleeve. "Hinton shot you."

"That was my bad luck. Well, actually, more of yours, now that I think of it." She fixed her gaze on Hinton. "Assault with a deadly weapon. Carrying a concealed firearm without a license. Illegal discharge of a firearm." She looked back at Griggs. "Aggravated assault with a firearm. And that's before the trafficking charges land."

Hale returned. "The Hawai'i Police Department is sending cars to meet us. There's a double track service road that comes in from Saddle Road and goes all the way through to Stainback Highway. Goes right over the lava flow, with a place to turn around. I have the GPS coordinates where they want to meet us, and I sent them to Kai. He and Makoa will meet us there too. It's a little over two miles from here, due east, and down about eight hundred feet." He wrapped an arm around Hinton's upper arm and hauled him to his feet, then Griggs, who groaned as his broken finger was jostled. "Due east means into the forest. You guys go first. Take it slow. You don't have hands for balance, and if you trip, you're going down face-first. We're not in a rush. But if you make a break for it, the dogs found you once—they'll find you again."

They moved into the forest, which thickened the farther in they went. Griggs led the way, followed by Hinton, and then Hale and Byrne, Meg, Todd, and Hawk, and then Brian and Lacey bringing up the rear.

Relief flowed warm through Meg. They'd found the beginning of the threads of this organization, from the transportation, to the company that owned it, to the frontline thugs. She knew McCord, knew he'd be tugging on that thread to unravel it and simultaneously follow it back to the beginning.

This was the first step in taking them down.

At her side, Hawk slowed, then stopped. Looking down at him, she froze as she took in his stance—legs splayed, head cocked and ears high, hackles raised. He looked up at her and whined, low and uncertain.

More distressed than before. What does he sense?

The earth shuddered, sending Meg stumbling. Then came a rumble, a grinding sound from deep in the earth, one that sent fear streaking through her like barbs of ice.

She couldn't identify the direction of the sound—it seemed to surround them—but Hawk could, his eyes glued to an area farther inside the trees as he backed away from it. A look at Lacey showed her scurrying backward as well, already in full retreat from something she couldn't comprehend.

Something to be truly feared.

"We need to move!" Meg yelled. "Talon, come!"

To her relief, he turned and ran with her farther into the forest as the rumble turned into a roar. Todd fell into step on Hawk's other side, and the rest of the group followed them, even Griggs and Hinton.

Could they move fast enough, get enough distance from what was coming?

Suddenly there was an explosion of sound, of earth rending and trees toppling as an ejection of steam, hot gases, rocks, and dirt shot into the sky, followed by an illuminated fountain of lava. A wave of pungent gas rolled over them with the stench of rotten eggs edged with the scent of fireworks.

Even in full retreat, the wave of heat that hit them was brutal, nearly knocking Meg off her feet. She took the time to glance back over her shoulder, only to wish she hadn't.

Lava fountained at least twenty feet in the air, hurling globs of deadly molten rock, burning everything it touched.

A monster come to kill them all.

CHAPTER 21

Pele's Tears: Tear-shaped droplets of lava thrown during an eruption.

June 1, 1:39 PM
Upper Waiākea Forest Reserve
Hilo, Hawai'i

Bits of superheated materials thrown by the eruption pelted them, crashing through the canopy above like deadly rain. Lacey yelped, and Meg heard Todd's startled curse, accompanied by a flick of his left hand as if stung by a bee, but he didn't miss a stride.

"If you can," Hale called from behind them, "keep pushing east! That will be the shortest distance across the existing lava field once we leave the forest."

The existing lava field.

Because Pele was apparently waking Mauna Loa from a thirty-five-year slumber to create fresh lava fields. But even the old lava field was a hazard to their escape. If they left the forest to hike the old lava field, it would be hard going. It would be potentially impossible for the two handcuffed men who, with their hands secured behind their backs, wouldn't be able to properly balance or catch themselves if they went down. That could lead to severe injury or death, depending on how they fell on the jagged rocks.

Worse, if a new fissure formed in the existing flow, a timely escape might be impossible for some or all of them.

Meg had just gathered herself to jump over a toppled fern tree—still green, so likely freshly fallen with the seismic activity—when another earthquake shook the kīpuka. She was already coiled to spring, but the tremor tilted her upper body off-balance, so she successfully pushed off but didn't clear the tree, catching one booted foot and going down face-first, just getting her hands down in time to catch her head from hitting the ground.

The rumble filling her ears washed a wave of terror over her.

Again?

With a roar, spitting heat and light like a dragon's flame, another fountain of lava exploded from the earth about fifty feet away.

Hands grabbed her arms, yanking her up—Todd on one side, Brian on the other—with less of a mind to care and more to purpose, which made her left arm sing with pain. They helped steady her as she got her feet under her in a run, forcing their way through the underbrush. A quick glance to her left showed her both Hawk and Lacey winding through bushes and tree trunks, keeping pace with them.

More heat, more putrid gases, and this time, ash rained down on them. Meg's throat and lungs burned from the overheated air and the acidic vaporized gases as she pushed through the forest.

They escaped the second eruption, entering a quieter area of the forest, where the air was cleaner and clearer, but they were conscious of the fact they were running downhill and the lava would surely follow them.

Her lungs burning, Meg slowed. "Can we take a minute?" She stopped, braced her hands on her knees as a spasm of coughing tore through her. "Is it safe?" She closed her eyes and let her head hang. Everything ached, pain pulsing through her muscles like she'd been put through a blender. She just needed a moment to regroup, to push through the pain, to get her breath back, then she'd be stronger.

Everyone gathered around, though Byrne and Hale stayed back a few paces with Griggs and Hinton.

"We can't take long," Hale said. "This whole area of the rift zone could crack under the pressure. I've never been close to a fissure when it blew, and I know some lava moves faster than others, but we don't know the flow rate. We have to assume the worst."

"We get trapped by it, we're done." Byrne was breathing hard and her voice sounded raspy, as if her larynx was scorched by the acidic gases.

"What's our safest option?" Brian asked. "Stick to the forest or head for the old lava flow? Could that be a harder crust for it to cut through?"

"This whole area, the whole island, really, is layered lava flows. Forested areas might be very slightly less stable just because of the root structure of the larger trees, but not enough to count when you're talking about molten magma."

"Escape will be too hard on the flow." Meg straightened and tried to pull in a deeper breath from an upright position. "If speed is what counts, we won't have it out there. Not without an already established path. We need to stay on the kīpuka."

"Our bigger issue is that rift faults tend to run in a roughly straight line," Hale said. "If more fissures form, from the two we've seen, it's going to be laterally along the kīpuka."

"Hopefully it's going to be behind us," Todd stated. "But if that's what we're looking at, we need to move before any more fissures form." He laid a hand against Meg's back. "You going to make it?"

"Definitely." She took a deep breath and straightened her shoulders. "Let's get out of here."

They delved into deeper forest; even the canopy overhead seemed tighter, plummeting the light levels in the forest below. They kept pushing, forcing their bodies through the dense tangle of heavily leafed bushes and ferns, around tree trunks, and through dead leaves.

The grunt and thump of someone falling made them stop to turn. Hale was hauling Griggs up by one arm, dragging his handcuffed hands to one side as Griggs swore at him. Hale's lips pressed into a tight line, but he bit back a response, simply ordering Griggs forward.

A slight tremor had them freezing in place, eyes scanning the surrounding landscape as the breeze fluttered the canopy above.

Silence . . . Not even the birds sang. If they were smart, they'd escaped the rift zone until things cooled down. Literally.

But no new fissure. *Aftershock? Or the harbinger of the next one?* Impossible to tell.

When they hit a slightly clearer, more level area, Meg pulled out her phone to check her map app to gauge their progress. And found a flurry of texts from McCord that she'd missed while they'd been on the run. She quickly scanned down the chat—messages of the HVO changing the volcano alert from watch to warning, the highest level. Then an update about an active eruption in their area. Finally two messages pleading for them to check in.

She activated voice-to-text and spoke into her phone without losing a step. **Sorry, busy outrunning active fissures. Two in our area so far. Caught traffickers. Hawaii PD meeting for support. We're all okay. Will contact when can.**

McCord's response came quickly. **Be careful. Be safe. Will wait to hear from you.**

She flipped over to her map app to find they were well past halfway to the end of the kīpuka and were down about five hundred feet.

She put her phone away and powered through the pain and exhaustion.

They trudged on, trying to keep going as quickly as they could, dogged by fatigue, and handicapped by an injured teammate and two suspects who had no hands for balance or to clear their own path.

When the rumble came, followed by a roar, they were ready. The shock factor had faded, so when the ground shook, no one lost their footing. This time, however, the fissure that opened was only visible in the distance in front of them as a dancing red-hot glow.

"That's going to be a problem," Brian stated. "That's between us and the end of the kīpuka. Think we'll be able to get around it?"

It was a surreal situation: There they were, in the middle of a volcanic eruption, contemplating skirting around a two-thousand-degree lava flow so they could stay on forest land instead of being driven out into a nearly impassible field of lava rock.

"We'd have to get closer," Todd reasoned, "but possibly? If not, we're going to be forced out onto the existing flow, at least until we can clear the new flow."

Byrne wiped sweat from the back of her neck. "Which we might be able to do, depending on the speed of the fresh lava, which will be affected by the downward slope at that location."

"Let's check it out, then," said Hale. "Hopefully with three fissures open, the pressure is being relieved and that will be it for now. But that could mean the pressure will still be relatively high, so the flow rate will be fast. Be ready for anything."

They continued hiking down Mauna Loa's flank.

"What is . . . ?" Beside Meg, Todd's words trailed off and he stopped dead. "Everyone, hang on."

The group turned to look at him, but his gaze was fixed to the east, toward the newest fissure, as he inhaled through his nose.

Meg closed her eyes and inhaled, concentrating. Then her eyes snapped open. "Do I smell smoke?"

"Yes." Todd's single word was clipped.

"There's a fire?"

"In a rainforest?" Brian's tone held disbelief. "Do you remember the puddles we hiked through?"

"Do you know how fast something can dry out when heated to two thousand degrees?" Todd scanned the forest. "We have a real problem. We have flows coming in from the west as the lava runs downhill. Each fissure is going to have flows with multiple arms following the path of least resistance, but all in roughly the same direction."

"There may be no path going back," Byrne said.

"We run the risk of getting trapped if we make the attempt. But fire moves uphill, so that's coming at us from the east. And then past that is another lava flow that's getting a head start." Todd met Meg's gaze. "We're in the middle."

"No one knows fire like you do," Meg said. "What do we do?"

"I know fire; I don't know volcanoes. The combined threat could be a killer. How badly do we not want to have to navigate the old lava flow?"

"For me, pretty badly." Meg scanned the group, saw nods of agreement. "If a fissure blows out there near us, I don't know how we'd manage to outpace it."

Hinton's arm jerked as he tested his cuffs. "You send us out onto the lava field like this, we're not going to make it." His eyes narrowed on Hale. "Or is that your plan?"

Hale matched Hinton's acidic tone. "No."

"We'll have to try to skirt the fire, but will need to be prepared to use the lava field as an escape route because there's nothing to burn there," Todd instructed. "Better to take our chances with a fresh lava flow out there than burn to death for sure in here. Who has a map handy? Where are we?"

Meg pulled out her phone. "Here. I checked our position not too long ago." She held out the phone for Todd.

They had covered almost two-thirds of the distance from their starting point to the end of the kīpuka, but as they moved east, the land mass narrowed to a point at its eastern end.

"Let's stick to the south end of the kīpuka, which will give us a straighter shot across, but be prepared to go north depending on the fire. Here's some quick pointers: Fire moves uphill, unless the wind drives it downhill. In here, there's little to no wind, but up top, it could move differently. Burning branches could fall from above, and then you have a new focus of fire. Even if we get past it, keep your eyes on the canopy. Hotshot firefighters who fight these fires all the time have a rule: Get no closer than four times the height of a fire for safety. If the flames are ten feet tall, you're safe over forty feet away from the fire. It's our bad luck we're in the hottest part of the day at midafternoon, so that's going to play against us, but nothing we can do about that. Last thing, as we get close to it, pull up your collar to cover your mouth and nose. Wood fires burn a lot cleaner than structure fires with all their synthetic materials, but the smoke can still kill you." He stared at Griggs and Hinton for a long moment, then slid his gaze to Hale. "Hinton is right, though. Keeping them bound could be disastrous if we need to run or take cover on the lava field. You need to consider freeing their hands. I know we despise what they're doing, but it's not our place to sentence them to death."

Hale's jaw went tight, and Meg understood his indecision. If he freed the men, there was every chance they'd take the opportunity to escape. If he held them, they might die.

Hell, even freed, they might die. They might all die if they couldn't navigate the hazards of this rift.

Hale nodded. "I'll keep it in mind."

Todd handed back Meg's phone. "Let's move."

"You take the lead. You'll know better than the rest of us when we need to compensate."

Todd took the lead, followed by Meg and Hawk, Brian and Lacey, then Griggs, Byrne, Hinton, and Hale. They'd only gone about fifty feet when smoke started to haze their view of what was in front of them. Assisting Griggs and Hinton, they pulled collars over their mouths, breathing through the material, their eyes watering with the acrid smoke. Soon, even through the smoke, they could see the blaze of the fire and hear its *snap* and *crack* as it gorged on the forest.

The land curved inward to the north as the fire intensified, flames shooting up one of the trees to set the leaves of the canopy aflame. The fire seemed to take on a living, breathing life of its own, producing its own terrifying roar. Or was that the fissure?

It could be both.

"I don't like this!" Todd yelled back to the group. "We're pushing it. We need to ditch for the flow before it's too late."

"Wait!" Hale yelled.

Everyone turned around to find him digging into his pocket before he pointed at Griggs. "Turn around." As the man presented him with his back, Hale said, "We know who you are. We know what you've done. You already have a stack of charges. Don't make me add evading arrest to the list just because I don't want your death on my hands. You run, I *will* find you. You stay, we'll work as a group to keep every one of us alive." The cuffs fell away.

Griggs turned his head to fix Hale with a slitted stare. Then he nodded and stepped aside so Hale could do the same for Hinton.

Hale stuffed both pairs of handcuffs in his pocket and turned to Todd. "Get us out of here."

Todd angled them south, fighting his way through the underbrush. But it was clear soon enough that they couldn't move as fast as the fire, especially overhead as Todd's gaze was drawn upward again and again.

"Todd?" Meg had to yell over the roar of the approaching flames. "Should we be heading back to the west? We're going to get cut off here!"

Todd held up a hand to stop the group and turned to peer through smoke to take in the flames licking even closer, even higher, clearly calculating the odds.

A nearby tree groaned, and then a horrible splintering sounded as the tree toppled.

"Run!" Todd yelled as the tree fell toward them, and then he sprinted in the direction of the southern border of the kīpuka.

There was no choice now between the lava flow and the flames: One was certain death, one was a chance at life.

Meg dropped the material from her nose and mouth. "*Talon, Athena, run!*" She pounded after Todd, Brian at her side, knowing the dogs would follow, and indeed, they shot between them to run closer to Todd.

Dogs and humans frantically pushing through bushes and over ferns, stomping on the endangered life they knew was only moments away from turning to ash. Life they had to sacrifice or they would join them.

All Meg could think was that if Hale hadn't loosed Griggs and Hinton, they'd likely already be dead. That fate still remained for all of them if they couldn't outrun the inferno.

The air thickened with smoke, and Meg's lungs, already burning, struggled even more to deliver enough of the oxygen she needed to keep going. Tears slipped from her stinging eyes, and when she wiped one away, her hand came away smeared with dark soot.

Heat built behind them as the fire raced along with them. Meg kept her gaze forward and nearly stumbled with relief when beyond the trees ahead, light flowed through the smoke.

Nearly there.

"Keep going!" Todd's yell floated back as he plowed through the underbrush, forging a path for the group. "We're almost there!"

Ahead, Hawk faltered, nearly tripping over a downed branch half hidden under fallen fern fronds. Meg slowed, letting Lacey and Brian move ahead as she reached for her dog. "Come on, Hawk." She paused to suck air into her starved lungs. "Stay with me, buddy. I won't leave you behind." Another gasp of air. "Stay with Lacey. You can do this."

Her dog seemed to find some hidden reservoir and poured on a burst of speed. Meg dug deep to find the same.

The light steadily increased, and then they were through, the smoke dissipating without a canopy of leaves to hold it in.

"This way!" Todd stepped off the grass and onto the ragged rim of the lava field. "Get away from the edge!"

Meg followed Brian and Lacey on the rocky surface, Hawk at her side as they moved ten, then fifteen feet onto the flow. Griggs and then Byrne followed.

It came like an arrow from the sky, dark and deadly.

With a shriek, an 'Io plummeted, heading straight for them. No, not for them as a group. For Hinton and Hale.

Hale instantly recognized the threat and dove to one side, rolling over the grass, and then clambering onto the lava flow.

Hinton knew it too. As the bird pulled its wings in, its talons extended toward Hinton's head, he turned and ran in the opposite direction, stepping back from the rocky edge of the kīpuka.

But the bird didn't stop, alighting on Hinton's shoulder, its wings beating his head and talons digging deep. Hinton punched at it with his fists, knocking it off, but the bird simply flew after him, readying its next attack.

Hinton ran directly toward the flaming forest, the only cover he could see.

Man and hawk disappeared into the flames.

Todd took two steps forward before Meg caught his arm, dragging him back, even as Hinton's agonized screams echoed over the lava field. "Todd, no. You can't help him. He's gone." Craig's long-ago words echoed in her head. "Bring home the ones you can."

His biceps were rock-hard under her hand, a sign of the struggle within. She totally understood—saving lives was an integral part of his psyche, even when those actions put his own life at incredible risk. Then his muscles relaxed, and she knew he'd accepted that this time, it wouldn't be enough. In fact, the price to pay would be much too high for those who loved him.

With a cry, the 'Io sailed out of the forest just as flames billowed behind it, singeing the tips of a few feathers. It soared into the brilliant blue sky, where it joined its circling mate, then they both turned to the south and glided out of sight.

Justice had been served as far as nature was concerned.

Todd nodded, and the muscle beneath her fingers loosened. She let her hand slide down his arm to his hand, where she intertwined her fingers with his and squeezed. She looked up into his face, smudged with soot, with pale lines radiating around his eyes from when they'd been squinted shut against the smoke. There was regret in his dark eyes, along with resignation, but also the determination to see the day through.

He squeezed her hand and then dropped it, turning back to the group.

A distinctive buzz from above registered through the thunder of the inferno backed by the eruption. Meg's gaze swung to the far side of the lava flow as a dark dot flew over the tops of the trees a quarter mile away, headed directly for them.

"Better late than never," Hale said, his eyes fixed on the drone as it flew in their direction. He waved one arm over his head as his phone rang. He dug it out of his pocket and answered. "Hale." His gaze returned to the drone. "Yeah, we see it. Thanks for making the attempt." Another pause as he listened. "Actually, there is something you can do. There are at least three fissures along this kīpuka. It's going to be harder to spot because of the amount of heat radiating from the eruptions and the fire, but check to make sure no one else is here who needs help. Thanks." A long pause. "Is HPD still waiting for us? Great. Tell them we're on the way, coming over the flow. They'll be able to see us shortly." He ended the call and put his phone in his pocket. "We have about three-quarters of a mile to go, but officers are waiting to meet us." His gaze slid to Griggs. "I'm going to leave your hands free because you're going to need them over this flow. A reminder that we're all armed. We'll get you there safely, but don't try anything stupid."

Griggs muttered something under his breath, but nodded sharply.

Hale turned toward the east. "Come on. I'm ready to leave this goddamn forest reserve."

"Amen," muttered Brian.

They pushed through the lava field, exhausted, covered in soot and ash, battered and bruised.

Finally, in the distance, three white, blue, and yellow Hawaiʻi PD SUVs sat facing Saddle Road, lights flashing, with a handful of figures and a dog backlit by the brilliant blue sky. The moment they saw the group round the edge of the kīpuka, they waved.

"Kai and Makoa are there." Byrne's voice was full of relief.

It felt like an eternity before they made it to the rough twin track road carved out of the middle of the lava flow. Hale cuffed Griggs again, and then two officers took him and put him into the back of the cruiser.

Meg knelt down and hugged Hawk as he wagged enthusiastically and tried to lick her face. "Hawk, down boy. That's my boy. Don't lick me. I probably taste like a charcoal briquette."

Brian came to stand next to her. "Damn. Look at that."

"At what?"

"Back to where we might have died." He held out a hand to her. "Need help?"

"Normally, no. But right now, every single muscle aches and all I want is a half hour in a hot bath. After a shower to wash off this grime." She slapped her hand into his, and he hauled her upright.

They stood side by side, flanked by their dogs, watching the conflagration rip through the kīpuka as fingers of fiery red lava spilled from both sides of the high ground to trail toward them.

Todd came to stand behind them, laying a hand on Meg's hip. As a group, they stared in silence at the place they'd only barely survived, the place where Miles Hinton had not.

There were times when nature's fury could not be denied.

It had been man versus nature.

Nature had clearly triumphed.

CHAPTER 22

Fallout: Volcanic ash and debris that fall to the ground following a volcanic eruption.

June 1, 7:53 PM
Waikōloa Beach Marriott Resort
Waikōloa, Hawai'i

They'd taken a corner table on the deserted patio, most of the other diners having long finished and moved on with their evening. If this was to be their last night at the resort, they were going to enjoy one final meal at the restaurant instead of takeout in their suite.

Meg and Todd had canceled the last leg of their trip to O'ahu days ago, and Craig had booked them all on a flight home the next day.

They'd said their goodbyes to Hale and Byrne at the vehicles they'd left parked off Stainback Highway with the promise to keep in touch about the case. McCord had assured them that just because the dogs were done and the Hawai'i chain had been broken, that didn't mean his part was over, and they'd be hearing from him once he was back in DC. He still had lines to tug—saving the species under threat in Hawaii was only part of the story, as far as he was concerned; if he could help get to the heart of the organization, he was all in.

They'd returned to the resort and had split up to shower sweat, dirt, and soot off both humans and dogs, check out bruises, and clean and bandage burns. Todd had taken the hardest hit there, having been hit with a rock ejected by the eruption, which had likely been well over a thousand degrees Fahrenheit when it left the earth, cooling somewhat as it flew through the air, but still striking with the heat of a brand. He had an angry-red, quarter-sized blister on the back of his left hand and Meg suspected he might be left with a scar when it finally healed—a permanent souvenir of what would hopefully be their only time tangling with a volcano. Definitely a honeymoon to remember.

Their server had taken their orders and delivered their drinks, and now they were relaxing as dusk fell ever deeper over 'Anaeho'omalu Bay.

"It's weird, not nailing down the end of the case," Brian said. "We arrested some of the people in this arm of the trafficking ring, and I know their base is back in the US, but it feels unfinished."

Meg set down her drink. "I know what you mean. But now it's agent legwork; no need for the dogs." She smiled down at Hawk and Lacey, lying together on the warm pavement between Meg's and Brian's chairs. "They worked hard and did a great job. We wouldn't have Griggs in custody without them."

"And that mated pair of 'Io are still together."

"The case isn't over as far as I'm concerned," McCord stated. "And I found out some enlightening new things today." He sent a pointed look in Meg's direction. "I would have told you earlier, but someone had a date with a soaker tub."

Meg returned his look. "By the time we got here, I could barely move. All my muscles had tightened up on the drive back. That tub soaked away a major part of my pain. And then someone needed to look after my arm again. And to confirm I wasn't hiding a concussion."

Todd toasted her with his tall, slender pilsner glass. "'Someone' wanted to make sure after all that action you weren't putting on a brave face."

Warmth flooded Meg's cheeks because they all knew she'd been guilty of that in the past. "I only do that when there's no time for me to be injured." She paused. "And I guess there wasn't today."

"Thus the double check. So, McCord, fill us in. What did you find out?"

"First of all, Hale had one of his fellow agents get in touch with me while you were still out in the field, about the new flight plan for N4814A. I'd been keeping an eye on all three planes and had looked earlier today, and none of them had flight plans logged. But I checked again after Meg said the suspects knew you were on to them, and that's when I found the flight for four thirty. Special Agent Sterling called to get all the information, as Hale was out of touch. He got a search warrant in the works while he was on his way here. When he landed at Kona, he went right to Waimea-Kohala, seized the plane, and searched it."

"They weren't keeping any birds they'd found there, were they?"

"No. But he tracked down the flight crew and questioned them. Sterling honestly thought they didn't know what was going on, the pilots especially. But the flight attendant was serving Griggs, Hinton, and one other man during the flight here, and she happened to catch bits and pieces of what they were doing. Not enough to figure out what was going on, but enough to help Sterling put it together. They'd rented an Airbnb in Hilo, and she heard the street name, though not the address. A quick search of the Airbnb website gave him a single possibility, and he was able to get a warrant quickly. Hawai'i PD backed him up on the search, and when they got there, they found an exotic bird expert and a rental four-by-four."

"The bird nerd we talked about earlier. He was the driver who got them in and out of their pickup spots," Meg surmised.

McCord leveled an index finger at her. "You got it. The bird nerd was happy to play second fiddle for a big payday to drive the vehicle and care for the birds."

"Wouldn't it have made more sense for him to be the one out in the field? They might have had better success rates with the mist nets."

"I asked Sterling the same question. Apparently, the guy was a raging asthmatic and there was no chance he could manage the exertion of getting to the required altitudes, so he taught Griggs and Hinton what to do. Then was extremely happy to sing like a canary and sell them out as soon as the impact of the charges became clear."

"He's cutting a deal with the US attorney?"

"Who knows? This one was apparently spilling the beans before he knew if a deal could be made. We'll leave that for the lawyers to settle, but it's going to be a big problem for Aviatronics because he sold them down the river. In any case, they found six birds caged and waiting for transport, all in good condition, so the bird nerd was apparently earning his keep. Sterling called in someone from the Hawai'i Wildlife Center, and they were going to get in touch with US Fish and Wildlife. Byrne was likely looped in as soon as she came back into contact. The wildlife folks didn't want to hold on to them; they wanted to get them back to the Puʻu Makaʻala area and release them ASAP. As far as I know, that's already been done."

"Thank God." Meg sat back in her chair to make room as the server appeared with her salad. "Thank you. So, in the end, there are the two birds still at the Wildlife Center and the one that died that we know of in Puʻu Makaʻala. Otherwise, they didn't make much of an impact on the local avian community."

"Thanks," McCord said to the server as she set a half dozen oysters on the half shell in front of him. "You ruined this trip for them. The organization not only lost this entire sale, but they lost two of their thugs. Sterling was going to meet Hale and Griggs to see what the two of them could get out of him."

"Good," Brian said, staring at McCord's oysters. "How can you eat that?"

"Oysters? Love them." He picked up a half shell, brought it to his lips, tipped the shell, and swallowed the oyster.

"Ugh." Brian shuddered and turned to his Pupu rib eye steak appetizer. "You take the surf. I'm sticking with the turf."

"Hey, I need to enjoy the *Post* picking up my tab while I can. Speaking of which, dinner is on me. Or rather, on Sykes." He winked at Meg, who grinned back. "Anyway, when we knew we were looking at Aviatronics Customs Brokerage, I did a deep dive into the company."

"Once it was clear it was them, so much of this case made sense," Meg said.

"Totally agree. I spent so much time today digging into the shell corporation and trying to tug on the thread of the local black market, I temporarily discounted a group that simply parachuted in from the mainland, took what it wanted, and sayonara'd out of here. Or tried to."

"Part of that could have been the nature of the capture," Todd reasoned. "They brought the bird nerd with them, but it doesn't sound like they needed any local support. Not like they wanted rhino horns and needed a big game hunter for hire or to find one who was already trading in black market animal parts."

"But this is a group with its fingers in customs pies all over the world. They were the perfect cover for this. When we get home, I'm going to keep working on tracing their activities. As far as I know, the local field office is already getting a warrant to search their offices, as well as the homes of select upper management. And then there's the money aspect. Now that we know where the money went, the FBI and FinCEN will trace it backward. I'm hoping that between what they can do and what I can do, we're going to bring down more arms of this trade."

"Good work, McCord." Meg touched her cocktail glass to his pint glass.

"Thanks. Oh, and by the way, that shell corporation? That's something I may continue to dig at because it's so tangled, there must be something nefarious there. But that's a project for another day." His cell phone rang and he pulled it out, a smile curving his lips. "Why is she still up? Let me get this." He accepted the call. "Hello? Hello? I can barely hear you. Let me call you right back." He hung up and sent a sideways glance at Meg. "I just lied to your sister."

"Why?"

"So I could do this." He placed a video call back to Cara. She answered, smiling back at him. "Hey, sorry about that. This seems much clearer. And while I have you, look who else is here." He turned the phone and passed it over the whole table.

"Meg!"

Meg snatched the phone from McCord to smile back at the face that looked so very much like her own. "Why are you up at this hour?"

"I'm just about to go to bed. I got stuck doing the books." Cara grimaced.

Meg laughed. Cara *hated* doing the books for her dog training school and usually put it off, so when she finally had to break down and do them, it was a huge amount of work. "Ah, that explains the insanely late hour."

"How's your arm?"

"Getting better."

"Todd's been keeping an eye on it?"

Todd leaned into Meg so Cara could see him. "Yes, ma'am."

"Good man. How's the case going?"

"McCord didn't tell you?"

"Clearly not." Cara's look said she wasn't impressed with her partner.

Across the table, McCord grinned at her.

"Well, we had an interesting day," Meg said. "Kind of an unbelievable day, when it comes down to it."

"Why?"

"Why don't I tell you tomorrow?"

"Tomorrow? Why not now?"

"Because I'm not sure you'd believe it. I'm not sure *I* believe it. But I have a better reason."

"Which is?"

Meg picked up her drink and took a long sip as she scanned the faces around the table—McCord, laughing; Brian, smug; Todd, amused. She set her drink down and took in her sister, whom she'd missed like crazy over the nearly two weeks they'd been away. She couldn't wait to see her again.

"So I can tell you in person." She couldn't hold back the smile. "We're coming home."

Acknowledgments

Crafting a novel is rarely a solo pursuit, and, as always, I was assisted by, and owe thanks to, an amazing group of people:

Kelly Vaiman, who saw an article about Kīlauea's June 2023 eruption and reached out with a concept of Meg and Hawk traveling to Hawai'i for a case. Having recently handed in *Summit's Edge*, which ended with Meg and Todd newly married, this suggestion struck a chord with me because a potential setting for the next book could involve Meg and Todd's honeymoon as long as they stayed within US jurisdiction. And with that suggestion, I was off to the races on planning *Deadly Trade*. Thanks, Kelly, for putting the kernel of an idea in my head that led to this book!

James Abbate, my editor at Kensington. James, we really perfected the art of the middle-of-the-night manuscript pass-off on this one. Teamwork, FTW! I may be getting repetitive, but I don't know how I'd manage this killer schedule without your unending flexibility and good-natured willingness to help me keep my head above water. So many thanks!

My husband, Rick Newton, who was a willing fellow traveler on a whirlwind trip to Hawai'i to ensure I could properly write the setting this book required. Some might say a trip to Hawai'i is no hardship, but it was definitely not a relaxing vacation. I had an agenda of things I needed to see and do—hiking Pu'u Maka'ala, visiting Volcanoes National Park, becoming familiar with the island and its culture—and he willingly chauffeured me around the island (so many trips back and forth over Saddle Road ... so many insanely early mornings so we could drive a hundred miles to the other side of the island for 9 AM hikes) and made sure that every item on that list was checked off before our week was over. Thank you for humoring me on yet another research trip. I don't know what I'd do with myself, but someday, we'll have to try a relaxing vacation for a change!

My daughter Jess, of Jess Danna Photography, for her enthusiasm and willingness to jump into any project where her skills might be needed. In this case, the concept of a map came up for this book, as so much of the story is spread from nearly corner to corner of the Big Island of Hawai'i. Jess immediately offered her assistance. It turned out to be a pretty big project, dealing with topography, lava flows, cities and towns, airports, protected forest reserves, and an author/mom who always wanted something just a little to the left. Thank you, Jess, for putting up with me, and for producing such a great representation of the story that will greatly increase readers' enjoyment.

Shane Vandevalk for his willingness to always brainstorm titles and planning angles with me. I will also forever appreciate the fact that I can ask you a gun question and you'll instantly go down a rabbit hole to get every detail I need. Thank you for always making sure that aspect of my writing is realistic and perfectly suits each scenario.

My critique team of Jess Newton, Rick Newton, Jenny Rarden, and Sharon Taylor once again took on the challenge of me and my extremely tight deadline with grace, good humor, and the precision to nail their edits in the shortest time frame yet. I am beyond grateful for your assistance and can honestly say that the book wouldn't be nearly the same without each and every one of you.

My agent, Nicole Resciniti, for always working so hard for me in every aspect of my writing life. Nicole, thank you for always being available, accessible, and so enthusiastic in your support. Additional thanks to the Seymour

Agency, including Lesley Sabga, Gaby Cabezut, Brittney Brunelle, and Mike Seymour, for all their assistance.

The awesome team at Kensington is, as always, a pleasure to work with. Lou Malcangi for another dynamic cover, Madeleine Brown for such enthusiastic, efficient, and energetic publicity support, Robin Cook for editorial support, Susanna Gruninger for her work on subsidiary rights, and marketing and communications support from Vida Engstrand, Kait Johnson, Alexandra Nicolajsen, Kristin McLaughlin, Sarah Beck, Catherine Kenny, and Andi Paris. One of the reasons I love Kensington so much is because of the universal support from the entire team and how everyone pulls together to bring such wonderful books to the world. Thanks to you all!